RISE OF POLARIS

THE OMNILOGOS SINGULARITY
BOOK 1

MICHELE AMITRANI

ISBN (ePub): 978-1-988770-52-9

ISBN (Paperback): 978-1-988770-57-4

First Edition 2022

Published by Michele Amitrani.

Cover Design by 100 Covers

PROLOGUE

2010

Wei had stolen the colorful toy from Dr. Fenberg's table. He'd succeeded without being noticed just a moment before his mother led him to the waiting room outside the doctor's office.

It had been easy to snatch the toy. When he'd entered the office with his mother, the doctor had given him a hasty look, a forced smile, and talked as if the child didn't exist.

Wei hadn't liked Dr. Fenberg from the get-go. The man treated him as if he were invisible, whispering the words *differently abled* and *slow learner* to Wei's mother twice, believing Wei hadn't heard him.

But being invisible had its advantages.

Wei turned the toy over in his hands. It had an internal pivot mechanism that enabled each of the six faces to turn independently, thus mixing up the colors. It was also the only thing that was keeping him from dying of boredom in that smelly, decrepit place while he waited for his mother to finish talking to the doctor.

"Are you okay, honey?"

Wei hid the toy behind his back and looked at the nurse who was smiling at him. It was a forced, hurried smile, the same type Dr. Fenberg had greeted him with.

"How are you doing?" The woman stepped closer, widening her fake smile. "Are you bored?"

Her eyes were circled with red and her expression was dull, as if she hadn't slept in days.

"Your mom's going to be done soon, okay?" The nurse fished something out of her apron pocket. "Look, I brought you a present."

It was a stuffed animal: a purple crocodile with yellow eyes and a smile more fake than the nurse's.

"Do you like it, sweetheart?"

Wei didn't answer.

"Isn't it nice? Take it. It's yours."

Wei withdrew a few inches when the woman showed the intention of giving him the toy.

"You don't want to play with it?"

The boy crossed his arms and shook his head.

"You sure? Come on. Look at him, this poor crocodile! I think he's sad. He's all alone. He needs a friend. Will you be his friend?"

Wei sighed. He pulled a blue marker and a small notepad out of his jeans pocket and began writing something on it.

"Oh, what do you have there? Are you drawing something? No, *wait*. It's not a drawing. You're writing! Look at you! Can you write already? That's awesome. Come on, show me what you're writing."

Wei showed her the notepad.

"'I can't breathe with you around.'" The nurse frowned as she read the message. "'You smell like a hospital. Get lost.'"

Wei pinched the bridge of his nose with his thumb and forefinger, then stuck his tongue out.

"Karen?" a nurse called from across the room. "Where'd you put file fourteen? Dr. Rea needs it. Right now."

Karen stared at Wei for a couple seconds, as if she wanted to say something but didn't know exactly where to start.

"Karen? You with me?"

"Coming, coming." The nurse straightened up awkwardly and walked away, taking the stupid crocodile with her.

When she was gone, Wei picked up Dr. Fenberg's toy and resumed moving its parts. He clicked one of the red-colored rows of the object forward and into place, then did the same with another row.

He liked the *click* sound the toy made each time one part was moved into place. *Click. Click. Click.* It felt like he was building something. Wei liked to build the most diverse things with whatever was available. It made him feel like he was doing something useful with his time.

He completed the puzzle game about ten minutes later, then took the blue marker and scribbled something on one of the sides. When he was done, he dropped the toy on the ground hoping someone would trip on it.

Wei tapped his fingers on the armrest and looked around, huffing. He was the only person in the waiting area, but the adjacent hallway seemed packed with people; doctors and nurses were coming and going, and the occasional patient in slippers trudged around holding IV poles with bored expressions.

Wei glanced toward Karen, who was busy talking to her colleague. At that moment, her back was to him.

It was now or never.

When he was sure the nurse wasn't looking, Wei stood up and headed down the hallway.

No one paid attention to him. The hospital staff was busy and didn't seem to notice the five-year-old kid walking purposefully down the corridor.

The wide hallway seemed to have no end. There was a myriad of identical white doors to the left and right. One of them caught his attention. It had the number 4 posted at the top. Four was Wei's favorite number for a simple reason: The world was based on it. Four were the cardinal points, the seasons, the phases of the moon, and the elements of the zodiac. Wei also liked the shape of the number. To him, it looked like an arrow pointing toward the sky.

Wei opened the door and entered without knocking. He found himself inside a spacious, well-lit room. The open window was letting in the fading afternoon sunlight. There was a large metal cabinet to his right, and a lot of machinery with red and orange lights that pulsed like fireflies.

A strong chemical odor mixed with the stench of urine hit Wei. He rubbed his nose and turned sharply to find out where the stinky smell was coming from. As his head moved, his eyes caught a row of toys lined up on a long wooden table.

Wei blinked, surprised. There were four of them, just like the number of the room, and each one sparkled like a gem. He did not know what they were doing there, or who they belonged to. Not that he cared.

He walked to the table and picked up the closest toy. It was as long as his forearm, thin like a cigar, and ended with a red, metallic tip. The object stood on a wooden trophy base on which were engraved the words *Mercury Redstone*. Wei put the toy back on the table and moved on to the next one, which was a little larger and slightly taller than the first. This one was called *Gemini Titan*, and it was white, gray, and black, with a shorter, flatter tip compared to the *Mercury Redstone*. Wei turned the bigger toy over in his hands, then put it back on the table too and moved on to the next toy, the largest of the four. It had to be at least five times bigger than the first two. It was black and white, with the words *United States* highlighted in red on the hull. Engraved on the base were the words *Apollo Saturn V*.

Wei moved on to the last of the toys displayed on the table and was disappointed by its shape. It differed from the other three; not shaped like a rocket, but like a stumpy airplane. It had a squashed fuselage that made it look like a penguin dropped on its belly. He picked it up and read the name printed on the fuselage: *Space Shuttle Atlantis*.

"Are you lost?"

Wei almost dropped the *Atlantis*. He turned sharply toward the voice, his heart racing inside his chest. He hadn't noticed the bed on the opposite side of the room, and much less the scrawny man lying on it. He was older than Dr. Fenberg—who had already seemed to Wei the oldest human being he'd ever seen—and wore an azure hospital gown. His skin was an intricate web of wrinkles that seemed to dig channels into his ancient face. His eyes were the light blue of ice.

"Well, kiddo? Are you lost?"

Wei glanced at the door, thinking to run away, but deciding against it. The man didn't seem like he could do anything to him. He looked weak and frail, barely able to sit up to look at him better.

Wei shook his head to answer the question. The *Atlantis* was still firmly in his hands.

"No?" The old man studied him. "You sure? Well, then you must be my new nurse." He made a grimace that could have been wry amusement.

Wei shook his head again.

"No?" The man smiled. "Kid, I'm confused. You mean *no*, you're not lost, or *no*, you're not my nurse? Which one?"

Wei hesitated. He glanced at the door again and shift his weight from one foot to the other.

"What is it? You eat your tongue?"

Wei was about to shake his head again, but had a better idea. He set the *Atlantis* down on the table and fished the marker and notepad out of his pocket. He scribbled something and walked a few steps closer to the old man to show him.

"'I'm not lost,'" the patient read aloud. "'And the nurses stink.'"

Now that Wei was closer to the bed, he realized that the urine smell was coming from there. He changed the page, wrote a new sentence, and showed it to the old man.

"'You stink too.'" The patient stared at Wei and pushed his eyebrows upward. After a couple seconds, he burst out laughing; a strange sound, somewhere between a grunt and a dry cough.

"Well, you're not wrong, kiddo," he said. "But if you think I stink *now*, wait a few weeks, when I'll be worm food.

What's the marker thing all about anyway?" He took a handkerchief from his pocket and coughed into it. "Are you tongue-tied or something?"

Wei wrote the answer and showed it to him: *Mom says I can't talk to strangers*.

"So you *write* to them?" the man said, frowning. "A clever way around the problem. How old are you?"

Wei wrote the number 5 on the notepad.

"Five?" He whistled, a long, high-pitched sound that made Wei wince. "I'd given you twice as many years for brain, and half as much for constitution. You're the smallest kid I've ever seen, I swear. Wait..." He leaned over to the nightstand and opened a drawer. He picked out something wrapped in a yellow and orange wrapper. "You want a chocolate?"

Wei scribbled on the paper: *Mom said I can't accept anything from strangers*.

The old man nodded gravely. "Your mother is right," he said. "She knows her stuff. You always do what she tells you, okay?"

Wei looked at the chocolate and moistened his lips. *However*, he wrote, *if I knew your name, you wouldn't be a stranger anymore*.

"Ah!" The old man managed to cough and laugh at the same time. "I said you were smart, didn't I? Well, call me Eltanin."

Wei wrote three letters on the notepad: *Wei*.

"It's done." Eltanin handed him the chocolate. "We're buddies now."

Wei unwrapped the chocolate and stuffed it into his mouth.

The old man stacked a couple pillows behind his back

and leaned on them with a sigh. "You know, the smartest people I've met didn't talk much, and I've met a lot of smart people. The smartest people in the country, perhaps in the whole world."

Wei picked the *Atlantis* back up from the table and turned it over in his hands. He wondered if there were any more chocolates left inside the drawer.

"Do you like it?" The man pointed to the model of the Space Shuttle.

Wei nodded.

"I helped build it." Eltanin pointed to the three models on the table. "I worked on those too, you know? Jeez, it's like I've been living a dream. My life went by in a flash." He snapped his fingers meaningfully. "If I close my eyes, I can see it, clear as day. God. The world has changed a lot in eighty years."

Wei pointed to the three models on the table. *Are these yours?*

"My niece gave them to me," Eltanin said. "I carry them around like some kind of good luck charm, I guess. They're beautiful, aren't they?"

Wei nodded.

"You don't know how much energy, hope, and resources we've poured into them. I'm talking about entire generations, kid. Thousands and thousands of people working toward the common goal of exploring space, unveiling its secrets, and mastering the stars. Take that beast there, for example." Eltanin nodded toward the *Saturn V*. "We launched thirteen of them in less than ten years. All the launches concluded successfully. We used them for the Apollo missions, which allowed twelve astronauts to land on the Moon. The Moon! Can you believe it? The only rocket capable of taking a man to another celestial body." Eltanin inhaled and exhaled, wiping sweat from his forehead with the back of his hand. He looked as if he had run a marathon. The light that had made his eyes glow went out like a dying fire. Suddenly, his gaze became dull and spent. "Then," he continued, dragging out the words, "it all went south. We stopped daring, became afraid of failures and setbacks and let the future slip through our fingers. It all turned to shit. Today people spend half their lives staring at a screen. You know, to 'surf the net' and all. Living in a world that doesn't exist. No one looks up to the stars, heart singing with possibilities. No one gives a damn. Old farts like me are about all that's left of those days of ingenuity, and us old geezers are dying like flies."

Wei studied Eltanin. There was something different about him, something that made him stand apart from all the adults he'd met. He couldn't explain it. Maybe it was the way he spoke, or the light in his eyes.

Suddenly, the *Atlantis* seemed much heavier in his hand, as if Eltanin's words had added weight to the small model.

"Listen to me." The old man settled himself better on the pillows. "Whining like a whipped dog to the only audience I have left. Am I boring you?"

Wei nodded.

Eltanin laughed. "Another thing I like about you, kiddo. You don't pull any punches."

Wei wrote on the notepad: *Do you have another chocolate?*

"I've got plenty, you little punk. One of the nurses likes me. She brings me truckloads of them. Look, I'll give you some more, but you have to promise me not to eat them before lunch, okay? You better not lose your appetite. That would make your mother mad, you know?"

Eltanin gave Wei a handful of chocolates, which the boy

put in his pocket, intending to eat them the second he left the room.

"Do you want that too?" Eltanin pointed to the *Atlantis*.

Yes, Wei wrote.

"Take it then." Eltanin paused, looking at the Space Shuttle with glassy eyes. "I mean it. It's yours."

Wei put the *Atlantis* in his pocket, then turned and looked at the table with the models of the three rockets. He wrote, *Can I take them all?*

The old man opened his mouth, then closed it. When he spoke, his voice was slightly lower than before, more labored. "Wow, kiddo. With you it's all or nothing, hmm? All right. Take them. They'll throw them away when I'm gone anyway. Here, take this."

Eltanin opened the drawer and pulled out a plastic bag. "Put them here so you can take them away."

Wei took the bag and put all the rockets inside it, except for the *Atlantis*, which stayed in his pocket.

"Well, Wei." Eltanin nodded toward the bag. "You're bringing with you the whole package. Literally. My whole life is in that bag. Take good care of it, you hear me?"

Okay, Wei wrote.

"And promise me one thing." The man asked Wei to hand him the notepad and the marker.

"I wish I'd have seen a place when I was younger. A place far away. Maybe, when you are older, someone will get there. Promise me that if that happens, you'll witness that moment with these models beside you."

Eltanin displayed the word he had written. The letters were so big they took up the whole page.

Wei stared at the word, then nodded without hesitation.

"Well then." The old man gave the marker and the

notepad back to Wei. "Shake my hand, boy. This is Texas; a handshake is as good as a notarial act here."

Wei shook his hand.

"Good. Now give me a big smile, for heaven's sake. You're way too serious for a kid who just robbed my room clean."

Wei thought about smiling for a couple seconds. Then, not without effort, he projected the corners of his mouth upward tentatively.

"Jesus Christ." Eltanin stared at him. "What's that? Is there a corpse in my room? You need to hit the bathroom? Come on, kiddo. Give me a real smile."

Wei laughed at the joke.

"There you go. Much better." Eltanin closed his eyes and leaned his head on the pillow, wincing. "Now you'd better go back to your mommy. She might be worried."

Wei looked at Eltanin and frowned. He changed the page of the notepad and wrote, *Why are you crying?*

The old man wiped his eyes with the back of his hand. "I've got something stuck in my eye."

Really? I can't see anything.

"It's tiny, but it's there. Trust me, okay?"

Okay.

"It was nice to meet you, Wei. Don't drive your mother crazy, and remember to smile once in a while. Don't be a grouch. Life's too short for that. Laugh. Make fun of people. Let friends make fun of you. Try everything at least twice. And for god's sake, stay away from candies. It lengthens your life. I promise."

Wei nodded absently, then checked that the chocolates were still in his pocket. He waved his hand to say goodbye, but Eltanin had closed his eyes and seemed asleep.

Wei left the room. Once outside, he started walking down the hallway.

"Here he is! Lady? Over here! I found him!"

Wei turned just in time to see Nurse Karen rushing toward him. She grabbed his arm and pulled him toward her.

"Where do you think you're going?" Her face was flushed and drenched with sweat, as if she'd been running for an hour.

Wei felt the woman's hand squeeze his wrist to the point of hurting. Her hand was cold and clammy against his skin.

She was making him dirty.

"You gave me quite a scare, little one."

Wei struggled, trying to free himself, but the nurse was too strong.

"Calm down. Don't you know you scared your mother? She almost died of—"

Wei stopped listening. Everything suddenly went blank. It was as if someone had flipped off a switch. His mind stopped working. The world became a confusion of sounds, colors, and shapes. He fell to the ground with a choked groan and began punching his head with a cry.

"A-a-a-a-a-a-a-a!"

Nurse Karen stared at him with eyes wide open. "Hey, what you doing? Stop it!" She tried to block his arm, but Wei kept hitting himself, again and again, until the pain became the only thing he could feel.

"Stop, kid! Stop it!"

"Let him go!"

Wei heard footsteps approaching. A familiar voice, someone he knew. The nurse let go of his arm and he recoiled, gasping for air.

"Wei?"

Wei opened his eyes.

"I swear I did nothing." Karen's voice was faint, distant,

like the echo of an echo growing weaker. "I just touched him and he started screaming like—"

"Move over. It's one of his fits. I need to be alone with him."

Wei smelled the familiar scent of orange and vanilla, the fragrance of his mother. He seized that feeling with eagerness, as if someone had thrown him a life preserver just before he drowned in the middle of the ocean.

But he was still scared, his heart pounding, sweat gathering on his forehead.

"Wei? Listen to me—"

"I can't breathe, Mom," he mumbled, wheezing. "I can't...breathe. I can't—"

"Close your eyes and focus on my voice. Pretend you're in a desert, far away from everything and anyone."

Wei closed his eyes, and the world went dark.

"Can you see it?"

Wei's breath slowed down. A glimpse in the darkness. A light. Flashes of images appeared in front of him. He saw a distant horizon, the gentle slopes of dunes in the distance. Sand. It was an ocean made of sand.

"I see it," he said.

"You're safe now, Wei. No one can reach you in the desert. Only I can. Do you want me to be there with you?"

"Yeah."

"Hold my hand."

Wei intertwined his fingers with his mother's. Her skin was cold and smooth. It felt like holding a piece of silk.

"Take a deep breath. Good, very good. Just like that."

Wei inhaled and exhaled. Slowly, the tightness in his chest loosened.

"That's good. Do it again. In and out the air goes. Again and again. You can open your eyes now."

Wei hesitated. He kept his eyes closed. "Do I...do I have green light?" His voice was fearful and uncertain.

"Yes, love. You have a green light."

Wei opened his eyes.

Sitting on the floor beside him was a smiling woman with dark brown eyes. His mother had a light sprinkling of freckles on her nose and cheeks that made her face look like a starry sky.

Only then did Wei realize he was still inside the hospital. Nurse Karen had stepped back a couple meters, her eyes wide with surprise.

She wasn't the only one. The hallway was full of people staring at him. All those adults, who until that moment had done nothing but ignore him, now saw only him.

"Let's go." His mother carried him in her arms. "Let's go home."

They left the hallway, went down the stairs, and out of the hospital.

It was only after his mother had started the car that Wei noticed he had left the bag with the rockets in the hallway.

Panic flooded him. He turned sharply to the window and stared at the hospital. "I left my toys in there."

"What toys? You brought no toys, Wei."

Right.

Wei remained silent. If he told his mother about Eltanin, she would not be happy. Not at all.

He leaned back in his seat and sighed. He felt something in his pocket and reached inside with his hand. It was the *Atlantis*. The model shone faintly in the sunlight, the pearl white metal of the spaceship cold against his hands. Wei clutched it tightly.

As long as he had the *Atlantis*, everything would be all right.

It was the last piece of Mr. Eltanin's legacy. He must not lose it.

"So, what happened out there?"

Karen looked at Dr. Fenberg and shrugged. "Mrs. Wang's son. I lost sight of the boy for a second and he disappeared. *Poof.* Just like that." She snapped her fingers, shook her head. "Well, I'll spare you the part where I almost had a heart attack... Anyway, I found him after ten minutes outside room four. He saw me and was about to run away, so I grabbed him and... Well, how can I put it? He started freaking out. He was screaming like I was butchering him or something. He started kicking and punching and..." Karen trailed off. She took a deep breath and said no more.

Dr. Fenberg patted her shoulder gently. "Well, you only had to deal with him for thirty minutes. His mother doesn't have that luxury. That poor woman is going to have her hands full with him. It won't be an easy life, I'll tell you that."

"Yeah," Karen said. "You were his second opinion, right?"

"The third one," said the doctor as he turned and put the last of his files inside his briefcase. "She came all the way from Orlando to get me to tell her something she already knew. She went to a couple other hospitals before ours. Told her the exact same thing. There's little that can be done for the boy."

"Gotcha."

"Other than this little accident, everything okay?"

Karen shrugged. "The usual. Nothing new."

Dr. Fenberg closed the briefcase with a *click.* "Wait. Didn't you say you had something for me?"

"Oh yeah. Right!" Karen fished something out of her coat pocket. "I found it just outside the door. Must have fallen out of your briefcase."

The doctor took the Rubik's Cube from Karen's hands, frowning. He stared at the six monochromatic sides as if staring at a flying pig. Someone completed the puzzle.

"Congratulations." Karen pointed to the cube. "You got it finally. How long did it take? A week?"

The doctor held the object in his hand, blinking.

"Doc?

Dr. Fenberg snapped to attention. "What?"

"This thing." Karen tapped a finger on the cube. "You bought it a week ago, right?"

"Um, yeah. I think so."

The nurse rested her hands on her hips. "I've been trying to get it done for two months, and I've barely completed two faces."

The doctor nodded absentmindedly.

"Doc? Is everything okay?"

"Hmm? Yeah. I was just... I was..." Dr. Fenberg scratched his chin and shook his head slightly. "Never mind. It's nothing."

"Okey dokey." Karen turned and opened the door. "I'd better get going. Bernard will kill me if I'm late for dinner again. See you tomorrow."

"See ya."

The door closed behind Karen, leaving Dr. Fenberg alone.

He stood awestruck, looking at the cube as if he expected the thing to start explaining to him who the hell had done it.

At last, he sighed. "Well," he mumbled, "you are a mystery that I'll solve tomorrow."

He began to put the cube on the desk when he noticed the small blue writing on the yellow side of the polyhedron.

"What is this?"

He brought the object closer and narrowed his eyes to read the message.

You are the slow learner.

PART I

WEI

1

ATLANTIS

CAPE CANAVERAL, STATE ROAD 401

2011

That day the roof of the world was covered by a thick blanket of clouds. The light, dimmed by the greyness dominating the sky, weakly illuminated earth, sand, and ocean.

Wei quickened his pace while greedily biting into a hot dog. On the third bite, ketchup slid down his arm.

"Wei! Look what you've done." His father suddenly stopped, pointing at the mess. He took a paper napkin from his pocket and wiped the child's arm. "Come on now, or we'll lose the best spots."

The boy trailed after him, still eating and splashing ketchup all over his clothes as if nothing had happened. To their left, the cars kept coming. The long line of people who were walking on the side of the road trailed behind them with chairs, umbrellas, and boxes packed with food.

Wei finished his snack and licked his fingers while they

were passing under the big billboard near the road where they had parked. *401 North Cape Canaveral A. F. Station.* A boy was pointing to the billboard as he asked a friend to take a picture.

They walked for a little while longer. Finally, his father stopped. He looked at a distant point on the horizon, scratching his head thoughtfully.

"Yeah, should be fine here," he said. Wei wasn't listening. He was busy taking the cookie and the can of Coke that a lady nearby was offering him. Wei loved sodas.

"Thank you." His father smiled, nodding toward the woman as his son ate the edges of the cookie with methodical precision.

Both sat on the towels they had brought with them and waited.

"How long?" Wei asked, folding his arms across his chest and tapping his feet on the ground.

His father glanced at his wristwatch. "Just a few more minutes. Be patient. Sometimes they have to delay."

"Why?"

"To be on the safe side. They gotta be sure everything is nice and dandy."

Just when Wei was getting bored, people around him began speaking louder, smiling at each other and pointing to a specific point in front of them. His father stood up and talked with the people nearby. Wei paid little attention to the growing frenzy and continued to focus on the stretch of water just a few dozen meters away, busy counting the waves.

"Come here."

Wei felt two strong arms around his waist. His father gently lifted the boy from the ground and put him on his shoulders. "Can you see it? That big launchpad? It's going to lift off from there."

Wei frowned. He saw against the horizon an L-shaped structure that was smaller than his thumb from where he was looking. He narrowed his eyes and finally distinguished the thing he came for. He recognized a spaceship shaped like a bulky glider, a dark orange-colored external fuel tank, and two white, slender rocket boosters.

"Yes!" he said, waving his hands. "I see it!"

"All right." His father laughed. "Just don't move too much, or we're both going down."

Meanwhile, the line of people who besieged the edges of the road was growing.

"Twenty-five seconds," a voice suddenly cried to their right. Another two or three voices echoed the first as the excitement grew.

Wei paid attention to the thrilled murmurs that saturated the atmosphere. People were pointing at the Space Shuttle, whistling and cheering. He could almost taste the electricity in the air.

An old man turned to him with a toothy smile and raised the volume of his radio to allow everybody around to hear.

"Go for main engine start. T-minus 10, 9, 8, 7, 6... All three engines up and burning."

The crowd stopped talking, captured by the message on the radio.

Wei looked around, admiring the mass of people—all strangers united to witness the historical event. Many were nudging friends or family members with their elbows. Other were jumping like crazy rabbits. He felt part of that incredible family of unfamiliar faces, bonded by an inexplicable sense of participation he couldn't really explain.

Time seemed to stop for everything except the voice on the radio that continued the countdown.

"...2, 1, 0...and *lift off*! The final lift off of *Atlantis*! On the shoulders of the Space Shuttle, America will continue the dream..."

The voice got lost in the sea of cheers and celebrations as a powerful spark ignited on the horizon. Wei, completely taken aback, stared breathlessly at the light lifting from the ground like a powerful firework that quickly became lost in the cloudy sky.

The crowd continued to cheer at the light for a few seconds.

When the show was over, people gathered their things and left.

"Did you like it?"

Wei swallowed. He felt his throat on fire. He realized at that moment he must have cried out with the rest of the people as the *Atlantis* soared to the sky. It had been a surreal experience, like living inside a dream. Exactly as Eltanin had said.

He lifted his eyes up, trying to catch a final glimpse of the *Atlantis* among the steel-colored clouds.

"Wei? Everything all right?"

Wei nodded. He was still searching for that one glimpse that might suggest the spaceship was still there. *There it was*. He saw it just for a second. It was as if the *Atlantis* had winked at him, a final farewell before the void and the stars.

"Time to go back, son. Pick up your things and thank the lady here." His father nodded toward the woman who had offered Wei the cookie and the Coke.

Wei didn't obey.

"Dad," he said, still looking for the *Atlantis*. "Can we see it again?"

"Again?" His father frowned. "What do you mean?"

"Can we see the light again?"

"This was the last time, Wei. I told you. Don't you remember? This was the Space Shuttle's last departure."

The boy reluctantly looked away from the sky and studied his father. "Why is it the last time?"

The man opened his mouth but said nothing. He looked surprised by the question, as if he had no real answer to offer.

"I want to see the light again!" The child's eyes shone with a magical fire as he pointed to the sky. "It was beautiful... No. It was awesome! Where will it go now? What was it made of? How could it be that fast? It'll be back, right?"

His father smiled. He covered the distance between them in a few steps, then knelt in front of Wei.

"You really want to know all these things?"

"Yes," the little boy immediately answered, "and I also want to see that light again."

"You will then, I promise," his father said with his hand over his heart. "Now let's go." He gently took his son's hand and together they walked back to their car. Wei obeyed, letting the man guide him, but continued to stare at the legacy left by the tall column of smoke in the fading light.

2

MICHELLE

ORLANDO, CURRY FORD ROAD

2012

Michelle Jordan dropped off the back of the ambulance carrying the stretcher along with her colleague. Police cars blocked the intersection of Semoran Boulevard and Curry Ford Road. Traffic was being diverted to one of the side roads by a pair of officers waving reflective signs toward the oncoming stream of cars.

"Mother of God."

Michelle turned toward the younger man beside her, who was staring in horror at the scene before them. Walter was just over twenty-four years old and this was his second shift on first line duty. He was a few inches shorter than her and walked as if he were constantly on the verge of tripping over something.

"Remember what I told you yesterday," Michelle said, picking up the pace. "Focus on your work."

"Right," Walter said. "The work. Good idea, boss."

"Don't call me that. I'm not your boss."

"Right. I'm sorry, ma'am."

"Now you make me sound old."

"I'm sorry. I didn't mean to—"

"Walter. Relax." Michelle patted his back. "Just remember to breathe."

Walter flashed a nervous smile. "Yeah, that's a good one. Breathe. Gotta remember that."

Michelle looked in the direction of the car that had blocked the bypass road.

An ice-blue Toyota had tipped over at the edge of the road, its front end—hood, windshield, and front wheels—reduced to an amorphous mass of crumpled metal. The two front doors had been unhinged and lay a few steps away from what remained of the car. Large pools of blood dotted the area.

A burly police officer with a thick, rust-colored beard and long, raven-black hair came toward them as he finished speaking into his walkie-talkie.

"We put the boy on a makeshift stretcher," said the officer, pointing to the right.

"Is he conscious?" asked Michelle, as she continued to carry the stretcher.

"He comes and goes." The police officer made a quick hand gesture, like a dismissal. "We've already sent the parents to the hospital." He hesitated for a second, then added in an almost inaudible whisper, "What was left of them."

Michelle continued to the spot she had been shown, Walter at her heels.

The boy lay on a long surfboard-like piece of wood that had been placed under one of the light poles.

"Okay." Michelle nodded toward Walter. She grabbed the end of the stretcher and said, "One...two...three." They pushed the stretcher down and lowered it to street level.

"Hey, champ," Michelle said with a crisp, clear voice, turning to the child who was opening and closing his eyes, murmuring something unintelligible. "Can you hear me? Tell me your first name." She turned toward Walter. "No responses."

"Not showing any head deformity," Walter said, doing his best to maintain a professional tone. "No bleeding."

"Okay." Michelle glanced at the boy's little body to confirm her colleague's assessment. "Let's put a C collar in place."

The boy moved his head toward her, as if following her voice.

"Hey, champ," Michelle said, snapping her fingers. "Does it hurt when I'm touching in your belly?"

The boy blinked. "N-no," he mumbled.

"No pain or rigidity," Michelle assessed. "Arms intact. Champ, we're going to lift you up now, okay? Walt? Three, two, one."

They hoisted the child onto the stretcher and carried him into the ambulance.

When the stretcher was secured to the hitching mechanism inside the vehicle, Walter closed the front door and signaled to the driver they were inside. After a few seconds, the ambulance activated its sirens and moved.

"Can you hear me?" Michelle snapped her fingers, but this time the child didn't respond. She tried calling him again, but had no better luck.

"Do a large-bore eighteen. Left AC. Go ahead and set me up a second line. Not showing injury to his chest. No deformity."

Walter inserted the IV into the child's arm and attached the tube to the fluid bag.

The boy moved. He opened his eyes and whispered something.

"Honey, can you hear me at all?"

"Wei," said the child. "My name's Wei."

"Wei." Michelle smiled. "It's a nice name. Short, easy to remember. I'm Michelle, and this is Walter."

The little boy looked at Walter, who waved at him.

"Wei, does it hurt when he touched you here?" Michelle touched the boy's sternum.

Wei shook his head.

"What about over here? No? It doesn't hurt? That's good. Very good. How old are you, Wei?"

"Seven," the boy said. He looked around. "Where... where am I?"

"You are in an ambulance, Wei. We're taking you to the hospital."

"Hospital?"

"Just to make sure you're okay. You don't have to worry about a thing. You're in good hands. I promise."

Wei blinked and looked around again. "Mom... Mom and Dad? Where are Mom and Dad?"

Michelle checked the IV. "They are in good hands too, Wei. You don't have to worry. Everything will be fine."

Wei's eyes rolled back, and he lost consciousness again.

"How long until we arrive?" asked Michelle.

Walter looked at his wristwatch. "Five minutes."

"Then let's call—"

"Where...where's the *Atlantis*?"

Michelle turned toward Wei. "What did you say, honey? Did you say *Atlantis*?"

"Yes." Wei started showing signs of restlessness. He tried to stand up.

"No, Wei." Michelle blocked him. "You gotta stay still. You can't move like that. You're going to hurt yourself. Do you understand?"

"It was here. I always keep it here."

"All right. Now I'm going to check your pockets, okay? But you gotta stay still. Promise?"

Michelle searched the boy's pockets but found nothing.

"There's nothing here, honey." Michelle glanced toward Wei, who had passed out again. "Wei? Can you hear me?"

"We're almost there, boss... I mean, Michelle." Walter pointed outside.

Michelle grabbed her walkie-talkie. "McLoyd Marion," she said. "Medferry omega 3-0-9."

"Medferry omega 3-0-9, McLoyd Marion, go ahead."

"McLoyd Marion, Medferry omega 3-0-9 inbound. Party, one. Seven-year-old male involved in a trauma, MVA, road accident, unwitnessed by pedestrians. Patient is showing a light head injury. He's sluggish, unreactive. Goes in and out of consciousness. Unresponsive at this time. ETA about four minutes."

"Copy that, Medferry omega 3-0-9. Over and out."

"*Atlantis*," Wei was murmuring, his brow furrowed. "I have to find the *Atlantis*. The last light. It's the last light. Can't lose it."

"We're almost there, champ," Michelle reassured him as she checked his pressure again. "You're going to be fine. We're almost there."

Michelle looked outside the window. They were approaching a large, light-gray building five floors high. "Okay, Walt. Let's get ready."

A couple minutes later, the ambulance pulled into the

bay area reserved for the emergency department. They lowered the stretcher and transported the boy inside the hospital.

They passed the lobby, headed down the first corridor on the left, and took Wei inside the intensive care unit.

"Seven-year-old boy," Michelle announced as she and Walter pushed the stretcher into the room. "Unknown trauma. Was involved with his parents in a car accident. Walt, go to the other side. Patient has superficial injuries to his arms and abdomen. Some abrasions to the right side of his forehead. We have an eighteen established, bolus in correctly. Pressure was sixty over twenty."

"Okay," said the doctor on duty, a big man with a duck-tail hairstyle and a frown that seemed sculpted into his forehead. "Let's move him on over."

Michelle and Walter moved Wei onto a gurney.

"Pressure?"

"Sixty over twenty."

"All right." The doctor turned to a nurse. "Margaret, keep that IV wide open. Okay, guys." The doctor nodded toward Michelle. "We'll take care of him now."

"Got it. We'll leave you to that." Michelle signaled for Walt to leave the room.

As soon as they were out of the hospital, Walter took a cigarette from his breast pocket and tried to light it. He couldn't. His hands shook so badly he almost dropped it to the floor.

"I'll get it," Michelle offered.

"Thanks."

Michelle used the lighter, then handed it back to Walt.

The young man pulled at the cigarette for a good three seconds, then he closed his eyes as he exhaled slowly.

"Better?"

Walter nodded. "Fuck yeah."

"Good for you."

The boy took a couple more puffs, then lightly tapped the cigarette with his index finger. "So, how did I do today?"

"I'm seeing progress."

"Yeah? What makes you say that?"

Michelle raised an eyebrow. "Well, for a start, you didn't throw up."

Walter let a nervous chuckle out. "Right, there's that."

"Look, it's okay to be nervous. I've told you. It gets easier after a while."

Walter nodded. "Promise?" he said, flicking his cigarette even though he didn't need to.

"Cross my heart."

"All right. Now that feels better." Walter pointed to the ambulance still parked in the bay. "Have you been doing this for long?"

Michelle shrugged. "Five years, give or take." She noticed her reflection in the ambulance's window. Even from that distance, she could see the deep shadows besieging her eyes, making her look ten years older. Her skin, usually a lustrous dark brown, was paler than usual.

She definitely needed a vacation.

"What did you do before?"

Michelle turned. "What was that?"

"Before the heart-pounding chase against time to save lives," Walter said, nodding toward the ambulance. "What did you do before that?"

Michelle glanced toward the hospital. "I worked in the

ICU, was a nurse for a couple years after my apprenticeship. You know, to get used to things."

"What made you want to work outside the triage room? Wanted a little more action?"

"Let's just say I preferred to breathe fresh air. Spending too much time in a hospital wears out your soul."

Walter made a half chuckle. Then he stared at his cigarette as if he'd suddenly realized something. "Hey, you want to take a drag?"

"Nope. Don't smoke."

"Really? Christ, you must be the first one in the whole team to nay a cigarette. What's that about?"

"My husband died of lung cancer."

The last drag went sideways for Walter. When he had finished coughing, he looked at Michelle with watery eyes. "Jesus. I... I'm sorry. I didn't mean to—"

"Relax." Michelle made a conciliatory gesture with her hand. "That was a long time ago."

Walter stared at the half-finished cigarette hesitantly. "Look, I can put it out in a half a sec if it bothers you."

"Nah. Don't mind me. Take a breather while you can."

Walter shifted his weight from one foot to the other. A long moment of silence followed, then the young man glanced toward the hospital entrance. "He didn't look too bad to me," he said. "The kid, I mean." He took another drag and waited for the cloud of smoke to disappear before talking again. "Remember the cop who talked to us on the street? You heard what he said about the parents?"

"I heard."

"And did you see the blood all around? Half the car was more pressed than a sardine can. If they were there in the..." Walter left the sentence hanging.

"Yeah." Michelle breathed in air that smelled like cheap

tobacco. She tried to swallow the lump in her throat, but couldn't.

MICHELLE FOUND the *Atlantis* two days later. It was the end of her shift, late in the evening. She was closing a retractable table from inside the service ambulance when she saw it.

"What's this?" She picked up the model from the ground and showed it to Walter. One wing was folded back, scratched and about to come off.

The young colleague walked over and studied the model.

"It's a Space Shuttle." He mimicked a shuttle lifting off. "You know, NASA's spaceships."

"Thanks, Walt. I know what a Space Shuttle is. What's it doing in here?"

Walter shrugged. "Don't know. Maybe someone dropped it when we were moving the stretcher or... Hey, wait a sec! Yeah. I remember. That kid we transported to the Saint Jones a few days ago. You know? Kind of small, dark hair, Asian traits. He kept saying the word *Atlantis*." Walter tapped the name *Atlantis* marked on the fuselage of the spacecraft. "I bet it's his."

"You mean the kid from the car accident?" Michelle said.

"That's him. The one we picked up on the interstate highway."

Michelle studied the *Atlantis*. "You're right. It must be his."

"Well, I'm pretty sure he forgot it." Walter pointed to the trash can. "Let's just dump it."

Michelle weighed the object for a moment. "No," she said. "I've got a better idea."

"Hey, Sasha." Michelle walked over to the nurses' station in the middle of the hallway and gave a big smile to the black woman intent on typing on the keyboard. "Did you miss me?"

Sasha looked up. Her brown eyes took a second to recognize her.

"My, oh, my." The nurse almost jumped onto her feet. "Michelle R. J. Jordan. The prodigal daughter is back. How are you doing, girl?" Sasha went around the counter and hugged her.

"Good." Michelle returned the hug. "What's the word?"

"Same old, same old." Sasha pointed to the other nurse who shared the small space in the middle of the hospital corridor with her. "Beth is still dumping half her salary on lottery tickets, hoping to buy her own island."

"Hilarious," Beth said dryly to Sasha, then looked at Michelle. "Hey, girl."

"Hey, Beth."

Sasha pointed to a nurse who was just coming out of a patient's room. "And Gloria here broke the world record for 'boyfriend's exposure.' It's what I call dumping a guy every other day. Right, Gloria? What number are you seeing now? Hmm? The seventh this month?"

"Ha-ha-ha, you're so funny, Sasha." Gloria rolled her eyes. "Brody is the third, if you need to know, and he's the right one."

"Believe it, sister," Sasha teased her. "Believe it."

Gloria raised her middle finger, then disappeared into another room.

"How about you?" asked Sasha, turning back to

Michelle. "Any news? We see less and less of you around here."

"Management has been treating us as rugs for the past couple months," said Michelle. "Double shifts and a crazy schedule. Between work and Ivory, I barely have enough time left to brush my teeth."

"Mm-hm." Sasha nodded sagely. "I hear you, sister. How's your little hurricane doing?"

"I'm struggling to keep up with her," Michelle said with a sigh. "She's growing at lightning speed. Bless the day God invented grandparents."

"Amen. Hey, if you need anything..."

"I know you've got my back. Thanks."

"Any time, girl."

Michelle rubbed her hands. "Look, are you busy?"

"Nah. It's been a slow day. What you need?"

"I brought you a child a few days ago. Seven years old, Asian. His name is Wei."

"Mm." Sasha looked into a thick binder. "Yes, he's still here."

"How is he?"

"Let me see." Sasha flipped through the pages quickly. "Here it is. Wei Wang. What do you want to know?"

"Is he stable?"

"Oh yes. As stable as a tripod. Passes all tests with flying colors. They stabilized him and did a CT scan. Nothing serious. Has a slight bruise, a broken arm, and a cracked rib. Physically, he's fine. Raya wants to do a couple final assessments before discharging him."

"You know anything about his parents? I think they were brought in just before him. Both involved in the same car accident."

Sasha shook her head. "They didn't make it," she said.

"Christ." Michelle cast a glance at the *Atlantis*. "Does he know?"

"Oh yeah," Sasha said. "Some guy from the Willom's Oath Institute told him yesterday."

Michelle felt a sudden heaviness at the base of her stomach. "Wait. Why did someone from the institute come?"

"The kid doesn't seem to have other relatives." Sasha closed the binder. "They've been looking for a while. Nothing. Complete void."

"Shit," Michelle said, putting a hand on her neck.

"I know."

Michelle cast a glance toward the hallway. "Can I see him?" she asked.

Sasha frowned. "Um, sure. What for?"

Michelle showed her the *Atlantis*. "On his way here, he kept asking about it. I found it a few minutes ago inside one of the rescue units."

Sasha's face lit up. "That's nice of you. Room twenty-two. He's alone for now."

"Thanks."

Michelle passed the nurses' station and walked through a less-trafficked section of the hospital. She entered room twenty-two and glanced around. There were three beds inside. Two were empty, with fresh sheets. Wei was lying on the bed closest to the window, on the opposite side of the entrance. His eyes were closed, his chest rising and falling slowly.

Michelle walked up to him, trying not to wake him. When she reached his bedside, she noticed his right arm was in a cast. He had a couple Band-Aids on his face and neck. Other than that, he seemed to be fine. When she thought about the state of his parent's car on the interstate, it was a miracle he was still alive.

She laid the Space Shuttle model on the nightstand beside the bed. She had tried to repair the broken wing with some tape, but the result had been rather depressing.

Michelle ran a hand through her curly hair and sighed. She was used to seeing bad accidents and people seriously wounded. It was part of her job, but no matter how many times she saw it, she never really got used to it. Seven years was not a good age to lose parents. That child's life would never be the same.

"Good luck," she whispered. She turned and headed for the exit.

"I remember you."

Michelle turned and found Wei's eyes staring back at her.

"Hey," she said. "Thought you were sleeping."

"You're the ambulance lady." Wei propped himself up on an elbow. "You're Michelle."

"That's right." Michelle retraced her steps to the bed. "I brought your toy, the *Atlantis*. It was in the ambulance."

"It's not a toy," the boy said stiffly. "It's a reusable, rocket-launched spacecraft designed to go into orbit."

Michelle stared at him. "Well, it sure sounds cooler when you put it that way."

The boy leaned out to pick up the *Atlantis*, then stopped abruptly. He shut his eyes and groaned.

"Hold on." Michelle picked up the model and placed it in the boy's hand.

"It's broken," Wei noticed, unblinking. He didn't look sad or disappointed. His face was devoid of emotions.

"I'm sorry," said Michelle. "The wing must have broken when it fell."

"Or in the accident," Wei said.

"Or in the accident," Michelle echoed.

The boy looked away from the *Atlantis* and stared out the window. "They're dead, you know." The sound of a siren broke the silence. "My parents."

Michelle nodded slowly. She cast a glance toward the hallway, then picked up a chair and placed it beside the bed.

"Mind if I stay? Chat with you a little?"

"Sure, you can stay," Wei said. "I like the way you smell."

Michelle raised her chin. "You like the way I smell?"

"Yes. You smell like petrichor."

"I'm sorry, like *what*?"

"Petrichor," Wei repeated. "It's an earthy scent produced when rain falls on dry soil. It's a good thing," he added, as if to reassure her. "Everyone likes the scent of rain because our ancestors relied on rainy weather for survival."

Michelle raised her eyebrows. "Wow. How do you know that stuff?"

Wei shrugged. "I don't know. I like to read."

Michelle settled on the chair. She let a few seconds pass, looking for reassuring words to say to him. She found none.

"You know, I don't talk to other people." Wei pointed to the hallway. "Mom told me I'm not supposed to talk to strangers."

"You are talking to me though."

"You're different."

"How so?"

"You have a green light."

"Green light?" Michelle repeated, confused.

"I know your name," Wei explained. "You brought me the *Atlantis*. You have a green light."

Michelle looked at the Space Shuttle with a broken wing and suddenly felt guilty. She didn't know exactly why; perhaps because she should have fixed the model before giving it to Wei, or maybe because she could have shown up with a brand-new one.

It was a silly thought, considering that the boy's parents had just died, but it was all she could think about.

"I'm sorry about your parents," said Michelle, her hands resting on her knees.

"Why?" asked Wei, as if finding her sorrow something strange and inexplicable. "You didn't even know them."

That was a fair question, and one who you wouldn't expect from a seven-year-old child. Michelle opened her mouth, but found nothing else to add except, "You're right. I didn't."

Wei stared straight ahead, his eyes glassy. "The man with the white coat said the same," he said. "That he was sorry. So did the priest, and a couple doctors who came here after I woke up. They were all sorry." Wei glanced at the broken wing of the *Atlantis*. "Mom says that being sorry won't get the spilled milk back inside the bottle."

Michelle stared at the boy. Another answer she hadn't expected.

He must still be in shock.

Experience told her that when it came to breaking bad news, such as the death of parents, children had to be treated like adults. The news had to be delivered clearly, without sugar coating. Each child absorbed the blow differently. Most ignored the facts for a while. They would ask for a cookie, or to watch television. Others, if they grasped the full gravity of what had happened, might cry or shut down.

However, judging by the way Wei was taking it, he didn't seem to react as most children would. He seemed to have already passed the phase of mourning, and was now analyzing the whole situation in cold detachment. Maybe it was his way of dealing with the pain.

"My parents also died in a car accident," Michelle said. "I was about your age when it happened."

By the time the sentence was out of her mouth, she didn't know why she had spoken it. It just felt like it was the best thing she could say. Maybe that was why she was there. Not to return the *Atlantis*, but because she knew how that child felt.

"Were you sorry?" Wei asked.

"No," Michelle said. "I was angry. Furious. And I was scared." She looked up and met Wei's eyes. "It's okay to be scared."

"Dad says fear is a compass. It marks the direction we need to follow to become a better version of ourselves."

"Mmm, yeah." Michelle rubbed her hands on her legs. "Your father was not wrong."

Wei laid the *Atlantis* on the bed. "A lady from L.A. is coming to pick me up in a few days," he said, as if making an observation about the weather. "Her name is Gloria Powell. She has other children in her institution..." Wei left the sentence hanging for a few seconds, then added, "You know, children without parents."

"I'm sure she will take good care of you."

"I don't need her to. I know how to take care of myself."

"I'm sure you do. Well, then she'll have less work. Look, I want to give you something." Michelle fished a business card from her wallet and handed it to Wei. "This is my private number. If you need anything, call me."

"Okay." Wei took the card and studied it for a moment, then picked up the *Atlantis* again. He studied it with a strange look, eyes twitching as if he was conflicted about something.

"If you want, I can buy you a new one," Michelle told him, interpreting his expression as sadness.

"No," Wei said. "I think it broke for a reason."

"What do you mean?"

"The *Atlantis* will never fly again," Wei said. "The space program we knew is dead. It represents the past. If we want to go back up there, we will need something else, something better."

"Wei, what are you talking about?"

"About space," the boy said, looking annoyed that Michelle couldn't follow him. "To get back there, we will need a better way."

"Wei?"

"What?"

"The *Atlantis*," Michelle said. "If you keep squeezing it like that, you're going to—"

The other wing of the model broke off with a snap. Wei looked at the Space Shuttle as if he realized only then that he had been holding it the whole time.

"Are you hurt?" Michelle leaned forward. "Let me see."

"I'm fine," Wei said. He threw the *Atlantis* into the garbage can.

Michelle stared at him in mute stupor. There was something in his gaze that she couldn't decipher. A sparkle, an unspoken resolution that seemed out of place on his child-like face.

Wei had been studying the *Atlantis* with his eyes narrowed to slits. It almost looked as if he was trying to solve a puzzle.

3

ANURADHA

LOS ANGELES, CLAIR SPRING CHILDREN'S
HOME

2013

The soft glow of the laptop faintly illuminated the room otherwise shrouded in darkness. Miss Gloria Powell settled back in her chair as she finished filling out a form full of graphics, letters, and numbers.

After a few minutes, she snorted with disgust and pushed aside a stack of papers so huge it took up one-third of the desk.

The woman absently moved her hand to grasp the cup on the table.

"Jesus Christ!" Miss Powell cursed after spitting out hot coffee. The brown liquid went all over the monitor. She cursed again and looked around in search of a paper napkin to sop up the spreading liquid. She found none.

After looking through her pockets, she used a blank sheet of paper from the table.

When she was done drying the last keyboard button, she threw the dirty paper in the trash can. She then stood and turned to go to the restroom—when the alarm she had set a few hours before rang.

"What time is it?" she asked, as if expecting an answer from someone. She scratched her frizzy hair, recovered the alarm clock shaped like a hamburger from the ocean of paper on her desk, and turned it off.

She moved the mouse and typed a password.

After a few moments, an icon on the desktop glowed. Miss Powell checked the time on her laptop. She shook her head, cursed once more, then clicked the left mouse button with a sigh.

The face of a woman with dark skin, grey eyes, and an aquiline nose appeared on the monitor. She had long, dark hair tied back in a long braid that stretched beyond the borders of the screen. Her skin was rough and hazel brown, as if she had worked for years under the hot midday sun.

"Miss Powell, can you hear me?" the newcomer asked as she adjusted her webcam.

"Yes, I hear you loud and clear," Miss Powell confirmed while clearing her throat.

"I'm Dr. Anuradha Galacta, from the Jet Propulsion Laboratory," the woman continued. "Thank you for your time. I really appreciate it."

"Of course. No problem," Miss Powell said, as she fidgeted in her chair to find a more comfortable position. "I read your e-mail last night and I must say I didn't expect to see you personally today. I mean, after checking your profile, I was expecting a call from your secretary or something like that."

"A secretary?" Anuradha repeated, looking amused. "Well, I can't say it wouldn't be nice to have one, but I assure you that NASA's funds don't justify such a luxury." She waited a few seconds and then added, indicating the stack of papers, "Judging from what I see there, though, it seems you could definitely use one. Did I catch you at a bad moment?"

"Not at all." Miss Powell shook her head while awkwardly moving a stack of papers. "So," she said when she cleared enough space to rest her elbows on the desk, "to what do we owe the honor? Your e-mail mentioned my kids' letters."

"Right," Anuradha confirmed while fiddling with a pencil, moving it back and forth from one finger to another.

Miss Powell scratched her cheek as she stared blankly at the screen. "You know, I remember when I was ten, I sent you guys at the JPL a letter with my ideas on how to colonize Venus: get to the planet's surface with a huge umbrella made of diamonds to protect us from the acid rain."

"Sounds like a promising start to me," Anuradha said. "Your suggestion has been noted. If you come up with similar solutions to overcome the lack of oxygen, the atmospheric pressure, and the impossibly high temperature, I see no reason why you shouldn't send us your résumé. We constantly need original ideas."

Miss Powell laughed heartily as she got rid of another stack of papers, pushing them into a drawer. "So they say," she answered, showing a white, toothy grin. "I never knew who he or she was, but a few days after sending the letter, I received a huge picture book with a description of all the planets of the solar system. I still have it tucked away somewhere in my basement. That book literally blew me away. I believe I've never written back to you guys to thank you for the gift."

"Don't mention it." Anuradha leaned forward in her

chair. "What an interesting story. I guess that's why you ask your kids to send us their ideas."

"Exactly, and some of your colleagues always send us something. You know—stickers, calendars, star charts, pamphlets, magazines, that sort of thing. It's nice to have that kind of attention, especially in places like this, if you get what I mean." Miss Powell looked around her, as if that gesture explained what she meant better than any words. "However, this is the very first time we've received a call from a PhD at MIT."

"Actually, this call is the result of a... Well, I guess *misplacement* is the correct word," Anuradha said as she kept her pencil moving between her fingers. "The package with your letters arrived on my desk by chance. Imagine my surprise when I found what was inside: a dozen proposals suggesting how to boldly go where no man has gone before."

"Are you serious? By chance?" asked Miss Powell. "Well, maybe at the JPL someone *really* thought that you needed new perspectives, *original ideas*, as you said. Don't you think?"

Both of them laughed, but Anuradha's face seemed to tense. Her smile was the first to fade.

"It may well be, yes," she said, drumming her nails on the arm of the chair, "and honestly I've called you because of one of these ideas. I hope... Well, I hope you can help me figure this issue out. To tell you the truth, this thing is giving me a headache."

"You're still talking about the kids' letters?"

"Absolutely."

"I have no idea what you're referring to, but if I can be of any help—"

"Thanks, I really appreciate it," Anuradha cut her off,

suddenly becoming serious. "I seem to understand that your institution sends the letters without the supervision of an adult. I mean, none of your staff usually puts his or her ideas in one of the kids' letters, right?"

"Dr. Galacta, my *staff* is composed of my sisters and I. And we're not included in the senders list."

"No one else corrects or checks their work?"

"Well, no. The letter is an assignment the kids complete in class in a couple of hours. When they're done, we collect the letters and send them on."

"I understand," said Anuradha, suddenly thoughtful. "If that's true, you've just made this conversation a lot more interesting."

"What do you mean?"

"Most of the letters you sent us were...let's just use the word *normal*. One portrayed a banana-shaped spacecraft powered by flatulence, while another mentioned a bunch of astronauts riding comets. The bolder among them suggested hitting a spaceship with a giant baseball bat to allow it to exceed the speed of light. All stuff you expect to hear from kids, nothing strange in this, and yet... There is one letter I just can't explain."

"Which letter is that?"

Anuradha took a sheet near her and read, "It's signed *Wei*."

"Wei?" Miss Powell repeated. "Oh, yes! Wei Wang. He arrived a few weeks ago here at the institute. What's so interesting about his letter?"

"First, let me ask you a question," Anuradha said, raising her hand. "The kids were supposed to send their proposals on how to travel among the stars. Is that right?"

"Yes, that was the point."

"Right. This Wei sent us ten reasons why we *can't* do it."

Miss Powell looked puzzled for a moment, then she said, "Let me get this straight. You called because an eight-year-old boy didn't do his homework properly?"

Anuradha shook her head. "Of course not. That's not the point. What I wanted... Wait a second! You said *eight-year-old*?"

"That's what I said."

"I thought your institute takes care of only ten-year-old boys or older."

"That's correct, but we are temporarily entrusted with some younger cases if the circumstances require it."

"I see," whispered Anuradha.

"But I don't," said Miss Powell, folding her arms across her chest and studying the other woman. "I don't understand what is—"

"Is it possible to see this boy, Wei?" Anuradha interrupted her.

"To see Wei?" Miss Powell slowly repeated. "How do you mean?"

"I'd like to see him. Can you arrange a meeting with the child tomorrow, maybe?"

"What? I... No, I'm afraid it's not possible. Wei will leave the institute tomorrow morning. I've already said his staying here was temporary. But why would you—"

"Excuse me, do you know where he'll be transferred?"

"Well...yes, actually." She paused. Anuradha's questions and pushy tone were making her uncomfortable. "The procedure in these cases is clear," Miss Powell continued after clearing her throat. "Wei will be transferred to an institution equipped to meet his special needs."

"What special needs?"

"Dr. Galacta, with all due respect, I think I've already

said more than enough. Excuse me, but we're dealing with confidential information here."

"My apologies," Anuradha said, looking embarrassed. "I shouldn't have been so pushy. I just got carried away. This whole thing made me curious."

"Never mind," said Miss Powell with a dismissive wave of her hand. "Just tell me why you're so interested in the child's letter."

"I'll show you why. Open the file I've just sent you. It's Wei's assignment."

Miss Powell did as she was told and started reading. After thirty seconds of silence, she said, "I don't understand."

"That makes two of us," said Anuradha.

Miss Powell continued to read the document in silence. When she looked back at the other woman, her expression was somewhere between surprise and disappointment.

"So, what do you think?" asked Anuradha.

"I think the kid's spelling is a disaster."

"That's it? What about the *content* of the letter?"

"I'd say that today's kids can give a whole new dimension to the term *plagiarism*. Isn't it obvious? He clearly copied sentences here and there and tried to make some sense out of them."

Anuradha shook her head. "No, that's not it," she said. "This is an original piece of work, with an introduction, a development, and a conclusion that complete each part of the paper. Despite the text's appearance, whoever wrote it shows remarkable knowledge and impressive analytic capabilities."

"What? Are you kidding me?" Miss Powell laughed as she nervously scratched her elbow. "I mean, are you suggesting that the child actually knows what he's talking about? Don't you think you're exaggerating this whole thing? Here I read terms like *muscle atrophy*, *microgravity*, *ion thruster*, and *nuclear fission*. Eight-year-olds have difficulty understanding the concept of a hot-air balloon, for God's sake!"

"Fine. Then tell me what to make of it."

"I don't know! Maybe one of the older kids helped him."

"Have some of them taken courses in astrophysics or nuclear engineering recently?"

Miss Powell snorted. "And I thought I was the funny one."

"You understand my dilemma now? I'm reading a six-page essay filled with specialist terminology. This is clearly an unfamiliar subject for the average adult and still, at the end of the letter, is the signature of an eight-year-old kid. Put yourself in my shoes. What would you do?"

"Look." Miss Powell shifted in her chair. "I understand the situation, but I assure you Wei couldn't have written that stuff. Not in a million years."

"Why not?"

"Because I know him. I've spoken with him, or at least tried to. He's been as talkative as a fish. He likes to stay by himself, away from other kids. He doesn't want to play or get involved in the institute's life and... Well, we had a couple incidents a few days ago involving him and two other kids." Miss Powell closed her eyes for a second. She waved her hand, as if dismissing a disturbing thought, then added, "Plus, to be completely honest with you, he doesn't seem to be very clever."

"Don't you see, all that you just said makes the whole thing more fascinating? Just think. What if Wei really wrote that letter?"

Miss Powell checked once again the file sent by

Anuradha, then nodded. "Well, if nothing else, I understand why you're so interested in seeing the boy," she said. "There is obviously something weird going on. If I were you, I'd want an answer. A damn good one."

Anuradha sensed the hesitation in her voice. She stopped playing with her pencil and inspected the screen.

"Look, I know I'm asking a lot. I know you have your rules to follow, and I realize I'm only acting out of curiosity, but *please* try to look at the bigger picture, try to do the right thing. Miss Powell... Gloria... I really just need to talk with Wei for a few minutes and—"

"I'm sorry, I can't." Miss Powell stood up from her chair, her expression set.

Anuradha bit her lips, looking uncertain about what to say.

"I can't just ignore the institute's rules," Miss Powell added as she grabbed the cup of hot coffee and walked toward the exit door. Anuradha said something, but the other interrupted her suddenly. "What I *can* do is get another cup of coffee from the kitchen downstairs and leave the door open to get some fresh air in the room. We will continue this conversation in exactly ten minutes." She blinked. "See you in ten, Doctor."

ANURADHA STARED at the open door for half a minute. When she snapped out of her surprise, she couldn't suppress a grin.

"Outstanding," she muttered while unconsciously continuing to fiddle with her pencil.

A minute passed that seemed to stretch into eternity. Then she heard footsteps approaching, followed by silence.

A figure appeared in the doorway, impossible to identify because of the dim light.

"Come on in." Anuradha's heart was slamming against her sternum.

The figure crossed the threshold of the room with a small jump, as if to avoid something on the floor. Anuradha leaned forward, almost touching the screen with her nose, then smiled.

"Hello. You're Wei, right?"

The little boy signified assent with a single vertical movement of his head.

"It's nice to meet you. Call me Anu." She waved both hands. "How about you sit down here and have a little chat with me?"

Wei didn't answer. He simply walked gingerly toward the laptop that was displaying Anuradha's smiling face. He stared for a few seconds at the woman's face with his small almond eyes, then tilted his head to the right, until it rested nearly on his shoulder.

"I'm Miss Powell's friend," Anuradha said, deliberately stressing each word. "I have read your letter, the one you sent to the JPL a few days ago, and I wanted to let you know that..."

The boy looked away from the monitor and started staring at the sheets spread all over the desk. He picked up a couple of them and read, apparently no longer interested in the speaking laptop.

"Wei? Can you hear me?"

The boy put the papers down, looked around, took the burger-shaped alarm clock from the table and put it in his pocket. Anuradha spoke, but something on the other side of the room attracted the kid's attention.

"Wei, where are you going? Wei?"

The boy disappeared from the screen, heedless of the woman's calls. She tried to lean forward to follow his movements, but without success. The boy had vanished.

For a few seconds she heard noises coming from somewhere in the room. Then something fell on the floor, followed by a sharp noise.

"Wei!" called Anuradha. The child appeared again on the screen. He was rummaging through Miss Powell's things, deaf to Anuradha's calling.

Suddenly the woman's cell phone came to life, filling the air with the bright notes of "*La donna è mobile.*" Anuradha jumped off her chair, taken aback, and looked around for the source of the sound. When she found the cell phone, she turned it off, annoyed. She then looked back at the screen. Surprisingly, Wei was returning her gaze. The boy cocked his head and stared at the woman, as if he was seeing her for the very first time. He sat down on the chair left by Miss Powell and started typing on the keyboard.

Anuradha read the message several times, but it took her several seconds to understand it. In a small window, the sentence, *I love Verdi,* had appeared.

Finally, a spark lit up in her mind. She could connect it with the ringing of her cell phone.

"You love Verdi?" she asked, puzzled.

The child nodded briskly.

Anuradha read the message again, but her thoughts were suddenly interrupted. Another message appeared.

Do you like him?

From her laptop a powerful, magnificent, and completely unexpected music broke out. Without even thinking, Anuradha whispered incredulously, "Richard Wagner?"

The child clapped his hands, visibly pleased. A new message popped up.

Your turn.

Anuradha was speechless. Willy-nilly, she found herself amid a musical competition against an eight-year-old child. This to her proved without a doubt that Wei was nothing like the average eight-year-old. She decided to treat him as the special person he had proved to be.

"Okay, listen up. If you can't guess the next tune, I'll win and you'll answer all my questions. What do you say?"

The boy covered his ears with both hands, closed his mouth and eyes, and stood for a few moments without moving. A smirk appeared on his face, then he typed one word: *OK.*

Anuradha fumbled for a moment with the mouse and keyboard. After a few seconds, she finally found what she was looking for.

Wei waited anxiously, as if someone was about to serve him a giant piece of chocolate cake.

Sweet, relaxed, and poetic notes flooded the room like a slow but inevitable magma of gentle sounds intertwining with each other. Wei held his breath. He was concentrating now, two deep vertical lines grooving his forehead just above his eyes. The unique melody soon captured the child. Anuradha imagined this tune was foreign to anything he had ever heard before. After two and a half intense minutes, the melody uttered its last note.

Wei wiped his eyes with his sleeve. *You won. Who made it?* the boy wrote.

"Ennio Morricone, an Italian composer. The melody appeared in my favorite movie, *The Legend of 1900.*"

The child nodded with a serious look on his face, as if he

was storing a fundamental notion. He settled back in his chair and waited. Anuradha knew it was now her turn.

"You have strange interests for a boy your age, Wei. Music seems to be only one of these. I imagine that on the list of things that you like there's also a place for astronomy, isn't there?"

Wei placed his forefinger on his right cheek, then nodded.

"Did you write that letter yourself?" Anuradha asked.

The boy nodded again.

"Well, if that's so, I'm really curious to know why you believe we can't travel to the stars."

Wei cocked his head to one side, then slowly tapped on the keyboard.

We can, but we don't want to.

That answer puzzled Anuradha. "I don't understand. Why wouldn't we want to? I work with thousands of people who devote their lives to this purpose. You should know this, everyone knows it. You know what NASA is? The people who work for it? What they've done? Miss Powell didn't explain all of this to you?"

The child looked at her straight in the eye. Anuradha looked back at him without blinking. After a few moments, the child leaned toward the keyboard and started typing again.

The woman watched the words forming quickly, one after the other. Without realizing it, she held her breath. Once she finished reading the answer, the pencil fell from her hand with a clatter. She didn't bother to pick it up.

"Well, well, well. Look who we have here!"

Anuradha shook herself out of her trance as she watched Miss Powell darting into the room.

"You should not be here, you rascal!" she said to Wei. "Come on, let's go back to your room."

Anuradha watched Miss Powell trying to hold Wei's hand, but the child pulled away, screaming.

"All right, all right." Miss Powell held up her hands. "Walk by yourself then. Come on."

Wei walked toward the door, as silent as the grave. Miss Powell sighed and followed him at a distance.

When she came back, she closed the door behind her. "So what happened? Did he do it? Did he talk? That alone would be a miracle."

"Not a word," said Anuradha absently as she kept staring at the last message written by Wei.

Miss Powell crossed her arms and shook her head. "Come on, don't be too hard on yourself," she said, misunderstanding Anuradha's expression. "It was predictable. I told you that the child clearly has issues. So, I guess the mystery surrounding the letter has been solved."

"I guess so," whispered Anuradha.

"So...he didn't write it, right?"

Anuradha looked at the other woman. Then she swallowed and shook her head. "On the contrary," she said, her eyes now bright with excitement. "Now I'm *sure* it was him who wrote it."

Miss Powell listened in round-eyed silence. "What?" she finally burst. "How do you know that? You just said he didn't say a word!"

"You're right. Wei doesn't seem very inclined to talk. But I assure you I established a connection. There's no doubt the kid is special, though I don't believe he needs the attention you spoke of. He's extremely knowledgeable and incredibly smart. I've never seen anyone like him."

Miss Powell threw her hands up in frustration. "All right,

all right... Let's say you've established a connection, what-ever that means. What are you saying, exactly? That the kid's good with equations?"

Anuradha bent down and picked her pencil up from the floor, again moving it from one finger to another, an enig-matic smile on her face.

"No, Miss Powell. What I'm saying is that with all proba-bility, I've just met the Einstein of the twenty-first century."

4

EVANGELINE

PASADENA, DANCES WITH WAFFLES
RESTAURANT

2015

Wei was sipping his hot chocolate while his fingers moved at the speed of light over his new tablet, a present he got the previous month for his tenth birthday.

After he finished drinking, he took a pen from the backpack, then a flashlight and a handful of white sheets. Although the restaurant was very well lit, Wei turned the flashlight on, pointed it at one of the sheets, and began to write.

After about half an hour, he put his pen and the flashlight down and rummaged once more in his backpack.

Eventually he found what he was looking for: an ivory-colored cap. He quickly put it on.

Around him the few customers inside the restaurant were busy talking about the weather, the government, and everything that the big TV over the bar showed on its flat screen.

The TV was now broadcasting a documentary that attracted his attention. The boy put down the tablet, moved the sheets aside, and folded his arms across his chest, his head resting nearly on one shoulder and his almond-shaped eyes wide open with sharp curiosity.

"Created with the intent of warning the public about the harmful impact that space exploration has had on human civilization, LAND is a fierce organization backed by politicians, journalists, scientists, and simple volunteers scattered throughout the states."

Wei's attention was captured by the symbol of the organization the reporter was speaking about: a man and a woman kneeling on opposite sides of a sphere enclosing the symbols of the four elements. The boy pulled a sheet toward him and wrote something as he continued to follow the documentary.

"When Douglas J. R. Woodside founded LAND in the financial district of Pasadena, he felt as though he was called to fulfill a mission. Born in Dallas, Texas, in November 1979, Woodside has spent much of his youth volunteering for the elderly and caring for disabled people. After completing his Master's in Public Relations and a PhD in Advanced Strategies of Communication, he dedicated his time to those whom he called *the forgotten*. He has since been involved in numerous projects around the world supported by FARON, Amnesty Confederation, and Global Nurturing. After living for some time on the five continents, comparing poverty and hardship in the most diverse peoples and cultures, Woodside developed the idea that humanity was at a crossroads, a moment in which our civilization must decide what is really important for its survival and what needs to be abandoned."

The face of a handsome man with big green eyes, high cheekbones, dark hair, and an intriguing smile appeared on the screen. Douglas Woodside seemed comfortable under the light of the studio that made him shine like the most prestigious piece of a diamond collection.

"Mr. Woodside, your organization—which some refer to as a movement—has lately grown larger and more powerful," a beautiful journalist sitting in front of him was saying, "and your message seems to gather more and more supporters and sympathizers every day. On the other hand, you have also made many enemies. Many of them call LAND the *anti-NASA*. These people find your message limited and wrong, or simply not making any sense at all. A few days ago, the astrophysicist Neil MacDonald Tyron called you, and I quote, 'a well-dressed snake oil salesman,' end quote. How do you feel about that?"

Douglas Woodside crossed his arms and put on a condescending smile. "Wendy, I think the contempt these people show toward me and my organization is reassuring."

"I'm sorry. You said *reassuring*?"

"I did. It means that my message has reached their homes, their families, and that it has become part of their lives. The first step in solving any problem is awareness. The second step is admission."

"I guess the problem you're referring to, and the main reason LAND exists, is space exploration."

"What I'm referring to, Wendy, is a dream that became a nightmare. A toxic fantasy that has clouded the intentions of some of our best minds and that has required the diversion of billions of dollars that could have been used for more constructive purposes. Things we really need."

"Such as?" Wendy pressed him.

Woodside breathed in and looked the journalist right in her eye. "What about homes, tractors, water wells, hospitals, a school in the Congo, a research center to cure cancer in California, a highway in Bangladesh, a pair of jeans that don't fade, automatic hair clips, or a longer and more resistant toilet roll?" Woodside looked up pleadingly. "For God's sake," he went on, spreading his arms, "any of these things is more valuable than giving a blank check to an imbecile with a white coat and asking him to build a twelve-million-dollar spacesuit for another imbecile who'll be satisfied when he looks like a giant snowman."

The reporter nodded. "So, what you're basically saying is that if we had not gone to the moon, we could have solved world poverty."

"It's never that simple," Woodside replied calmly, with a wave of his hand. "The money invested for the *Apollo* program wouldn't have met the food needs of Zimbabwe, let alone those of the hundreds of millions of people who still eat only once a day and will continue to do so for the rest of their lives."

Woodside paused for a few seconds. Then he looked straight at the camera lens that had a flashing red light, as though that object was his last friend left on Earth. "And yet, try to think of the energy, the tenacity, and the resources of the thousands of people that have made the *Apollo* program an undeniably massive undertaking, albeit completely useless and expensive. Try to re-invest these resources in everyday problems, problems that we face here on Earth, and I'm sure that today we would have a lot more than a handful of useless lunar rocks."

Wendy, the journalist, took her glasses off and looked directly at Woodside. "Is it possible that for you there's nothing to be salvaged from what many believe to be humanity's greatest achievement?"

"My grandma used to say that the meat that fell on the floor shouldn't be trashed, but given to the dog. I think it was her way of saying that we can see the bright side in every situation, if we try to look carefully enough." Woodside smiled grimly. "Let me think. You first mentioned NASA. Well, I feel compelled to admit that if, up to this point, we hadn't spent around six hundred billion dollars to finance it—that is, more or less Saudi Arabia's annual GDP —surely we would not have microwave ovens."

Those who were following the interview burst out laughing. Wei was frowning. While listening to the television, he took an object that looked like a large walnut out of his backpack. He turned it in his hands for a while and then put it back with a strange grimace on his face. When he turned to continue watching the interview, a tall woman with broad shoulders, massive cheeks, and eyes as big as ripe cherries obstructed his view.

"Would you like another glass of chocolate, honey?"

The server had appeared to his right. She had a wide and bright smile on her face, the dull expression that people use with small, helpless, cute creatures in the zoo.

Wei touched his tablet a few times and showed the stranger the screen.

"'No,'" the server read, frowning. She placed the coffee pot she was carrying on the table and looked closely at Wei, further widening her already generous smile. "Are you sure, honey?" she asked in a shrilly voice. "Next one is on the house."

Wei gave up trying to follow the documentary. He glanced at the big woman with annoyance and then turned his attention back to the tablet, touching it occasionally.

"Are you all alone?" the server asked suddenly, not noticing Wei's attempt to completely ignore her. She looked around, her expression a mix between concern and curiosity.

Wei did not answer. He just continued what he was doing while hoping the server would eventually leave him alone.

"Where is your mother, honey?" In an unexpectedly bold act, the woman moved with the clear intention of sitting down in front of him. It was in that very moment that the boy couldn't take it anymore. He wrote something on his tablet and showed it to the intruder before she could sit down.

"'She's six feet underground,'" she murmured. She didn't immediately grasp the meaning of the sentence. Then she gaped at him.

The server stood for a moment in a strange position, her bottom almost on the seat with her knees already bent but her back still straight. She seemed bewildered by the boy's answer, too surprised to decide what to do next.

Wei was staring at her with a severe, almost disgusted expression, as though she were the biggest cockroach on the planet. He waved his hand, pointing insistently at another table.

After seconds of complete silence, the server finally grabbed the coffee pot and began moving away from the seat with a dazed expression, like someone looking for a quick way to get out of an embarrassing situation.

Wei was happy to help her out. He pulled a ten-dollar bill from his pocket and quickly put it in her apron. She watched without saying a word as the boy nodded and gave her a pat on the butt that made her squeak.

"'Keep the change, honey,'" read the speechless server

before leaving his table, looking around embarrassed and confused.

Wei turned to watch the TV but realized that the interview was over. The screen was now showing what seemed like a huge construction yard, with countless cranes that crowded the horizon and an army of hardhats swarming around everywhere.

"...and the Korean government decided earlier this year to speed up the construction plan. We spoke with several engineers here and most of them are confident that Saemangeum City will welcome its first family long before..."

Suddenly the restaurant's door slammed open. A slender teenage girl with long, straw-colored hair appeared in the doorway, panting heavily. Heads turned to watch the newcomer. She looked around with urgency, pointed to a guy sitting at a nearby table, and darted toward him.

Wei, distracted by the frenzy, saw her speaking to some customers, but none of them seemed interested in what she was saying.

After a few minutes, the boy lost interest in the strange girl and turned to watch the TV. The report about the city in construction was over, replaced by news describing a new foundation that was gaining legions of teenage aficionado in Japan. Wei shook his head, closed his eyes, and returned to his reading.

Meanwhile, the girl kept walking around, her face tense and impatient. Whatever she was trying to do, she didn't seem to have any luck. After speaking with half a dozen people, she finally found someone who nodded with a smile and pointed to Wei.

The girl thanked the customer and quickly headed toward the table where the boy was reading. Wei was so concentrated that he didn't even notice her sit down with a sigh in front of him.

"Hey. What's up? You're the climber guy, right?"

Wei nearly jumped out of his skin. The girl was looking at him with beautiful blue eyes.

Wei's throat felt swollen. He opened and closed his eyes, his mouth half open. He studied the girl's freckles, a constellation of small brownish spots gracing her nose and cheeks. Her hair was a waterfall of pale-yellow lines flowing over her shoulders.

Wei swallowed. His ears were red and itchy, as though an invisible needle was piercing them repeatedly. Without really understanding why, his stomach felt weird—somehow heavy—and his mouth was dry. He cleared his throat and scratched his ears, looking away from the stranger.

"Look, I really need your help!" the girl went on, looking at him with a pleading expression. "I'm Evangeline. Kruscha was following that stupid bird and... Oh, I'm sorry! Kruscha is my chinchilla, you know, a very stupid chinchilla, but still... Well, that moron followed the damned bird up a tree. I don't even know how the hell he got there on his own. He's short and fat and... Anyway, now he's over there on that branch. He can't get off on his own and he's scared to death. I'm afraid he'll fall if we don't do something quickly. Nobody wants to help me! Please, please, you're my only hope!"

Wei realized that the buzz coming from Evangeline's mouth was probably some sort of request, but other than that, he didn't understand a single word of what she had said. And he didn't care.

After pulling himself together from the initial surprise, his brain worked hard and fast to forget her gibberish.

He touched his tablet and showed it to the girl without a word, waiting for a response.

"'I'm deaf and dumb'... What does that mean?" Evangeline asked, pointing to the screen.

Wei shrugged and went back to his reading.

The girl didn't move.

"Look, he told me you'd listen! Aren't you Wei?"

The boy stopped reading, his eyes wide open.

Who told you my name? immediately appeared on his tablet.

"I thought you were deaf. I hate liars!" Evangeline scoffed. "I'll forgive you only if you get up on that branch and save Kruscha. That's all I want."

Wei bit the inside of his cheek, then took a deep breath, picked up his pen, and began to write fast, his forehead almost touching the paper.

"Well?" Evangeline said, impatient. "At least say something!"

I'm busy, typed Wei, waving the tablet under her nose.

"It's a matter of five minutes. Kruscha is right outside and—"

Get lost!

"He needs you, don't you understand?"

Not listening.

Evangeline stood up, took off one of her shoes, and beat it on the table.

Wei and everyone around turned to look at her.

STOP IT! The boy's face was both angry and frustrated.

Evangeline stopped, took off the other shoe, and slammed both of them on the table.

"Hey, what the hell is going on over there?" asked the server who was serving a nearby table.

"It's a matter between me and my boyfriend," Evangeline shouted in reply, indicating Wei with a shoe. "Stay out of it!"

Wei's face and neck went completely red, his jaw wide open. He couldn't believe what the crazy girl had just said.

However, it seemed to the customers a normal enough reason. They turned away and went on with their own conversations.

"I can go on forever, you know?" Evangeline said with a triumphant smile.

Wei could have just picked up his belongings and left the place, but he didn't want to be forced out by the girl's nonsense. It would have been like giving up. He covered his ears, closed his eyes, and waited for the girl to go bother someone else.

He remained still for a minute and a half. After a while, he no longer felt the girl's presence and slowly opened his eyes.

Wei smiled, satisfied. There was no one in front of him. He was finally alone.

The boy breathed a sigh of relief and settled back in his chair to go back to his reading, but he realized that there was nothing on the table. His tablet had disappeared.

"'The Pheno-phenomenology of Spirit'? What the hell is this?"

Wei turned his head and saw Evangeline holding his tablet, absorbed in the reading.

"Hey!" shouted the boy, flustered.

"Mute, is it? You're the worst liar I've ever met!" Evangeline looked at him with contempt.

Wei stood up so fast he almost jumped. He tried to grab the tablet, but stumbled on something and fell hard to the floor.

Evangeline laughed. "If you want it back, you'll have to

help me, asshole." She left the restaurant in the blink of an eye.

Wei, sprawled across the floor, realized that the strings of his shoes had been laced together. Evangeline had kept herself busy while his eyes were shut.

Creeping like a worm, he slowly got back to his seat, grabbed his backpack, and pulled out a pair of scissors that he used to snip the knot.

Once he was on his feet, Wei collected his things and rushed out of the restaurant, stumbling twice on his way out.

It was late afternoon outside, and the streets were almost empty. Evangeline was waiting for him near one of the trees that lined the sidewalk.

"Hurry! He's here!" said the girl, the stolen tablet clasped tightly in her arms.

Wei clenched his teeth and charged toward the thief, trying to grab his tablet, but Evangeline dodged him just in time, causing the boy to lose his balance. For the second time in five minutes, he found himself with his face on the ground. He grunted and spat.

"Don't get smart with me, moron!" the girl warned him, batting at his head. "Now come on and save Kruscha if you don't want me to destroy this damn thing."

Wei rubbed his aching head, wiped his mouth, and sat up. The girl was too tall, too fast, and too determined. He couldn't hope to take the tablet away from her by using force. Frustrated and helpless, he pushed himself up to look at where she was pointing.

On one of the branches of the tree, over twelve feet above the ground, a small rodent with long ears and thick greyish fur was watching them, immobile and scared.

"Looks like you need a ladder," Wei said slowly, considering the distance that separated them from the frightened thing.

"Kruscha is dying of fear. Can't you see? I don't have time to look for a ladder! Come on, climb up. And be quick about it!"

"Are you kidding me? How am I supposed to get up there? You think I've been bitten by a radioactive spider?"

"You're just a liar. I know you can do it! Don't make me ask you again or I swear I'll break your stuff!"

Wei stood up and dusted off his pants. Clearly, the girl had issues. It was impossible to reason with her. But he really wanted his tablet back in one piece.

For a few seconds he seemed to estimate the distance that separated them from the chinchilla. Then he licked his forefinger, exposing it to the wind.

"What's its favorite food?" the boy asked.

Evangeline looked at him, confused. "What? Its favorite food? I don't—"

"What does the damn rat like to eat?"

"You mean *Kruscha*?" Evangeline asked, taken aback by the question. "Well, raisins. What does this have anything to do with—"

"Have you got any with you?" Wei cut her off.

"Sure, but what—"

"Just shut up and give me some if you want my help!"

Evangeline considered the boy for a moment, his hand held out toward her. She reached into her pocket and gave a little bag to Wei.

The boy turned it over in his hands, considering its weight. He tossed it in the air and caught it. He mumbled something, then threw the bag up in the air again, this time higher. Wei knelt down, took off his cap and, with the scissors from his backpack, made four holes equally spaced on each side of the hat. After that, he took a long string out of his pocket, made a couple knots to secure it with the four holes in the cap, and put the half-opened bag full of raisins in the middle of it.

"What are you doing?"

Wei didn't answer. He fumbled for a few more seconds with the string and made sure it was tied to the four sides of the cap.

Meanwhile, the chinchilla seemed to show signs of restlessness. Perhaps because it had noticed Evangeline, it turned on itself, almost falling half a dozen times.

"Kruscha! Stay still, you idiot!" Evangeline, her eyes bright and wide open, looked as though she was about to burst into tears.

"Go under that branch and be ready to catch your rat," Wei said, urging the girl to move.

Evangeline opened her mouth, but Wei stopped her by raising his hand.

"Get under that branch. *Now.*"

Evangeline did as she was told.

Wei stood motionless for a couple seconds. Then he suddenly threw his cap toward the tree and over the branch with the chinchilla.

"What the hell are you doing? You almost hit him! Do you want to kill him?"

"Just look!" Wei silenced her while pointing to the branch.

Evangeline saw the boy's cap dangling in the air, held up by the twine that he firmly held from the other end.

The chinchilla stopped moving and sniffed the air, its head dodging back and forth, looking for something. Soon it noticed the cap a few inches away, and in no time, the little thing dove in, lured by its content. The boy felt the weight of the rodent on the twine.

Slowly and steadily, the cap came closer and closer to the ground. When the rodent was finally within Evangeline's reach, Wei tied the string to a light pole nearby. While the girl was busy rescuing Kruscha, he could get back his tablet.

"Kruscha! Gosh, are you okay?" Evangeline was ecstatic, her eyes swollen with tears.

The rodent was happily eating one of the raisins scattered inside the hat. It raised its head for a second, then went back to eating.

Wei snorted and shoved the tablet inside his backpack. He then untied the string, eager to put as much distance as possible between him and the crazy girl, but something grasped his shoulders, forcing him to turn around. Before he could realize what was happening, Evangeline kissed him on the lips. Wei was petrified, unable even to blink.

When she was done with him, she put her arms around his neck.

"You saved Kruscha! Thank you!"

Wei gasped, his face as red as a tomato. "Disgusting!" he blurted, taking a couple of steps back and looking like he was about to throw up.

"Thanks, thanks, thanks," Evangeline chanted, grasping Wei's hands.

"I..." Wei stopped, searching for something better to say that would shut her mouth and get rid of her. "My...my plan was to hit that *stupid* rat with my cap. Got it? Now get off me."

Evangeline laughed out loud—a laugh that seemed to Wei as fresh and crisp as a sweet melody. Again, he felt that strange heaviness at the bottom of his stomach. All of a sudden, the psychopathic thief was surrounded by inexplicable charm.

"Come on, you moron, today's dinner is on me. You're officially my guest."

"Your guest?" Wei looked around, bewildered. "Are you kidding me? You don't even know who the hell I am!"

"Who cares?" the girl answered, humming happily while spinning into a strange dance. "You're cool."

"Listen," Wei said, taking another step back. "You're totally nuts. You hear me? You're totally, utterly nuts! I'm not going to—"

"Oh, shut up, brat, or we'll start all over again. We have to celebrate Kruscha's adventure!"

Wei found out soon enough that Evangeline was incredibly strong for a girl. His attempts to free himself were useless and painful. Tired, he finally gave up, letting the girl guide him.

The boy touched his head and suddenly realized he'd left his cap behind him, still hanging in mid-air.

"Wait. I've left my—"

"You're a smart boy for your age, you know? Weird, but smart," Evangeline said while patting Kruscha. "How on earth did you come up with that idea? I mean, the elevator thing back there you pulled off with the cap. It was brilliant!"

Wei remained silent for a few seconds, looking absently at his cap lolling lazily in the breeze that spoke of the approaching sunset.

Wei looked at Evangeline, and then at the little creature she was holding in her hands.

Again he watched silently with a blank expression as his cap dangled lazily at the side of the tree, swinging in the warm wind.

"I..." Wei said absently, studying the chinchilla and the cap; first one, then the other, over and over again.

Finally, before completely losing sight of it, he looked at the string that was holding his cap in the air for the last time. His eyes lit up for a moment, as if he had caught the last spark of a firework.

"Yes," he whispered. "That really was a brilliant idea."

5

TIAGO

PASADENA, QUEENSBERRY ROAD

2017

"2360 Queensberry Road. Destination is fifty-eight feet northeast. Estimated time to..." Tiago turned off the device and put it in his pocket.

With a slow and deliberate pace, he continued walking along the road, carefully looking at the numbers painted on the sidewalk's edge.

After a few minutes, he stopped in front of a house similar to the others that faced the street. A dry and twisted plant partially covered the number 2360.

Thirty people were waiting in line in the driveway, speaking with each other and occasionally glancing around. Tiago followed their gaze and saw a tall, burly man opening the door and coming out of the house. He carried a wooden table and two chairs. The man set the table down at the beginning of the driveway and the two chairs on opposite sides of the table, facing each other.

Without further ado, Tiago walked toward the man.

"Hey, you!" someone shouted at Tiago. "The damn line starts here!"

Tiago paid no attention to the shouts and simply continued on his way.

When he reached the heavily built man, he held out his hand and put on his best smile.

"It's a pleasure to meet you, sir. My name is Tiago Melo and—"

"Max Lewis," the other cut him short without shaking his hand. "Now do us all a favor, boy. Turn your ass around and move to the back of the line."

Max moved toward the house, but Tiago quickly blocked his way, standing in front of him.

"Excuse me, Mr. Lewis. I'm from L.A. I study at USC Annenberg. I just wanted to make sure that this is the right place—"

"Yes, this is the place," Max said unceremoniously, his eyes glaring with menace. Tiago stepped back, intimidated by the man's look. "The *magic* will start shortly," Max continued. "I suggest you find yourself a nice spot. This place will be crowded in no time. Now get the hell out of my way."

"Hey, Max! The line starts—"

"Oh, shut up, Josh!"

"But that asshole skipped the—"

"He's just a parrot, goddammit!" Max called back to the bald man, who kept complaining. "He only came to sniff around, like all the others."

"Parrot?" Tiago muttered to himself as he watched the big man quickly going back into the house, cursing under his breath. He imagined Max meant *press*.

He noticed that in a brief interval of minutes, the line had grown in length, and a few dozen people had already occupied the garden that surrounded the driveway. All eyes were staring at the bare table that Max had carried out earlier.

Tiago decided it would be wise to follow the man's advice and found himself a good spot by the garden.

Five minutes later, Max came out of the house with a big sign that he put up in front of the door so that everybody could see it.

Tiago leaned forward to read it.

Straight questions, straight answers in 10 seconds.
$10 against $1,000.
Complaints are not accepted. No refunds.

The student took his smartphone from his pocket, ready to take a picture, but a growing racket forced him to turn around.

The people waiting in line gradually fell silent. Tiago craned his neck to see what was happening.

"Okay, guys, make way. Move! Let him through!"

A couple men in yellow t-shirts were yelling at the crowd gathered around the house and in the garden, pushing to make way. People slowly moved aside. From the passage, a kid emerged who could not have been more than twelve years old. He wore a red cap and a large pair of dark sunglasses that hid a third of his face. He was very short and thin.

The kid was not walking; he was swaying, as if he was staggering on the deck of a ship caught in a storm. His hands were clasped tightly behind his back, and he seemed completely uninterested in the crowd of people watching and pointing at him with growing excitement.

Tiago watched the short figure approaching from the

street. The kid took a seat on the chair that Max had earlier prepared and waited in silence. The other chair in front of him was empty.

"*That* kid is the Omnilogos?" whispered Tiago, bewildered.

The two men in the yellow t-shirts had taken places on both sides of the line of waiting people, looking around to make sure everything was going smoothly. People had resumed their excited chatter, insistently pointing to the kid with the red cap.

Tiago decided to take a picture of the boy and noticed something weird. His smartphone no longer responded to his commands. Tiago shook it, turned it over and repeatedly touched the screen, but nothing happened. The device was dead.

"Outstanding," Tiago huffed. He tried to reboot it. It didn't work. "This is just awesome."

Meanwhile, Max Lewis came out of the house carrying a small box. He walked toward the kid and reached to shake his hand.

The two talked for a few moments. Max laughed heartily as the boy said something that Tiago could not catch because of the increasing noise from the crowd. After a while, the big man took some bills out of the box, placing them on the table.

"One thousand dollars!" Max called out loudly while showing the money to the crowd. He then put the bills on the table, on the right-hand side of the kid.

"Who's first?"

Tiago turned his head toward the voice. He noticed that Josh, the bald man who had yelled at him, was talking with someone else, indicating the very first man waiting in line.

"Dunno. Some new guy, I think. They told me he

camped around here a day ago, the poor bastard. He's probably just a junkie who smelled easy money."

"Yeah, and what about you?" asked Josh, showing a line of yellow teeth. "You've come prepared today? Got any surprises for Mr. Genius there?"

"You bet. This time, I'm going to squeeze that little shit. Oh yeah. I've spent an hour on the damn question. You'll see."

Max clapped his hands, and everyone fell silent.

"Okay, folks, let's start!" He pointed at the first person waiting in line. "You. Yes, you! Don't be shy. Come on."

Tiago tried to turn on his smartphone again, but it was pointless. He cursed, realizing he could do nothing but watch in silence as the first in line sat in the empty chair with his back turned to the audience, reached into his pocket, and put ten dollars in front of Max's one thousand. The little box was laid open and empty amid the two contenders.

Max took something from his jacket and, while watching it closely, he chanted, "Three...two...one. Start!"

The first competitor cleared his throat and asked with a wry smile, "What is the square root of 857,965,847?"

Immediately after he spoke, most of the people waiting in line broke out into laughter.

"29,291.05404385441," the boy replied.

Max took the ten dollars and put it in the box.

"Next!"

A young woman with long hair sat in front of the Omnilogos.

"How to lose ten dollars in two seconds," said Josh, looking with contempt at the first contender who was leaving quietly. "What an idiot."

Everything happened so fast that Tiago's brain had no way of processing it.

Max's voice, inviting the second contender to start, suddenly interrupted Tiago's thoughts.

The woman asked, "What was the name of the second vessel of the Kaiser class of battleships built by the German Imperial Navy?"

Two seconds of absolute silence.

"SMS *Friedrich der Grosse*," was the Omnilogos' answer.

"Thank you, thank you. Okay. Next!" Max bellowed to overcome the indistinct noise from the crowd.

An old man stepped forward. Max nodded. "Go on," he said.

"What is the name of the fifth book of the Jewish Torah?"

"Deuteronomy."

Max took a step forward. "Thank you. Next?"

The chair creaked dangerously under the weight of the fourth participant, a short but fat man whose face was covered in sweat.

"To which animal family does the western capercaillie belong?" asked the contender.

"The western capercaillie is a bird belonging to the grouse group, which is a subfamily Tetraoninae in the family Phasianidae."

Max invited yet another competitor to come forward.

Tiago watched speechlessly as dozens of people, one by one, challenged the Omnilogos with their questions and inevitably lost.

Tiago had heard of what some called the *human database* or *Omnilogos*, but nothing could have prepared him for this. Omnilogos was a compound word made up from the Latin word *omnis*, meaning *all*, and the Greek word *logos*, meaning *a principle of order and knowledge* or *word*. Although it was unclear who crafted that word, it immediately became the most widely used to describe the genius boy.

"Next in line!"

Tiago snapped to attention and returned focus on the competition. It was Josh's friend's turn.

"How was the chemical element lawrencium synthetized for the first time?"

The Omnilogos absently scratched his nose. "The first atoms of lawrencium were produced by a team led by the nuclear scientist Albert Ghiorso. They bombarded a three-milligram target consisting of three isotopes of the element californium with boron-10 and boron-11 nuclei."

Max took the ten dollars and put it in the box.

"Come on, Josh. It's your turn."

The bald man rubbed his hands as he sat on the chair.

Looking at the boy, he asked with a malicious smile, "What is the perihelion of the dwarf planet called Haumea?"

"The perihelion of Haumea, or 136108 Haumea, is about 35.164 AU."

Josh looked at a notebook he had in his hand. When he finished reading, he slammed his fist on the table. "God-dammit! That's impossible!"

"Next!" Max bellowed, staring at the bald man still sitting on the chair. "Get out of the way, Josh. I won't ask again."

Josh cursed as he slowly got up. After throwing a look of animosity at the boy, he left without saying another word, moving aside everyone who was in his way.

Time passed quickly, and with question after question, the money in Max's box never stopped increasing.

While studying the Omnilogos, Tiago's brain worked to

figure out how he could possibly answer all of those questions. For the people around him, cheering and chit-chatting, it was nothing more than an exciting show to enjoy. For Tiago, however, it became a challenge—a puzzle to solve.

He turned toward a group of people who were muttering to each other and asked, "Hey, guys, is this your first time here?"

A girl shook her head. "Nope," she said. "It's the third time actually."

"Look, I'm new here," Tiago said. "Doesn't it seem odd to you, this whole thing? I mean, there must be something going on here. That kid must be cheating. Someone is giving him the answers. It's probably a buddy around here, or maybe he has a portable device. I don't know...*something* is happening. Don't you think?"

"Oh, well... Yes, that's what I thought the first time I came here. But it's not what you think."

"How can you be so sure?"

Another girl from the group answered, "Try to turn on your cell phone."

"Beg your pardon?"

"I said, try to turn on your cell phone or any other device you have with you."

Tiago blinked. "Well, I'd do that if I could. My cell phone died on me and I—" Tiago cut himself off. He stared at the girl, his eyes wide open.

"Got it?" said the girl, noticing Tiago's expression. "Calling, taking pictures, making videos, getting information, or anything that involves the use of technology is impossible during the competition. We think there could be some sort of electromagnetic field that blocks any device. The only thing that works is the stopwatch Max is using, and a couple guys have already checked it several times. There's no weird stuff in it."

Tiago looked at his smartphone, baffled, and then at the girls, who looked back with a grin.

"But how can—"

He never finished the sentence. The audience was pointing out the last participant in the line who was about to sit down. The excitement in the air seemed to grow exponentially.

"Who is he?" Tiago asked the girls, forgetting the last question.

"That's Professor Otto Von Bauer, from the University of California, Los Angeles. He's what we call a regular competitor. The professor is always one of the last and usually his questions are the most...entertaining."

Professor Otto Von Bauer was a short, middle-aged man with a long, thick moustache that made him look like an old walrus. Before sitting, he held out his hand. The Omnilogos shook it.

"Make yourself comfortable, Professor," Max said respectfully, ready to push the stopwatch's button.

Professor Von Bauer crossed his arms and asked, "When did Albert-Pierre Sarraut hold the office of prime minister in the French Third Republic?"

One, two, three, four seconds. There was no answer. The audience held its breath while mentally counting the handful of seconds left to the Omnilogos.

The boy settled back in his chair and slightly cocked his head, almost touching his shoulder.

"The question has been poorly worded," he said after what appeared to be a seemingly endless time. "The correct question should have been: In what *periods* did Albert-Pierre Sarraut hold the office of Prime Minister of France? This is because he was prime minister twice, the first time from October 26, 1933, to November 26, 1933, the second time from January 24, 1936, to June 4, 1936."

The professor smiled. "That is correct," he said.

An ovation shattered the heavy silence that had prevailed. In the uproar that surrounded him, Tiago could hear the professor ask the Omnilogos, "Son, have you had time to think of what I told you?"

"Professor, your persistence is admirable, but the answer is the same." The boy stood up and outstretched his hand. "Have a safe journey."

Von Bauer shook the boy's hand and said something else that Tiago wasn't able to grasp. Then the professor disappeared somewhere in the crowd.

Tiago turned to watch the short man walk away, and for a moment he had the distinct feeling that the Omnilogos was watching him from behind his glasses.

"You're not from here, are you?"

Tiago turned and saw one of the girls who'd asked the question.

"N-no, I'm from L.A.," Tiago replied absently. "I am... I study at USC Annenberg."

"Oh, you're a parrot!"

Tiago sighed. "Apparently I am."

"Pleasure, I'm Sonia."

Tiago offered his hand as he glanced around. The Omnilogos was talking to Max, and the two were heading together toward the house. Before the door closed, Tiago was almost certain that the boy had pointed to him.

"Hey, are you listening?"

Tiago, completely uninterested in what the girl was saying, took his leave abruptly and tried to make his way through the crowd that was quickly dispersing. He reached into his pocket and made sure that his smartphone was working again. The device turned on with no problem. Unfortunately for him, the table, the chairs, and the big board with the rules of the game were all gone.

When he finally reached the door of the house, all that remained of the competition were a couple beverage cans left on the ground by the crowd.

He closed his eyes, took a deep breath, and knocked. No one answered.

"Mr. Lewis!" he called out in a loud voice. "It's Tiago Melo. Remember?"

There was still no answer. He waited a minute, then knocked again and again.

"Mr. Lewis? Can you hear me?"

At that point, it was impossible that no one could hear him. Tiago thought they were deliberately trying to ignore him. He didn't give up and knocked on the door with both fists.

"I just want to ask the Omnilogos a few questions! Mr. Lewis?"

When the door opened, Tiago almost fell forward.

Max Lewis loomed in the doorway, his jaw clenched, his hands clasped tightly.

"Listen to me, jackass. Back away. Keep backing away till you're off my property. Then back away some more," said Max slowly, calm and as menacing as a nest of giant hornets.

"Look, I just want to ask him some questions."

"What?"

"I just want to ask the Omnilogos—"

"What are you blabbing about?" Max cut him off, raising a big hand. "What the hell is an *only goes?*"

"The Omnilogos," Tiago repeated, "the boy that was—"

"Boy? What the hell are you talking about?" Max said, rubbing his knuckles. "There's no *werdy goes* or boy here. You understand?"

"I...I saw him. I saw him going inside this house a few moments ago."

"Fine. Listen. Listen very carefully." Max hit Tiago with a rapid kick to the knee. Before the student even realized it, he was kneeling on the ground, with Max's strong arm around his neck.

"This won't end well if you don't pay attention. Now, this is Terry." Max showed him a Colt Anaconda, a double action revolver he had kept hidden behind his back. "She's specialized in keeping stubborn parrots like you in line. Now do as I said, and be quick about it."

Max pushed him away. Tiago coughed, then he took a step away from the porch.

He gazed at the mountain of muscles in front of him and swallowed hard, but he didn't go anywhere.

"This...this would be a threat?" he said, touching his neck. "I wonder what the police would say if I—"

Max spat on the ground. He put a hand in his pocket and showed him a sparkling police badge.

"I am the police, asshole," he said. "Now get lost."

Tiago looked surprised, but he didn't move a finger. He remained as still as a stone, exactly where he was.

"I get it. You really prefer the hard way, don't you?" Max started moving toward him, but suddenly he stopped. He searched in his pocket and came up with a cell phone. He looked at Tiago while answering the phone.

"What?" Max said after a moment. He touched his gun.

Tiago stepped back.

"No...no. Yes, I understand. I do." Max put his cell phone back in his pocket.

"Your guardian angel must be working overtime today." He got closer to Tiago, who could now smell his heavy breath. "Do what you want, fucker, but if you touch my door again, I'll tear you apart with my bare hands! Got it?"

Max turned away, moved up the steps to his porch, and vehemently shut the door without waiting for an answer.

"Tell the Omnilogos I'll be out here waiting for him," the student insisted, talking to the door.

There was no answer. Tiago moved away from the door and wandered around the porch for a few minutes while massaging his sore neck. He realized his hands were shaking only when he looked at his smartphone to check the time. He breathed in, then looked around to make sure that the house didn't have any back doors.

Once he had done that, he sat on the grass and waited, legs and arms crossed.

Ten minutes passed and nothing happened.

Tiago took a few pictures of the house and of the neighborhood. He checked the street occasionally to see if anybody was around to ask some questions. In fact, the place now seemed deserted, completely empty. No one would have thought that fifteen minutes before there were dozens of people swarming around.

After more than an hour, no audible noise had come from the house. The building was silent, as if everybody inside had gone to sleep, waiting for him to go away. He refused to give up and remained planted on the grass.

His mind was stormed by a legion of questions he couldn't even begin to answer.

Discouraged and bored, he grabbed a thin blade of grass and chewed on it while lying on his back with his hands behind his head, watching the clouds lazily dance in the sky.

Another half an hour passed in boredom.

Tiago took his smartphone from his pocket and played a hip-hop tune.

After a few minutes, he picked another blade of grass as he reached up to stretch, and it was at that moment his hand struck against something.

"Ow!"

Tiago, surprised, quickly drew his arm back and looked to his right, eyes wide open.

"What the hell—"

A little boy with a crew-cut was rolling on the grass, rubbing his head with both hands. "Geez! You hurt me!" he muttered with tears in his eyes.

"What? I... I'm sorry," Tiago said, blinking. "I didn't see you. Who...who are you? Where did you come from?"

The boy suddenly stopped complaining and jumped to his feet.

"Never mind. My name is Wei Wang. Nice to meet you." He held out a hand that was covered with grass and dirt.

Tiago looked at the boy's smiling face and then at the filthy hand.

"Yes, well. Pleasure...kid," said Tiago, without shaking his hand.

"You're not introducing yourself," the boy said, looking both surprised and annoyed.

"Okay, my name is Tiago," he answered. "Now, could you just—"

"T-I-A-G-O," repeated Wei, as though he was memorizing a nursery rhyme. "Gosh, that's quite a name, isn't it? Short, easy to remember... Sounds like a fruit, or a flower. Yeah. What other names do you have?"

Tiago looked carefully around, searching for parents desperate to find their lost child.

"I've just got this one. Listen, are you lost?"

"Let me guess," said Wei, without answering the question. "Tiago Bernardes. Is it?"

"No. Listen—"

"Cardoso."

"No."

"Conceição."

"All right, all right! Tiago Melo, my name is Tiago Melo. Okay? Now, would you just—"

"I bet you've also got a Tavares somewhere in between."

"NO!"

"Vasconcelos."

"I said no! Can't you just shut—"

"Villa Lobos."

"Tiago Silva Abreu Melo!" Tiago burst out. "Are you happy?"

Wei nodded, paying no attention to the annoyance on Tiago's face. "I wish I had a name like that. With such a name, you can do whatever you want. When you show up, you must leave everybody speechless, right? Of course, if someone urgently needed you, he or she would be really fuc—"

"Listen, kid," said Tiago while looking around. "I'm busy here, okay? Why don't you just go home and—"

"What are you doing here all alone?" Wei interrupted him, pointing to the garden.

"I'm busy!"

"Busy? Busy doing what? Digesting the grass?" he said, pointing to the blade of grass Tiago was holding in his hand.

"What?" the student said, letting the grass slip away from his fingers. "No, I'm...I'm waiting for someone."

"Really? Who are you waiting for?"

"It's none of your business! Now get lost!"

"How can I?"

"How can you *what?*"

"How do I get lost? I know this neighborhood like the back of my hand."

"Damn! You're annoying, kid."

"Speak for yourself. I don't say my name in bits and pieces."

"Fine!" Tiago threw up his hands. "Stay, but stop talking!"

Tiago sat back on the grass and stared at the door. Wei sat down beside him.

After a few moments of silence, Wei hummed.

"What did I say?" barked Tiago.

"Fine. Stay, but stop talking," Wei repeated, mimicking Tiago's annoyed tone. Then he went back to humming.

Tiago jumped up and yelled, "Officer! Open the door!"

Wei looked at Tiago, who kept on yelling. When the student started walking toward the door, Wei said, "Hey, who are you yelling at?"

"I'm yelling at a cop with issues. Now would you just—"

"You mean Max?"

Tiago whirled on the spot and turned toward the boy. "You know him?"

"Sure. He's one of my best friends."

"Yeah, sure." Tiago snorted. "All right, one of your best friends. If that's so, why don't you ask him to open that damn—"

"Nobody's home."

Tiago looked puzzled. "Say that again."

"Max went out an hour ago. He had some errands to run."

"What? Gone? Where? *How*? No one left this house."

"He didn't use the door, you moron."

"He didn't? And how on earth could he possibly have left this house? Using a secret passage?"

"Precisely," Wei said, dead serious.

Tiago was speechless for a good half a minute.

"You're kidding, right?"

"No. But if you wanna laugh, I know a—"

"You're saying...you're saying that this house has a secret passage? I mean...a *real* secret passage?"

"Yes, you know? Like those castles in the Middle Ages when people *really* needed to get out before someone captured them and chopped their heads off. That kind of secret passage."

"How could you possibly know that?"

"I do because I used it ten minutes ago."

Tiago stared at the boy as if he was seeing him for the first time.

"You used a secret passage to get out of there?" he finally asked, pointing to the building.

"Stop repeating what I say. It makes you look stupid, you know?"

Now that Tiago was paying attention, Wei was not much taller or shorter than the Omnilogos, but on the other hand he was wearing completely different clothes. He had dark hair, sure, but that alone didn't really mean anything. It could have just been some kid who was making fun of him.

"So, you're the Omnilogos?"

"Omnilogos?" the boy repeated, frowning. "No idea what that means."

"If you're the kid who answered those questions, prove it."

Wei shrugged. "Okay, ask me a question. Any question. I have ten seconds to answer."

Tiago had already prepared a question that came to his

mind while looking at the row of competitors dwindling before his eyes.

Years before, his grandfather challenged him to finish the most boring and difficult novel he'd ever laid his eyes upon. He never finished the book, but he exactly remembered one of its sentences. The book was a classic but not an easy read, nor particularly popular, and almost a century old. There was no way a kid like that could have ever heard about it.

"Okay. Can you tell me in which book appears the sentence: 'Because no battle is ever won, they are not even fought. The field only reveals to man his own folly and despair, and victory is an illusion of philosophers and fools.'"

"Easy," Wei said, scratching his buttock. "*The Sound and the Fury*, written by William Faulkner."

It was as if someone had hit Tiago's face with a baseball bat.

"No way," he murmured. "It's really you."

"Are you happy now? Good. It's time to pay up, buddy."

"I'm sorry?"

"You heard me, Tiago Silva Abreu Melo. You owe me ten bucks." Wei outstretched his hand.

"What? You suggested that I ask a question."

"I never said it was for free. Now pay up if you don't want me to scream that you're harassing me."

"What? Are you high? I won't give you a penny, kid."

"Now, now, don't be a smartass," Wei warned him, smiling a wicked smile. "Do you have any idea what could happen if a kid started shouting the word *pedophile* in the middle of the street?"

"I...I...I don't believe this!" Tiago said, clasping his hands behind his head. "Is this really happening?"

Wei moved his fingers impatiently. "Come on. I don't have all day."

Tiago looked at Wei. Wei looked back at him. Blowing air through his clenched teeth, Tiago put his hands in his pocket. "I don't even know if I have enough cash."

His hand finally came out with a pair of crumpled five-dollar bills. Wei grabbed them before Tiago could add anything else.

"Well, now that we have completed this transaction—"

"You mean this *robbery*," Tiago said, tight-jawed.

"May I ask, Mr. Melo, what business brings you here?" Wei asked, paying no attention to Tiago's expression.

Tiago's heart was pounding. He steadied himself with a couple deep breaths. After all, he thought, ten dollars was a reasonable price to pay for what he came for.

The Omnilogos was in front of him, at his mercy. He just had to play the part of the friend, ask the right questions, and he would go back home with a story with a capital S.

Tiago smiled, trying to sound less hostile. "I am a student at USC Annenberg and—"

"Ah! So, you're a—"

"Yes, I know, a *parrot*," Tiago anticipated him, closing his eyes in frustration.

"I was going to say a wannabe journalist."

"Oh, well...yes, exactly," Tiago said, taken aback by the kid's answer. "I came...well, I think you know exactly why I came here."

"You're not the first and certainly will not be the last," said Wei, patting Tiago's shoulder. "The only difference between you and everyone else is that *you*, my friend, will get exactly what you came for."

"Really?"

"Really," Wei confirmed. "Even better, you'll have the

unique opportunity to follow me on my typical day. What do you say? Sound good?"

"Absolutely!" Tiago waited a moment, his excitement suddenly subsiding. Something felt odd. It was too good to be true. "Wait a sec," he said. "How much will it cost me this time?"

"Not a penny."

"You mean you'll do it without asking for something in return?"

Wei laughed. "Now, don't be naive, my friend. There ain't no such thing as a free lunch. At the end of our day, you'll return the favor. Don't bother," Wei said, raising a hand, "you'll know exactly what it is at the right time."

Tiago closed his mouth. He didn't like the idea of being held hostage by this twisted little boy, but he would have done anything to unravel the mystery surrounding the Omnilogos.

"Agreed," the student said.

"Good, because we've already lost too much time chit-chatting. We have a long day ahead."

Wei picked up a small backpack from the ground that Tiago hadn't noticed before, and together they set off.

"Do you have a car or something else we can use to reach the city center?" Wei asked, staring at his wristwatch. "I've left my bike at home."

"Yeah, of course. I came with that." Tiago pointed to an old motorcycle parked a few meters away.

"Curious and courageous," Wei said once in front of the motorcycle. He touched the tank and the wheels. "This thing would make the fortune of a museum."

"This *jewel*," Tiago pointed out, patting the seat, "works just fine. It's convenient, considering its age, and it consumes close to nothing. A great motorcycle."

"If we don't blow up on our way, it'd be more than enough for me. Okay then. Let's go!"

The two climbed on.

"Where are we going?" Tiago asked as he started the engine.

"Go straight. When I tell you, turn left. We'll go down Allen Avenue for a while till we get to Colorado Boulevard. Our destination is the Old Town."

THE TRIP LASTED LESS than fifteen minutes. Neither of them spoke on the way, except for Wei who gave some pointers. When they arrived at their destination, Tiago parked his motorcycle and examined the landscape: they were surrounded by strong smells, beggars, and passersby who swarmed around the shops lining the main street.

"Come on. This way." Wei motioned for Tiago to follow him.

For a few seconds, they walked in silence.

"So," Tiago finally began, going over in his head the speech he made up on the ride. "That question-answer show you put up in Queensberry was remarkable, wasn't it?"

Wei didn't answer. He kept walking, occasionally looking around.

"I'd like to know how you did it," concluded Tiago in a neutral tone, trying not to betray any emotion.

Wei's face suddenly brightened. "And I'd like to eat chocolate grapefruit," he said, looking straight at Tiago. "Of course, it would have to be dark chocolate, not milk. That would ruin the contrast between the bitter of the fruit and the flavor of the cocoa."

Tiago frowned. "I'm sorry. What is that supposed to mean?"

Wei shrugged. He looked confused. "I thought we were playing *I Wish I Could.*"

Tiago stared at him.

"It's a game," Wei explained. "You know, when you talk hypothetically and the player who imagines the most absurd thing wins. Don't you guys play this in L.A.?"

"What?"

Wei waved his hand to dismiss the matter. "You parrots just don't know how to have fun."

"How did you know all that stuff?" Tiago asked, ignoring his comment. "Are you, like, some kind of genius?"

Wei shook his head. "Don't think so," he said. "It's the rest of you who are stupid."

Tiago started to reply, but Wei suddenly raised a hand. "That's it. This is our first stop."

Wei stopped in front of a store with a big black sign shaped like a vortex.

Before Tiago could say anything, the Omnilogos took off his backpack. After a moment of rummaging around inside it, he came up with a small mirror and handed it over to Tiago.

"Take this."

Tiago grabbed the mirror without understanding. "What are you doing?"

Wei wasn't listening. He took a small case out of the backpack. When he opened it, Tiago stared at what appeared to be two contact lenses.

"Hold the mirror," he said to Tiago. "I need to put these in."

Tiago reluctantly did as he was told while watching the boy moisten both contact lenses and put them in his eyes.

"Well, now let's try."

"Try *what*?"

Wei approached the shop window. He put his face close to a zone marked by a black and orange rectangle and waited.

A beam of light erupted from the window and surrounded Wei's face, as motionless and impassive as a stone in the desert. Suddenly a voice announced: "Welcome to the Dark Matter Store 54 West Colorado Boulevard. By accessing the Matter-Quick service, you allow us to process your personal data in the government's database. Your data will be used for marketing purposes only. Please wait."

Tiago crossed his arms, waiting. He didn't understand what they were doing.

The automated voice resumed talking. "Welcome back, Mr. Bernard Pascal. We are pleased to inform you that you have accumulated one hundred and twelve Matter-Trust points. Please select—"

Wei moved away from the window and the beam of light instantly turned off. He had a huge smile on his face.

"Done and done. Let's go."

"Wait a minute!" Tiago indicated the window. "Didn't the voice call you Bernard Pascal?"

"Yes it did, so what?"

"And what's Wei Wang, hmm? An alias? Is Bernard Pascal your real name?"

"Does this seem to you the face of a Bernard Pascal?" Wei pointed out his almond-shaped eyes. "Of course it isn't, genius. That's the name that belongs to its rightful owner in France."

Tiago looked at the boy who was pointing at the contact lenses.

"Two plus two?" Wei said, putting the mirror and lenses back in his backpack.

"Whoa, whoa, wait a minute! You mean you have impressed on those contact lenses the reticular imprint of a guy who lives in France?"

Wei pointed with his thumb and index finger to the sky, simulating a machine gun that hits an enemy aircraft. "Hit and crashed, baby," he said with a grin.

Tiago was speechless. He couldn't understand how such a thing could be possible. What some called the reticular information industry had only recently started up. The services and the technology related to it were still poorly developed. A few days earlier, his university discussed the possibility of creating a course focused on this fascinating but still largely unknown subject. Yet Tiago realized as he watched the Omnilogos in awe that he had just witnessed a real robbery perpetrated with that very experimental technology. Wei didn't steal money, but he did steal something valuable: information.

Tiago rubbed his forehead and then looked at his hand, which had come away wet.

He wanted to express his amazement, ask Wei how on earth he did it, but he realized other major implications of what he had just witnessed.

"This is illegal," Tiago finally said, lowering his voice and looking around as if expecting the police to show up any minute.

"Illegal," Wei repeated, dismissing Tiago's worried tone with a quick flick of his hand. "The right word is *awesome*."

"Do you even realize you've just committed a crime?"

"Try not to shit your pants, Heidi."

Tiago got closer to the Omnilogos. "A security camera could have recorded you...recorded *us*!"

"Relax."

"It's not funny."

"I don't believe it." Wei looked straight into Tiago's eyes as he continued walking. He seemed annoyed. "What kind of journalist are you? Oh, sorry, *wannabe* journalist."

"What's that supposed to mean?"

"Do you think you'll get your best stories legally? Blackmail, deception, theft, extortion, stalking, these are all essential tools for any Pulitzer Prize winner."

Tiago felt humiliated. How dare this suckling little prick talk to him like that?

"You don't even know what you're talking about," he said, outraged. "A journalist is a respected, independent, and decent person."

"As was a money-lender in ancient Rome. You know, the kind of guy who asked fifteen percent interest on loans? These days, they call him a loan shark."

"Journalists are socially useful and, above all, *legitimate*," Tiago insisted, emphasizing the last word.

"So too were hangmen," Wei threw back, speeding up his gait.

Tiago felt as though he was in the middle of a tennis match where he invariably lost set after set. The boy always seemed to be one step ahead of him.

"So, is this the strategy you've used with the other *parrots*?" Tiago asked, not willing to give up. "Did you just send them all to the local nuthouse?"

"You kidding me? You're the first one who has the honor of speaking to me. You'd still be grazing grass outside of Max's house if it weren't for me. Now stop whining. We have to get into that restaurant."

Wei stopped. On the sign in front of them, *Sapori & Sentimenti* was written in beautifully crafted letters.

"What does it mean?" asked Tiago, looking at the foreign words.

"It's Italian. It means *Flavors and Feelings*."

"Why are we here?"

"Are you hungry?"

Tiago hadn't eaten in a long time. An unmistakable growl erupted from his stomach.

"You want to stop to eat here?" Tiago looked puzzled.

"I have some matters to discuss with the owner," Wei said, checking his watch. "In the meantime, I'll ask the chef to cook something for you."

"Right." Tiago rolled his eyes. "*You* will ask the chef? Sounds like you own this place."

"Don't be ridiculous," Wei said, smiling a toothy smile. "I'm only twelve."

He grabbed the handle and then stopped, lingering in front of the restaurant door. "Oh yeah," Wei said, scratching his forehead. "I almost forgot. The chef, Tonio, is a bit like... hmm...particular. Keep that in mind, please."

"What do you mean by *particular*?"

"Well, don't get me wrong, he's a genius. Personally, I think he's the best chef I've ever met, but...you know, he's one of those *compassionate* Italians. There have been some misunderstandings where he worked before. And there are stories...you know..." Wei trailed off.

Tiago narrowed his eyes. "What stories?"

"Let's just say that his former boss didn't appreciate some of Tonio's recipes. Tonio didn't take it very well."

"Come on, don't tease me. What happened?"

"Word is... Well, it seems he filled the owner's car with tar." Wei looked straight at Tiago. "With the owner inside."

Tiago opened his mouth, but no sound came out.

"Well, anyway, you keep a low profile. Promise me?"

Before Tiago could answer, Wei opened the door and took a couple steps forward, spreading his arms as if he was waiting to catch a huge ball.

"Uncle Matthew!" the Omnilogos cried out at the top of his lungs.

Tiago winced. He entered just in time to see a fifty-year-old guy wearing a suit and tie—he started running like a madman toward them.

"*Disgraziato! Ma tu mi fai penare!*"

The man, a giant six and a half feet tall, embraced Wei like a son, lifting him off the ground with one arm. The boy laughed and laughed.

Every head in the place turned to watch the scene.

Once he was back on the ground, Wei pointed to Tiago. "Uncle Matthew, this is a very dear friend of mine who is visiting. He's hungry. Can we give him something to eat?"

Tiago didn't say a word. He just put on a weird grin that he hoped looked like a smile.

The restaurant owner studied him carefully. Finally, he made a half bow and held out his hand.

"Matthew Bonati, here to serve you. Wei's friends are my friends."

"Tiago Melo, sir. It's a pleasure," he said, nodding at the giant.

Matthew Bonati snapped his fingers. "Rodolfo!" he called, looking around the room.

One server hurried to him immediately. The owner indicated Tiago.

"Prepare the twenty-four for our special guest," ordered Matthew, putting a hand on the server's shoulder. "Also, ask Tonio to prepare something appropriate for our friend Tango here."

Tiago held up a finger and opened his mouth, about to

say something. He looked at Wei, who was shaking his head. Tiago lowered his finger and closed his mouth, resigning himself to the Italianization of his name.

Matthew smiled at Tiago and Wei. Then he lowered his voice a little and continued giving Rodolfo instructions. "After that, you go straight to table forty-one and clean up that mess, all right? *Dai, dai!* Go on. I pay you by the hour, not by the minute."

Rodolfo nodded meekly and invited Tiago to follow him.

"I'll see you in an hour," Wei said, as he walked into the kitchen with the owner. "*Buon appetito!*"

Tiago was sat at the table with the best view of the whole restaurant. The place was well maintained, clean and elegant. He realized only then that he was in a very fancy restaurant.

"Mr. Tango," Rodolfo said with a strong Castilian accent. "Do you have any allergies that I should be aware of?"

"Tiago. The name is Tiago. No, no allergies. Thanks for asking."

Rodolfo nodded as he picked up a basket of bread and a saucer of oil from a nearby table, setting them to his right.

"Sir, would you like a bit of bread with caramelized onions and tomato bruschetta with olive oil?"

"Wow, thanks, Rodolfo."

"It's my pleasure, sir. This is our wine list. Our sommelier—"

Tiago shook his head. "No thank you, Rodolfo. I don't drink alcohol."

"I'm sorry, sir? What did you say?"

"I'm a teetotaller. I don't drink alcohol."

Rodolfo repeated the word *teetotaller* as though he had never heard it before.

"Just...just water?" he asked slowly.

"Yes, please."

Tiago ate while the server filled his glass with some sparkling water.

"Sir, Chef Tonio wanted to know if you prefer a vegetarian, fish, or meat-based menu."

"I'm easy," Tiago said. "Whatever he decides."

Rodolfo nodded and disappeared into the kitchen. While he waited, Tiago read the menu on the nearby table. He could find nothing priced less than thirty dollars, except bread and water.

"Here you are, sir. Squid and shrimp meatballs covered in a sweet cheese sauce. Would you like some fresh pepper?"

"That'd be great, thanks."

What followed was probably the best meal of his life. He couldn't even pronounce half the things that Rodolfo served him, but they were all masterpieces. Wei was right after all. The chef might have been a psychopath, but he knew his stuff in the kitchen.

Rodolfo was wiping some crumbs from his table. "In a moment, Chef Tonio will come over to make sure everything was of your liking."

Tiago spat out the water he was drinking.

"Sir, are you okay?"

"Fine...fine, thanks, Rodolfo," said Tiago, coughing as he wiped his mouth with a napkin. Mr. Tar was really coming?

A man strode out of the kitchen. He was very thin, in his forties, with no hair and no beard. He had huge bulging eyes, a sharp chin, and a nose so long that it would have been disqualified in a fencing match.

"I'm Tonio," the chef said. "Glad you're here."

"Tar... I mean, Tiago!" Tiago shook the chef's hand. "It's a pleasure, sir."

"Oh, you can drop the formalities, young man. Just Tonio is fine. So, how did you like my—"

"I've never eaten so well in my whole life," Tiago cut him off, showing the table. "Your dishes...your dishes are masterpieces. They are truly works of art. If there was a Nobel Prize for cuisine... I mean... You know, what I'm trying to say is that—"

"Slow down, buddy. I got it." Tonio smiled. "Wei told you the tar story, right?"

"Wha—? No, no... It's just... Wei said... Look, I don't—" Tiago was wheezing. "I think I'm going to throw up."

Tonio exploded in laughter.

When he finished, he wiped his eyes and said, "Yes, it's typical of that rascal. Look, I've done nothing like that. I swear."

"You mean you've never drowned your boss in tar?" Only after he finished the sentence did Tiago realize how incredibly ludicrous it sounded.

Tonio laughed again.

The chef sat at his left while describing the dessert that Rodolfo was bringing them. "Lemon sorbet with mint and slivers of candied orange."

Tiago thanked him. He picked up the spoon and let the flavors linger for a few seconds in his mouth before swallowing. His taste buds sung with joy.

"Outstanding," Tiago murmured, complimenting the chef. "Every bite is a blessing, really. If I may ask, how do you make things so...well, exceptional?"

"I have no idea," Tonio said with a shrug.

"I mean," continued Tiago, watching the man with interest, "where did you study? How long have you been doing this?"

"To tell you the truth," said Tonio, "I started this job nine months ago."

Tiago wiped his mouth. "You mean you started working *here* nine months ago?"

"Oh no, you got it right. Before working for Matthew, I was a government employee, a tax collector. It's the only work I've done over the last fifteen years."

Tiago looked at the chef. He couldn't tell whether he was serious or simply joking.

"Are you saying you've never cooked professionally before?"

"I finished my evening course exactly one year ago. Before that, the only kitchen where I was allowed to set foot in was my house's."

Tiago shifted in his chair. "Sorry, I don't think I understand. I mean, your dishes are truly exceptional...seriously. I thought it would take years to learn to make this kind of food."

"So they say," Tonio said, rubbing his chin.

There was a moment of silence. Tiago finished his dessert and put the spoon down. "You said you were a simple employee, right?" he asked. "What made you wear the apron?"

"Wei," Tonio answered at once. "It was that sweet little rowdy kid who convinced me to turn what I thought was a hobby into my profession. Before then, I never even thought I was cut out for the job."

"Wei convinced you? Wait a second. You quit your job on a twelve-year-old kid's say-so?"

Tonio looked at him without blinking. "Damn straight. He talked me into quitting that awful job and getting my diploma. He even introduced me to Matthew, who hired me on the spot, thanks to his recommendation."

Tiago nodded thoughtfully. The chef looked like the kind of person who loved to talk, if he could just ask him the right questions.

"How long has this restaurant been open?" he asked, trying to keep a neutral tone.

"*Sapori & Sentimenti*? It's quite new. Not even three years old." Tonio crossed his legs and looked around. "Matthew told me that at the beginning, it was little more than an inn. Then Wei came with his advice."

"Advice?" repeated Tiago, craning his neck.

"Well, from what I've heard here at the restaurant, *Sapori & Sentimenti* would not be what it is today without him. Don't ask me how, but Wei introduced Matthew to the right people, counselled him on what to invest in and what to save on. He revolutionized this place."

Tiago frowned. "Really? You're still talking about the twelve-year-old kid in the orange t-shirt and sneakers?"

Tonio nodded. "The one and only."

"Look, I'm not saying... Okay, the truth? I really have a hard time believing that. Put yourself in my shoes. It sounds like you're talking about a super manager, not a kid whose idea of transportation is a bicycle. Wei is smart and clever, nothing to say about that, but you know..." He left the sentence hanging in the air with a skeptical smile.

Tonio drew his chair closer to Tiago's.

"Let's not play games, young man. If Wei brought you here, it means he trusts you and that you know him as much as I do."

Tiago nodded, dead serious, even if he had known Wei for only a few hours. He felt his heartbeat speeding up. Beads of sweat dotted his forehead. This conversation was heating. He smelled the distinct fragrance of revelations in the air.

"That kid's got something special," the chef continued in a low voice. "It's something you understand as soon as you start speaking to him. But that's just the tip of the iceberg, trust me. That kid is not just damn precocious, erudite, and monstrously clever. It's the way he literally reads people, as if they were an open book. Sometimes, when I see him talking to other people, well... I get goosebumps. It's almost scary. You should see the way people seem to drink up what he says, as if it were pure nectar."

Tonio looked around. He crossed his arms and nodded toward the kitchen.

"My two cents?" Tonio continued. "That kid has a gift."

"Yes, I know," replied Tiago. "I've seen what he can do with his brain and—"

Tonio held up a hand and shook his head. "Forget his brain. There are others out there younger and smarter than him. No, Wei's special for another reason...something less visible. That kid has a gift for finding talent. It seems he feels compelled to find special people. His gift is in finding these linchpins and... I don't know how to explain it with words, but, well, once he finds them, his magic is to *empower* them."

"Honestly, it seems that Wei also feels compelled to make a lot of money," Tiago said. "I saw what he did in one of his morning shows up at Queensberry. You know what I'm talking about, right? Do you have an opinion on that too?"

"You mean his *Ten Against a Grand* contest?"

Tiago nodded.

"Yeah, that's one of his favorite pastimes, from what he tells me."

"A rewarding pastime," Tiago said, rubbing his thumb against his forefinger. "He made ten dollars every twenty seconds for an hour. Call me stupid, but I see no interest in helping anyone but himself in that case."

Tonio shook his head as he wiped some crumbs from the tablecloth.

"Trust me, young man. That show, as you called it, has little to do with money. The little thug has a dozen other ways to make more money in less time."

Tiago didn't reply to that. He felt that the conversation was taking an interesting turn. He let the chef go on talking.

"Take *Sapori & Sentimenti*, for example. Each week, Matthew puts an envelope in a safe box here at the restaurant; a paycheck destined to a certain *Mr. No One*. He and Wei are the only ones with the key to that box."

"And what would the amount in this safe box be?"

"Well, I don't know how much there could be in a paycheck that doesn't exist," Tonio said, waving a hand as if to ward off invisible smoke, "but I'm sure you've had a look at our menu."

"I understand," Tiago said. "I wonder why Mr. No One is using all his skills to help those who need it, as you said, and at the same time making a considerable amount of money."

"Don't let appearances mislead you, boy. Money is only a means to achieving a goal. Wei has a goal, that's as certain as death and taxes, but money is only a part of the answer. That kid likes to surround himself with useful people, people with potential, but in need of help. Look at me and Matthew. Matthew was on the verge of bankruptcy before Wei arrived, and I was unhappy with a life that didn't give me anything important. I'm going to return the favor when he asks me to do so. I owe him, as does Matthew."

"He said something like that to me too," Tiago said, looking at the chef, "but I don't have the slightest idea what he wants from me. I have nothing special to offer him."

Tonio shook his head. "If today you're here, it means he can use you. That makes you a special person in some—"

"Tiago Silva Abreu Melo!" a shrill voice interrupted their conversation. "Time's up. Gotta go. Now!"

Tiago saw Wei open the restaurant's door and leave without another word. The young man jumped up from his chair and stretched out his hand to the chef, who shook it.

"Thanks for everything."

"You got it." Then Tonio added, "You're not from around here, are you?"

"L.A.," Tiago answered.

"Enjoying the tourist's tour?"

"Let's just say that more than a tourist, I feel like a taxi driver. I'm thinking he just needed a cheap means of transportation."

"It's a good thing, my friend. It's a good thing," said the chef.

"Really?" Tiago asked, leaving his napkin on the table. "You bet it's a good thing for *him*. He's got a chauffeur for the rest of the day."

"No." Tonio grinned. "It means he really likes you."

"Move your ass, motor boy," Wei shouted from a nearby window.

"Yeah, I agree," Tiago said, making a face. After thanking Rodolfo, Tiago walked quickly toward the exit.

"Finally!" Wei exhaled when the restaurant's door closed behind Tiago. "We're late, you know? Chop-chop!"

Tiago quickly joined him.

"You know, I had a very interesting conversation with Tonio," he said, indicating the restaurant.

"I'm sure," the boy replied. "That spaghetti-eater is a motor-mouth."

"I'd like to ask you some questions."

"By all means, my friend."

"Oh, really? All right. Tonio told me a bit about your... your interests, what you've done for him and Matthew, for the restaurant and many other people. It looks like you're using your skills to create a kind of...network of people you trust. Is that so?"

Wei crossed the street as he checked his watch.

"Is that so?" Tiago repeated.

The Omnilogos just kept walking without even looking at him.

"Are you deaf all of a sudden? You don't have any answer to that?"

"Answer?" Wei asked, turning toward the student. "I thought you were talking about questions. You can ask me as many as you want."

"You mean you won't answer them?"

"No," Wei said, smiling. "See? I just answered."

Tiago stopped just before they reached his motorcycle. Wei stared at him blankly.

"I have no reason to continue this charade if you don't give me something back. You understand?" Tiago pushed his hands deep into his pockets.

Wei walked up to the student and looked him straight in the eye. "I understand that, since you came out of that restaurant, you know more about me than you knew starting out this morning in Los Angeles, chasing mere rumors. I understand that by continuing to follow me, you could keep sniffing around—and figure out some answers to your questions. But I also understand that you don't like the idea of being the chauffeur of a twelve-year-old kid and that you probably have much better things to do than trying to unravel the mystery of the Omnilogos." Wei paused and raised a hand, pointing at the motorcycle parked nearby.

"Now you have a choice. Either you decide to go back home or you keep collecting material for your Pulitzer. What do you say?"

Tiago knew his bluff had been called even before Wei finished speaking. "Come on, boss. We're late," Tiago said, starting the engine.

Wei followed him onto the motorcycle. "Go straight and turn left when I tell you."

FIVE MINUTES LATER, they were in front of a four-story building in the middle of the financial district.

As soon as they got in, Wei asked for information at the reception desk.

"Fourth floor," the receptionist said to Tiago, pointing to the stairs.

When they reached the fourth floor, Wei stopped in front of the men's room.

"Wait here. I'll be back in no time." He pulled out a plastic bag from his backpack and went in.

A few minutes later, the Omnilogos came back wearing new clothes: shirt, jacket, tie, and black shoes. He put the old clothes in his backpack. Tiago studied his new outfit.

"Don't ask," Wei said, putting his finger to his lips.

"Asking questions is my job," Tiago said, "and an answer costs nothing. I'd appreciate even a lie. A lie is something I can work with."

"Some answers need to be earned."

Tiago huffed in frustration. He studied the green and yellow tie that the Omnilogos was wearing. It was a very particular piece of cloth: smooth, shiny, small, and very colorful.

"Ken won't be happy to know you've been sacking his wardrobe," Tiago said, indicating the tie. "I'm no expert in fashion, but a blind man could tell you that's not exactly the best style choice of the century."

"A Barbie fan," Wei announced, looking around as if he was talking to an imaginary audience. "Now I understand many things." The boy put his hand on his hip, then walked away waddling like a model on a catwalk.

Tiago blushed purple.

They soon found themselves in front of a wooden door. Wei knocked, and the door opened almost immediately. A middle-aged woman with big glasses and sagging cheeks greeted them and invited them in.

The two were escorted into an empty waiting room with a television fixed on the wall.

"Mr. Banks will see you in a moment."

"Thank you," they said in unison.

When the secretary left them, Tiago asked, "Can I at least ask what we're doing here?"

"I have stuff to do," Wei simply said, smoothing his tie.

"What stuff?"

"If I tell you, then I'll have to kill you."

"Well, I tried." Tiago exhaled. "For the sake of conversation, I think you should know that the jacket should be unbuttoned when sitting. Since you want to look like an adult, you might as well act like one."

Wei looked at his jacket. "This is my style, Barbie-boy," Wei said with a wink.

Tiago started to reply, but the secretary entered the room at that very moment.

"Mr. Banks will receive you now. Come this way."

Wei followed the secretary, and the door closed behind him.

Tiago stared at the wall of the room.

The television was broadcasting a documentary about the recent expansion of an organization called LAND. A reporter was interviewing a certain Douglas Woodside, a tall and handsome man with a hell of a smile. On his chest, the *Landist*, as the reporter called him, had a pin that showed a man and a woman kneeling on either side of a sphere containing the four elements. Tiago imagined the sphere represented the Earth.

With nothing better to do for the following half hour, Tiago listened to the reporter describing the proselytizing that the Landists were carrying out in California, Texas, Washington, D.C., and Florida. The last scene showed a dozen Landists shouting slogans inside the Kennedy Space Center, at Cape Canaveral, as they were being taken away by security.

Wei left Mr. Banks' office just when the documentary was getting interesting.

"Done and done." The boy snorted, apparently exhausted. He took off his tie. "Let's get out of here."

Tiago followed the Omnilogos.

Once in the hallway, Wei stopped again in the men's room to change clothes. He came back after a couple minutes, half naked and still putting on his t-shirt.

"Nice," Tiago said, pointing to the odd-shaped pendant that Wei had around his neck. "Why eight?"

Wei looked at Tiago as if he didn't understand what he was talking about. Then he saw the pendant. His face paled instantly. He put it hastily under his t-shirt.

"It's not an eight, you moron." He walked away without looking at him.

Tiago smiled. The Omnilogos was embarrassed, he

thought, intrigued. He would want to find out more about the pendant.

When they were both out of the building, Tiago noticed the shadows were lengthening as the afternoon wore on.

"Next stop?" the student asked, mounting his motorcycle.

"Wait here," Wei said. "I'll be right back."

Tiago turned off the engine and waited, looking at his smartphone.

Wei came back shortly after, holding a large bouquet of flowers.

"Look at these," Tiago said, smelling the aroma. "Any point asking for whom—"

"For my girlfriend," Wei said without hesitation.

"Oh...you have a girlfriend?"

"Something wrong with that?"

"No," Tiago said quickly, "and no comments on the matter."

"Good." Wei climbed on and placed the bouquet under his arm, careful not to squeeze it. "We're late," he said, glancing at his wristwatch. "*Vámanos.*"

Tiago started the engine and drove off. "So," he said, stopping at a traffic light. "Has your girlfriend got a name?"

"Evangeline."

The tone of Wei's voice, Tiago noticed, had radically changed from contemptuous to soft and slow.

"What is she like?" Tiago asked while passing a car.

The Omnilogos smiled. "She's tall and lean, fair hair and fair skin, eyes the color of the sea. She is witty, intelligent, cheerful, charming, and incredibly sweet. Loves cheeseburgers, starry skies, hearty breakfasts, the scent of Pelargoniums, Monet's paintings, and nights with a full moon. You know, she has a natural talent for..."

Tiago smiled as he listened to the Omnilogos describing Evangeline in every detail with growing excitement. For the very first time, he remembered that Wei was only a kid, and when it came to girls, he was not very different from most his peers.

He seemed almost normal.

~

"THAT'S IT," Wei said, nudging Tiago with his elbow and pointing to a small house painted in white.

Wei climbed off the vehicle and looked in the sideview mirror, fixing his hair. "How do I look?" he asked, visibly nervous.

"Insecure and damn funny," Tiago said, teasing.

Wei made a face and then looked at the house.

Tiago was contemplating a completely different person from the sharp, brilliant, and ruthless Omnilogos that he had come to know. At that moment, Wei seemed to him just a clumsy little boy, eager to make a good impression.

When they were in front of the door, Wei took a deep breath and put his bouquet in plain view. He knocked three times.

"Michelle will skin me alive," Wei said in a low voice, ignoring Tiago's questioning look.

The door wasn't opened; it was almost thrown off its hinges.

A black woman with long, frizzy hair and hands as big as baseball mitts stared at them with bloodshot eyes. "*You*," she said with a hiss, pointing to the Omnilogos with her finger. A large, bluish vein protruded from her forehead. "You're late."

"Geez, I know Michelle, I'm so, so sorry!" Wei seemed

about to kneel and beg forgiveness. "I had some unexpected... I tried to get things done as soon as possible, but... Look, I got these for..."

"Let me see," she said, snatching the bouquet.

"Roses, tulips, daisies, lilacs..." Michelle chanted, inspecting the Omnilogos' gift, "...and red geraniums."

There was a long moment of silence. Tiago was sure that the woman would throw the bouquet on the ground, trampling it without mercy.

"At least you know your flowers," said Michelle instead, showing a row of white teeth. The vein in her forehead narrowed and her gaze became gentler. "Hurry and step inside, you punk, before I change my mind."

Wei sighed, then showed Tiago. "This is my friend. Tiago, Michelle. Michelle, Tiago."

The two shook hands.

"This would be the guy you were talking about?" she asked, eyeing Tiago from head to foot.

He answered with a shy wave of his hand.

"Yes, he is."

"All right," said Michelle, moving from the door and letting them in.

"Is she awake?" Wei asked, passing by a small living room full of flowers, paintings, and books before heading up the stairs.

"The last time I checked, she was sleeping," Michelle said, staring at the young man from L.A. and indicating the stairs.

Tiago approached Wei, trying not to be heard by Michelle. "The guy you talked to her about?" he whispered in his ear.

Wei didn't answer and kept walking. At the top of the

stairs, they found themselves in front of a simple yellow door. Wei pushed his hair back. He breathed deeply.

Tiago didn't understand what was happening. Rather than going to meet his girlfriend, Wei seemed about to start a marathon.

Swallowing hard, Wei put his hand on the knob and opened the door. Tiago crossed the threshold, followed by Michelle.

The dark room they found themselves in pulsed with red, blue, and yellow lights. Holoposters were scattered all around, on the ceiling and on the walls, creating images and sounds that made the room look like an ancient sanctuary.

Tiago needed a few seconds before he could distinguish the forms that surrounded him. Eventually he recognized some of the evanescent objects that swirled about: planets, comets, asteroids, nebulae, and bright stars. The young man had the feeling of being at a show offered by a planetarium, if not better. These three-dimensional projections had the best resolution that he had ever seen.

Tiago walked through what seemed a reproduction of Saturn and moved quickly to follow Wei's fast pace. There were so many of the three-dimensional reproductions that sometimes they overlapped each other, mingling with the shapes and profiles of real objects. As he followed the Omnilogos, Tiago nearly stumbled twice.

"Watch out," Michelle warned him just in time.

"Thank you," said the student, dodging the edge of a table at the last moment. He also instinctively avoided a comet that appeared to his right.

Tiago watched the comet cross the room and bounce off the wall. He shook his head, confused.

Surely he had just imagined that. Holoposters were decorations often used at parties and receptions or large gatherings. They were three-dimensional projections of objects that moved within a room, created by a projector that could be programmed at will. They were very expensive items, the latest rave of the entertainment industry—but they could not possibly bounce off the walls.

"What are you doing?" Michelle said, gesturing to him to move ahead. "Wei is waiting."

Tiago snapped to attention and kept walking.

Wei was putting his flowers in a vase surrounded by a small asteroid belt. He was humming the tune of a song that Tiago didn't recognize.

The sudden explosion of a supernova brightened the pale face of the girl lying on the bed, silent and motionless. Tiago closed his hand over his mouth as he looked at the girl, studying the details that until then had remained hidden by the wonderful and misleading holographic shapes and lights.

Evangeline was sick. Wei did not include that detail in his rich and passionate description. The tiny body, the small veins that wandered up her neck like an intricate network of cables, and the face beset by shadows gave Tiago the impression of weakness, sadness, and resignation. She was so pale that her lips were bloodless.

He carefully scrutinized her from top to bottom. The shape of the thin white sheets suggested an amputated leg just above her knee.

On the bedside table, a prosthesis covered by dust made him realize Evangeline hadn't left that room for quite a while.

Tiago's initial surprise, soon replaced by annoyance because of the Omnilogos' omission, turned into bitter anger. Why hadn't Wei said anything?

"What's wrong with her?" Tiago whispered to Michelle.

"Osteosarcoma," Michelle managed to say, sniffling.

"What is that?" Tiago had never heard that word before, but he suspected it wasn't good.

"It's a cancer, a...a common form of childhood cancer."

"A cancer? Why... I mean, what's the cause?"

"No one knows."

"Good God," Tiago murmured, watching the diminished figure lying before their eyes. "And she's... Evangeline, I mean... She'll recover?"

Michelle had no time to answer. Evangeline's eyes opened.

Wei smiled at her. "Don't you ever tire of sleeping?"

The girl licked her dry lips and cleared her throat. She seemed confused and disoriented. Her eyes caught another small explosion, caused by the clash of two comets. A smile enlightened her face. "Hmm..." Evangeline tried to get up, leaning on her elbow, but Wei gently placed a hand on her chest.

"Some water first," he suggested.

Evangeline nodded and let Wei help her drink. When she finished, the Omnilogos took a handkerchief from her bedside table and wiped her chin.

"As a nurse, you suck," Evangeline whispered.

Wei took her hand in his. "I know, I'm hopeless," Wei said, shrugging. "I'm still stuck with First Aid. Mouth-to-mouth, you know." He blinked.

Evangeline smiled. "You moron."

Wei continued to hold the girl's hand, then pointed to Tiago. "Look, I brought you a guest."

Tiago was trying to look as natural as possible. After a long silence, Evangeline beckoned him to come closer.

Cursing Wei under his breath, he walked slowly to the

bedside, unsure of what to do. No one had told him what to expect or how to behave.

Just smile? Maybe shake her hand? Smile and shake her hand? Tiago glanced at Wei for help. He found none.

"You don't look in great shape," said Evangeline, watching Tiago approach.

It sounded like an odd joke coming from someone without a leg, as pale as death, and with trouble breathing.

"Tiago Melo," he introduced himself. Then, fearing that was not enough, he lowered his head and bent his knees slightly.

"A bow," Evangeline said, turning to Wei. "Here's someone who knows good manners."

"A bow?" Wei said, genuinely surprised. "You're kidding me? I thought he was going to stumble on something."

From where he stood, Tiago could see the girl's clouded face. Although lean and altered by the disease, she could not be older than sixteen. A bandana covered her head, so he couldn't see her hair. Although clearly ill and under-nourished, Evangeline was a girl who suggested a kind of simple and universal beauty, like dawn's first light.

"So, you're the chosen one," Evangeline said with a strange finality in her tone.

Wei started to say something, but she raised a hand to stop him.

"Leave us. I want to talk with him for a while. Alone."

"Honey," Michelle immediately replied. "I don't think it's a good—"

"Michelle, I'll be fine. I promise."

Wei stood up from the stool where he was sitting, and without another word he left the room. Michelle looked to Evangeline first, then to Tiago. She finally followed Wei, reluctantly closing the door behind her.

"Make yourself comfortable," Evangeline said, gesturing to the stool near her bed.

Tiago obeyed. Another sudden light lit up the room again. Evangeline smiled. Sparks of scarlet light brightened her blue eyes.

Only then did Tiago fully realize that he was alone with a girl who was fighting death in front of him, surrounded by the wonders of the galaxy that moved, glowed, and exploded all around them.

Something told him he was going through one of those rare situations where you feel you are in a place you know you shouldn't be, with a person you thought you'd never meet, and without the slightest idea of what's going to happen next.

"I was sure he would have chosen a woman," Evangeline said, looking thoughtful. "He always says that they tell the best stories, the richest, the ones that make you want to read all over again."

Tiago shook his head. "I'm sorry, I don't understand."

Evangeline turned and looked at him in the eyes.

"Never mind. Tell me about yourself. Do you study or do you work?"

"I'm a student of USC Annenberg."

"No way," Evangeline interrupted him, surprised. "You're a parrot?"

"I am afraid so," Tiago said apologetically. "I have no idea what it means or why they call me that, but it's been my second name since I came here."

Evangeline shrugged. "You know, it's the word we use for guys like you. Journalists, paparazzi, etc., etc."

"I see."

"Wei always comes up with new ways to avoid them, especially since he decided to...well, to go public, I guess."

"Yes, clearly we are unworthy parasites, the scum of society," Tiago admitted. "Extortionists, criminals, liars..."

Evangeline laughed a sweet, crystalline laugh. A bad cough forced her to stop. She leaned forward, as if about to throw up.

"Are you okay?" Tiago asked. He looked around. The door was closed. No one came running. He was really alone.

"No, not at all," replied the girl, wiping her mouth with a handkerchief. "Could you pass me that glass please?"

Tiago whirled around and almost brought down the glass full of water that was on the bedside table. Cursing silently, he took the glass with both hands and gave it to her.

A long moment of silence followed.

"Are you here for him?" Evangeline asked, handing him back the half-empty glass.

Tiago nodded. "Yeah, just out of curiosity, I guess. I wanted... I just wanted to know."

Evangeline stared at him. "What do you think of Wei? Tell me the truth."

"The truth?" asked Tiago, raising an eyebrow.

Evangeline pursed her lips, looking at Tiago's conflicted expression. "Don't worry. I know the guy. Go ahead, shoot."

"If you insist." Tiago crossed his arms and stared at the white sheet covering Evangeline. He thought about what he saw and of Wei's omission regarding Evangeline's situation.

"The first impression I had was that of a greedy, conceited, manipulative little prick. Now I think he's also a criminal, an opportunist, and a liar."

There was another long moment of silence.

"It's much better than I expected," Evangeline said, absently touching her bandana, as if making sure it was still there. "Wei hasn't always been like that, you know? Before we met, he was a very different person; isolated, quiet, full of anger. He never spoke to anyone. He was closed in on himself in a way that I would call dangerous, trapped in a world different from ours. A person limited and frightened. But things have changed."

"Changed? In what way?"

Evangeline thought before answering the question. Finally she said, "I guess it all started with a mouse."

"What?"

Evangeline shook her head. She smiled. "Forget it, it's a long story. Let's say that over time, we have discovered a common passion that helped us get to know each other better. I like to think that our relationship has transformed him. Slowly, Wei has learned to trust people, or at least some people. And he stopped being afraid."

The girl seemed to have recovered. Tiago leaned toward her. "Before, you told me he has chosen me. Chosen to do what?"

"It's not up to me to answer that question. If he hasn't said it yet, it means it's not the right time for you to know."

"He also said that I'll owe him a favor."

"You bet. It's the way he thinks. He does nothing for nothing, but he's very picky when it comes to choosing the people he believes useful."

"Useful for what?" Tiago said, unable to conceal his impatience. "Look, I followed him all day and I've got nothing to show for it. I need help. That kid...he's driving me crazy. I don't even know how to say it. It's like an enigma wrapped in a puzzle hidden in the most intricate maze of the world. The quirks I saw today have been enough to make me sleepless for the next decade. I need to know more. What does he want? What is he trying to achieve?"

Evangeline looked into Tiago's hazel eyes. "You are handsome," she said. "You have a beautiful amber-colored skin, very dark hair and a very short beard, shaved with an almost maniacal neatness. And you are tall; very tall."

Tiago cleared his throat. "Ahem, thanks."

"However, that's not the first thing I noticed when I saw you. And I think Wei noticed the same thing."

"At the risk of sounding like a broken record, I don't understand what you're hinting at."

Evangeline focused on his eyes. "I sense kindness, curiosity, passion, and determination in you. I am beginning to understand what Wei saw in those eyes."

Evangeline let the stellar show surrounding them lull her senses. What seemed like a small galaxy was flying over her bed. A pair of planets shaped like tiny rugby balls were following the concentration of stardust and lights a short distance away.

"Wei is a gift," Evangeline said finally, drowning her eyes in the light show. "I think he was born to amaze people. Look around you. Isn't it amazing?"

Tiago looked at the stellar objects swirling around the room. "Are you talking about the holoposters?" he asked, a little surprised by the sudden change of subject. "Well, yes. I guess." He followed Evangeline's gaze. "I don't think I've ever seen such vivid projections. But what does all this have to do with Wei?"

Evangeline smiled. "These are not holoposters."

Tiago was motionless for a few seconds, trying to grasp what he thought was a joke. Then he turned abruptly. Understanding dawned upon him.

He looked around for a minute, bewildered by the revelation: there was no projector in the room, no energy source that nourished the stellar shapes, no device that would explain their fluid and hypnotic dance.

"He made them for me, for my birthday," she said,

pointing all around her, as though hugging the entire room. "The best analgesic I've ever been prescribed."

Tiago followed the downward spiral of an arrow-shaped asteroid, unable to look away. Whatever those forms were, he now knew they were not sold in stores. They were unique, personal gifts crafted by a visionary mind.

"I'm weak. I'm afraid our conversation ends here," Evangeline said, touching Tiago's hand. "It was a pleasure to meet you, Tiago Melo. Before calling the others, do me a favor. Wei may seem only like a big mouth with a brain above average, but know this: behind him there is a huge project, something that involves us all. Please, have an open mind, be patient, but above all, have faith. I think he made a good choice with you. Show him he was right. Promise that you will take care of his dream, that you will become part of it."

Tiago didn't know what to answer. In fact, he didn't even understand what Evangeline was talking about. He remained silent for a few seconds, trying to grasp the meaning of those words.

"Are you putting a dying girl on hold?"

Tiago snapped to attention, caught staring at the amputated leg. Without further hesitation, he nodded. "I promise," he said.

"Thank you."

Evangeline revealed a white bracelet tucked under her pajamas. She touched it and the door was opened by Michelle, who was the first to reach her bed.

Wei appeared at Tiago's left and looked at Evangeline. Evangeline nodded. She gave a thumbs up and smiled.

"Come with me," Wei said, gently tapping Tiago's shoulder and then leading him out of the room.

Tiago followed him while looking at Evangeline for the

last time. The girl put her hand on her lips, made a kiss, and blew it to Tiago.

When the door clicked into place behind them, Tiago had completely forgotten to be angry with the Omnilogos. He simply felt a great emptiness inside.

Both went down the stairs, crossed the living room in silence, and quickly left the house.

Outside, it was getting cold. Afternoon was quickly turning into evening and the sun was reduced to a flattened ball on the horizon. Tiago's mind was busy with thoughts, haunted by doubts and uncertainties. He felt tired—bone-tired.

He found himself in front of his motorcycle. He could not remember how he got there.

"You'll find a message in your inbox," Wei said, interrupting his thoughts. "Inside there is the information you came for, plus a small gift."

Tiago frowned. He picked up his smartphone. In the inbox folder, there was a message that had arrived three minutes before from a certain...

"Kruscha?" Tiago asked, not understanding.

Wei pointed to himself theatrically.

"What does that mean?" Tiago asked, reading the e-mail. "You want me to publish in thirty days' time a story of this day without mentioning the real names of the people and referring to you as...as the Omnilogos? What for?"

"Well, I've decided that I like that name after all. The Omnilogos is a name unlike any other."

"I wasn't talking about that," Tiago said, annoyed by the answer. "I don't understand why you want me to publish an article about you under these conditions. Why... What do you need it for? Is this part of your big plan?"

"Big plan?" Wei repeated, puzzled. "No. No big plan. I only have many small projects."

"I still don't understand what you're talking about. If you want to write today's diary, do it by yourself."

"I can't do that. I suck at writing."

"What?"

"You heard me. I don't do words."

"Wait a minute. Are you serious? You want me to believe that a living encyclopedia, able to crack experimental technology and to build those flying things, can't write?"

"You're a champion in pointing out your lack of tact, buddy."

Tiago read the message again. "This would be the favor that I owe you?"

"Exactly."

"That's it? You're basically allowing me to do what I wanted."

"Yes, the only condition attached is that you must wait thirty days from today before publishing your piece."

"Why?"

"Because I say so."

"Oh yeah? And what happens if I publish my piece tomorrow?"

"You won't."

"No? How can you be so sure?"

"Because you've got green light, my dear Tiago Silva Abreu Melo."

Tiago tapped a foot on the asphalt, frustrated. "Enough bullshit! I want real answers! What do you expect to get from me? Why do you want *me* to write this story?"

"Because I read your article on the social inequalities plaguing Los Angeles ghettos, and I found it mind blowing. Because I studied your research on the applications of the

Cloud and they made me think. Because I've seen your photo exhibition on the evolution of the greeting and I was speechless, and because you showed an innate talent in public relations when it came to sponsoring the Web space of one of your classmates. When I saw you today in front of Max's house, I felt you were different from the others. You've proven to be resolute and stubborn when you waited for an hour and a half until I showed up. And I saw the spontaneity in your work only by exchanging a few words with you. Does this answer your question?"

Tiago gasped. "I...I can't believe... How could you... How do you know all these things? We've never seen each other before!"

"Tiago, don't be naive. In the fantastic and frightening era we live in, anyone can know what you had for breakfast the day before yesterday."

"You..."

Wei nodded. "I surfed the Net while you were grazing in the garden, made some calls, dotted all the Is and crossed the Ts. You passed my test with flying colors."

"You knew...you knew who I was all along?"

"Of course I knew. Haven't your parents told you never to talk to strangers?"

"Shut up! Evangeline told me you have chosen someone to tell a story. She was referring to this? This is what you need me for?" He indicated his phone.

"No, she always thinks big. She was referring to the broader picture. The reason I have chosen you is very selfish, you know? I chose you because in the future someone will look back, and in front of a bunch of people ask: 'What kind of person was Wei Wang before it all started?' I want you to be the one answering that question."

A TINY COMET the color of ice lit Michelle's face. The woman bit her lips as she clasped her hands behind her back.

"I gave her hot soup and something for the pain," she murmured, gazing behind her. "She said...she said she wants to see you."

Wei nodded and started to move, but Michelle grasped his arm, holding it tight.

"You remember what you told me about your father when I came to see you in the hospital right after the accident?"

"I remember," Wei said. "I told you that fear is a compass. It marks the direction we need to follow to become a better version of ourselves."

Michelle nodded. Her face was inscrutable. "I know what you want to do. Evangeline told me."

"Of course she did."

"Wei, it's dangerous. It's not about doing something that scares you. It's a huge risk; you could lose everything. You don't have to do it."

Wei shook his head. "I appreciate your concern, but you're wrong. I have nothing to lose. If I fail, it will be the most glorious failure in the history of humankind. How can I say no to that?"

Michelle opened her mouth but closed it almost immediately. She glanced toward Evangeline. "She's dying," she whispered, tears in her eyes. "I...don't think she's got much more..."

Wei put a hand on the woman's arm. He smiled.

Michelle let him go. The woman sniffled and continued, "She needs to rest. Five minutes. You have five minutes."

Wei nodded. "Thank you."

Michelle closed the door behind her.

The Omnilogos closed his eyes. He breathed deeply, trying to slow down the uncontrolled hammering of his heart, then he walked forward.

As he sat on the stool near the bed, he looked at Evangeline's chest, slowly rising and falling.

"I like Tiago," Evangeline said suddenly, her eyes closed. "He's got a nice ass."

Wei raised an eyebrow. "I don't know if I feel like laughing or throwing up."

"Do both things, please. That'd be funny."

Evangeline coughed. Wei gave her some water.

She moistened her lips. "Think you can trust him?"

"Absolutely."

"Good." Evangeline nodded. "Very good."

They sat in silence for a few minutes. Then Evangeline turned toward him. "What did Matthew say?" she asked, opening her eyes.

Wei sighed. "He didn't take it very well."

"You mean...you think he won't help you?"

"At the moment, he's worried about the new branch in Los Angeles and the one under construction in New York. When he figures out that *Sapori & Sentimenti* is not on the verge of doom, he won't refuse. He'll see sense."

"He'd better," Evangeline said. She seemed annoyed. "His little Italian oasis wouldn't even exist without you."

Wei didn't answer to that.

"And how is Tonio coping with the new...ingredients?" Evangeline sounded curious and amused at the same time.

Wei tried not to laugh. "I think his scorpion's nest in spicy sauce is improving, but he's still struggling when handling all the stuff that Nok puts in front of him. He shivers like a child. Right now, his fried grasshoppers are the only decent dish he can cook."

"How do you know that?" Evangeline asked, covering her mouth with one hand. "Have you tried it...personally?"

"Sure." Wei shrugged.

The girl made a strange face and stuck her tongue out, as if she had just drunk a bitter medicine.

"I'll never kiss you again."

"Is that a promise?"

They both laughed.

Evangeline brushed the bandana with her index finger. "What about Banks? Did you go meet him?"

Wei nodded. "Yes. That's the reason for my delay."

"And?"

The Omnilogos rubbed his forehead. "Well, he said that it is legally possible. He'll introduce me to someone who could give me those kinds of documents. The visa will probably be the hardest thing to get."

Another long moment of silence followed. Wei noticed Evangeline was dozing off.

"Wei?"

"Yes?"

"Can you turn the lights off? I'd like to dream."

Wei stood up from the stool and walked toward the middle of the room.

He raised his right hand in the air, and then he clenched it.

The projections stopped in unison, motionless like frozen fish in a tank.

Wei swung his arm, as if waving a lasso.

The projections moved toward him, inexorably dragged by an invisible force.

Wei stopped and opened his hand again. The projections lost their shapes and quickly became simple beams of light that threw themselves toward him. For a fraction of a second, Wei saw galaxies, comets, stars, and planets shining in the palm of his hand. It was a tiny universe peeping through his fingers.

He touched the bracelet hidden under his sleeve and the last remnant of light disappeared at once.

The room was now dark, silent, and infinitely smaller.

"Thank you," Evangeline said.

Wei took his place by her side. The girl would be asleep soon.

He looked at her. "Eva," he called softly, brushing her hand. "I've decided on a name."

"Really?" murmured Evangeline. "Finally. Let's hear it."

The Omnilogos leaned forward. He kissed the girl on the forehead and whispered something in her ear.

Evangeline smiled with her eyes. "Polaris," she murmured, visibly happy before dropping her head on the pillow, following Morpheus' call.

That night, she dreamed of an ocean of grass that looked over an ocean of stars and two familiar shadows in the midst of that infinite.

In that place without time and space, she remembered Polaris.

PART II

POLARIS

INTROLOGUE
LOS ANGELES, GRIFFITH PARK

2015

Kruscha spun for a few seconds before noticing Evangeline's open hand beckoning the little animal to come closer. The chinchilla sniffed at her moving fingers, then took a little hop, climbed up her arm, and ended up snuggling on her shoulder.

Evangeline absently stroked the rodent's small, furry head. After a few seconds, Kruscha raised his tail and ears and jumped to the ground, wandering around her without ever getting more than a couple meters away.

The evening was cool and quiet. Evangeline opened her arms and whirled a few times, as if to greet nature's beauty all around her.

A light breeze from the west washed over her. She looked at the sky and smiled. Then she closed her eyes, breathed in, and stretched her arms, murmuring with pleasure.

The stars were an unending succession of bright spots that gave life to the timeless blackboard of the night sky.

Evangeline started counting them. She stopped at thirty and lost count. She began again, using a finger to keep track, but got lost again at fifty stars. She laughed heartily and laid down on the ground, folding her arms behind her head. The grass bent under her weight, turning into a soft mattress that smelled of leaves, bark, flowers, and wind.

She looked to her left. "Wei, the grass will not bite you," she said, sighing. "I promise."

The little boy glanced around, rubbing his elbow. He seemed uncomfortable and had the look of someone who, from some unfortunate set of circumstances, found themself naked on a stage in front of a wide audience.

He took a step forward, hesitated, took two more steps, then stopped completely. First he looked at Evangeline, who was inviting him to lay down beside her. Then he noticed Kruscha trotting around the girl, happy as a clam.

Wei snorted but approached the girl, keeping a distance of about ten feet. He looked at the ground and wrinkled his nose.

"It's wet?"

"No, it's fantastic."

"I don't want to get my pants wet."

"Then take them off and sit in your underwear."

Wei was about to reply, but in the end, he said nothing.

After finding what he believed to be the least dirty piece of land, he bent his knees and slowly sat down.

He felt uncomfortable. The ground was hard and gritty and the grass tickled his buttocks. Several ants invaded his legs the moment he touched the ground. Wei took a stick and, for a few seconds, fought off the little invaders.

It was a useless battle. His clothes were still besieged by

platoons of ants, relentless and numerous as the stars above his head. Even the stick, he realized, was full of insects. He gave up and threw it away with a frustrated sigh, wrapped his arms around his knees, and glanced at the girl beside him. She was gazing silently at the sky.

Wei swallowed hard as he watched Evangeline absently tucking her long, shiny hair behind her ears. He looked away and tried not to think of the annoying itch that was growing at the base of his stomach.

"Look! That's the constellation of the Dragon!"

Wei snapped to attention when the girl shouted, excitedly indicating the night sky.

Wei followed her finger and raised an eyebrow. "Actually, that's Cassiopeia," he replied, as dry as a desert. "The constellation of the Dragon is right there."

Evangeline looked at him with an expression that Wei could not decipher. The girl looked back at the sky, and a moment later outstretched her arm again, pointing to another group of stars.

"That's Gemini! Isn't it beautiful?"

Wei cleared his throat as he followed the girl's index finger. "Gemini? I don't think so. It's not visible in the northern hemisphere at this time of the year."

Evangeline seemed to ignore his remark. Five seconds later, she said again, "Look, look! The constellation of the Pelargonium." The girl was beside herself with excitement.

"What?" Wei exclaimed, completely caught off guard. "There's nothing like that!"

Evangeline approached him, crawling on the grass. She was looking at him carefully, as if she was about to make one of the most important decisions of her life.

Wei instinctively drew back a few more inches. That look made him uneasy.

"Can you show me the constellation of the Radiator?"

"Wha—? No, of course not, because it doesn't exist!"

"And what about the Little Underpants?"

Wei started to reply, but was preceded by Evangeline. "And what about the constellation of the Hangman, or that of the Royal Palace, the Bill, the Sea Storm, the Flamingo, the Crucifix, the Keychain, the Avocado, the Lover, and the Immortal?"

Wei shook his head without answering. He didn't know if she simply wanted to tease him or was just making fun of him. Probably both, he thought.

"You're weird," Wei said, without looking at her.

Evangeline stared at him for half a minute before returning to her previous spot without saying another word.

The two remained silent for a long time, rocked by the simple but impressive show offered by the night sky. The wind created a subtle symphony of sounds around them, moving the grass and dry leaves as if by direction of an invisible dance conductor—a dialog between Mother Nature and the universe.

"You know, I don't think that the constellation of the Dragon looks like a dragon after all," Evangeline said, examining the roof of the world with a serious look on her face. "No. It looks more like a river. Yeah. I think I'll call it that from now on, the constellation of the River."

Wei looked at her and sighed. He'd had enough of the childish game.

"That's so stupid," he said. "You can't just change the name of a constellation."

"Why not?"

"The names of constellations are convention," Wei replied. "You can't suddenly change the name of a constellation and expect people to take you seriously."

Evangeline seemed to reflect on those words. Finally she said, "Wei, what are the brightest stars in the constellation of the River?"

Wei rolled his eyes. "If you are referring to the apparent magnitude of those stars, the brightest in the constellation of the Dragon are Eltanin, Aldhibain, Rastaban, and Altais."

Evangeline got closer while he was talking, so close now their shoulders touched. Wei could feel the heat of the girl's body and the distinct smell that she emanated—a mixture of vanilla and peach blended with something sweet and alien, like a bouquet of exotic flowers gathered in a meadow at the edge of the world.

"Wei?"

"What?"

"Which of them is the brightest star? In the constellation of the River, I mean."

Wei swallowed hard as he spied on the girl, trying not to be noticed. For a fraction of an instant, he got distracted by the slow and steady dancing of her hair that moved like the hypnotic ripples of a jellyfish's tentacles, bright and beautiful in the ocean's vastness. Wei looked away and closed his eyes. Then he cleared his throat.

"Th-the brightest star in the constellation of the Riv— of the Dragon, in the constellation of the Dragon, is Eltanin."

Evangeline nodded.

"Wei?"

"What?"

"If I changed the name Eltanin to Aquamarine, do you think that the constellation of the River would be less bright?"

Wei was about to reply but when he opened his mouth, his eyes found Evangeline's waiting for him. They were shining like polished diamonds crafted by the world's finest artisan.

For the first time since the beginning of the conversation, those eyes forced him to be quiet. He then started to think. Something lit up in his mind.

He thought back to the strange questions that the girl asked him, and a precise pattern formed before his eyes.

Changing the name of a star does not deprive it of its brightness, or of its position in the sky, he realized. A convention is the common way humanity interacts with itself. It doesn't describe the reality of things, but only the need of humankind to find an order, a pattern to follow; a way not to be afraid.

Despite himself, his lips slowly parted and formed a smile. Evangeline sure had her own way of explaining things.

"No, I don't think so," Wei finally said, looking at the constellation of the River from a new perspective. "I don't think that would make much difference."

"That's the first sensible thing that came out of your mouth today." Evangeline smiled.

"You know," Wei said, "I met someone called Eltanin."

"Really?" Evangeline blinked. "I've never met someone with that name. It sounds original."

"I don't think it was his name. I mean, I guess it was just a nickname or something."

"What kind of person was he?"

Wei shrugged. "He was very old when I met him. I think —I think he was about to die."

Evangeline studied him in silence for a few moments. "Was he afraid?" she asked, her voice little more than a whisper. "Of dying, I mean. Was he afraid of dying?"

Wei pondered the question. "No," he answered. "I don't

think he was afraid. He seemed more interested in telling me the story of his life, what he had done, why he had done it. Maybe he wanted to pass me a flame, you know, like an Olympic torch relay. Maybe he didn't want to be forgotten. I don't know how to explain it."

"You just did, Wei," Evangeline pointed out to him. "And I'd say Eltanin has succeeded."

"What do you mean?"

"We're talking about him, right? He'll never die as long as he lives on in our memory."

Wei thought about that, then nodded. "Yeah," he said. "I guess you're right."

Another island of silence closed the conversation and they both got lost in their own thoughts.

Kruscha rolled on the ground, sniffed the air, and then responded to Evangeline's call since she was holding a small stick of willow. The chinchilla took it eagerly, put it in his mouth, and gnawed at it.

"When did we meet for the first time?" Evangeline asked suddenly, looking at Kruscha chewing happily on his stick. "Was it last week?"

"Two weeks and two days ago," Wei answered without hesitation. His cheeks flushed. He cleared his throat and added, "I think."

"Two weeks," Evangeline whispered, looking at him as if the kid was some sort of strange sculpture.

"Wei?"

"Yeah?"

"What are you working on?"

Wei shook his head, surprised by the sudden change of subject. "What am I... What do you mean?"

"You know what I mean. I always see you taking notes, listening to people's conversations, reading huge books with weird titles, studying things that would make Einstein puke, and doing a bunch of other strange stuff for a kid your age."

"I'm not a kid!" Wei protested, realizing at once that he sounded like one.

"What are you working on?" Evangeline insisted, staring at him.

Wei hated that look. It made him feel as naked as a worm. He didn't answer, but his cheeks blushed. Now his face looked like a ripe tomato.

A minute passed...two. Evangeline continued to stare as Wei turned to look the other way. The boy moved slightly, as if he wanted to shake off the discomfort caused by her look.

"I think you want to change things," Evangeline said after a while, as if she finally found a way to read his thoughts. "I think you're trying to build something."

Wei kept his silence, staring stubbornly at the night sky.

"Fine, keep it to yourself," Evangeline said, rubbing her hands against her knees. "You know what? Whatever you want to do, I don't think you're going to make it. In fact, I'm sure you won't."

The statement made Wei's head spin. He turned to face the girl. "I have no clue what you're talking about," he said, digging his nails into the earth, "but if I *really* wanted to build something, I could do it with no problem."

"No you couldn't."

"What do you think you know?" Wei snapped. "You know nothing!"

"I know you, Wei Wang," Evangeline said. "Admit it. You're a stubborn kid, closed off in your little, complicated world, impossible to reach. You treat others with contempt and disgust. Don't look at me like that, you know I'm right! You insult me, Kruscha, any person around you. I'm sure today you insulted someone before breakfast. Insulting is what you do best, your way to keep people at a distance, your way to feel yourself."

"I don't... You are..." Wei began, getting knotted up in his words. He was angry, outraged, and impressed at the same time. He didn't know whether to hide from the girl's look or just slap her. "You know nothing about me. *Nothing*," he managed to say, stammering, his heart pounding heavily. He had no idea how the conversation had degenerated, but at that moment it didn't matter. He felt attacked and humiliated, treated like a stupid little kid with no brain.

Wei started to get up. He wanted to get away from this arrogant girl.

"I know you," Evangeline repeated, still staring at him.

Wei stayed where he was, staring back, challenging her pretentious look.

"If you keep doing things the way you're doing them, you'll never, ever get anything done."

"How can you be so sure? You...you don't know what I can do, the things that I know and—"

"Everything is useless, don't you see? All your knowledge and all your confidence are worthless."

"Why do you even care?"

"Wei, I want you to understand."

"You don't even know what you're talking about."

"Yes, I do."

"Okay, let's hear it then," Wei pushed her, pointing to himself with a thumb. "What do I need, hmm? What's so important that I don't have?"

"You'll need other people."

Wei widened his eyes, confused. "Other people?" he repeated. He wasn't expecting that answer. He felt like someone who had just shown up in the middle of a conversation, without the slightest idea of what others were talking about. "What do you mean?"

"You'll need people like yourself if you hope to make a difference, or to succeed in your project, or build what you want to build, or whatever you want to do. Don't you see? Only someone stupid would think they could do it alone."

Wei challenged the girl's eyes, trying not to blink. He pointed at her with his finger, almost as though he was pointing a loaded gun, ready to fire.

"Other people slow me down," he finally said, releasing a flow of magma from his mouth. "People are stupid!"

"I am a person."

Wei looked at Evangeline. The burst of heat that warmed his neck disappeared instantly, becoming a shiver that ran down his spine.

"You...you're different," Wei said, his voice unsteady. "You're not like the others. You're weird. I can't understand you. You have...a sparkle. I don't know how to explain it. Sometimes...sometimes you scare me."

Evangeline laughed. "Really?"

Wei nodded. He lowered his head and stared at the grass.

The tension between the two of them slowly dissolved, like snow under the sun.

Evangeline put her hands on her hips. "Dummy," she said, smiling.

Wei looked at her, but he didn't answer.

"Listen," the girl said, getting closer to him, "you're incredibly intelligent, that's true. I've seen you do things I've never seen anyone else do before. I admit it, you're special, but you're not all powerful. Now, try to consider the people around you. They are human beings, Wei, with passions, weaknesses, and strengths. They're resources.

Resources you can use. If you want to change things, if you have an idea, you will need other people to make it happen."

"Why?" Wei asked stubbornly.

Evangeline's face lightened up with a smile. "Because only people can change people."

Wei paused, reflecting on that phrase.

In the end, he looked away and tore the grass from the ground, muttering something that never went beyond his ears.

"Listen," Evangeline said, "even though I met you just a couple weeks ago, I am convinced you are a gift from heaven. A gift locked in a safe box. To open that safe box has become my mission; something I want to devote my days to. A task I accept with joy."

"A gift locked in a safe box." Wei tore off more grass, his eyes cast down. "Is that all I am to you?"

Evangeline rubbed her hands. She seemed uncomfortable. "Wei?"

"What?"

"Sorry. I didn't mean to yell at you or...tell you that stuff."

Wei opened and closed his mouth a few times. The third time, he shrugged and simply said, "Apologies accepted."

Evangeline got closer to him. Wei moved away a few inches. She laughed, poking him with her elbow.

Evangeline continued to bother him for a while, tickling or trying to hug him. Wei responded with varying degrees of irritation and indifference.

After a few minutes, Evangeline lay back on the grass. There was silence for a few heartbeats.

"Wei, where's the North Star?" she asked after a while, looking blankly at the sky. "Where is Polaris?"

Wei considered a sour and sharp answer, but when his

gaze lingered on the girl's dreamy face, he forgot what he wanted to spit at her.

A constellation made of tiny freckles dotting the girl's face made him swallow. Eventually, he turned away and searched the firmament.

His eyes followed a well-known pattern. He studied the sky and quickly found the constellation of the Big Dipper, bright and familiar, like few others. He focused on the two stars at the edge of the formation, Dubhe and Merak. He drew an imaginary line segment from Merak to Dubhe and multiplied the distance for five times the space between the two stars. At the end of the segment, shining and stable, was Polaris, the North Star.

Wei pointed it out to Evangeline, who nodded.

"How did you find it?" she asked, looking at him with admiration. "I would have never spotted it among so many lights."

Wei shrugged. "It's easy. You just need to rely on the constellations."

"Really?"

"Yes."

"So even *you* need to rely on something sometimes?"

Wei didn't answer, but he acknowledged to himself that he was the loser of that exchange. It was in times like these that he both hated and admired the girl. That was also one of the reasons why he felt so uncomfortable around her. No one could make him feel that way. So...stupid.

The girl searched in her pocket. "I've got something for you."

Wei saw Evangeline holding an object. It was a pendant, as strange as its owner. It was silver colored, streaked in a particular shade of blue.

It had the shape of a horizontal eight.

The girl gave it to Wei.

"The symbol of infinity?" he asked, studying it carefully.

"It's a good luck charm. You'll need it."

"I don't believe in luck."

"That's why I'm giving it to you, moron," Evangeline said, chuckling.

"Okay. Thank you," Wei said, finding nothing else to add.

"Do you like it?"

"It's...it's girl's stuff," he ascertained, turning it over in his hands. It was thin and bright. It caught one's eye.

"Of course it's girl's stuff, you idiot. It's mine! And if you lose it, I'll kill you. Got it?"

Wei put the pendant around his neck. "Got it," he said, smiling.

6

AVALON

SOUTH KOREA, SAEMANGEUM CITY

2022

Saemangeum skyscrapers offered an impressive sight, a unique mixture of frenzy and magnificence. It was the unfinished work of a newly born settlement, without a clear shape, where hundreds of soaring towers made of steel and concrete stood isolated and incomplete. The sparks that joined their metal bones shone like the heart of the Milky Way itself.

Beams, cables, and titanic scaffolding dominated the skyline. They looked like a rugged and intricate spider web, ready to support the very foundation of the world.

Roads and bridges under construction linked the different parts of the city, most of them still ruled by water and mud.

The city was a beast ready to wake up, a masterpiece of human ingenuity brought to life by technology's latest wonders. Most of the buildings were naked, with profiles just hinted at, like a painter's immature sketch struggling to take on a clear shape. The scenery was chaotic and lively, and the urban environment expanded minute by minute.

The unfinished city was in constant motion, swarmed by a never-ending army of hard hats in emerald-green uniforms, busily adding height, texture, and thickness to the many unfinished buildings.

Avalon Moon put down his fork and wiped his mouth with his sleeve as he watched the glowing city coming to life before his eyes. The smell of wet earth, wet cement, and dust mixed with humid air filled his nostrils. He breathed in deeply and closed his eyes. The city had a particular smell, like the scent of a beast, sweaty and breathless, that had just finished its hunting.

From the top floor of one completed building, Avalon realized, looking at the scenery, how lucky he was. He could see the world below him slowly taking shape before his eyes.

The noises from the city, too, had their own special charm. They were swift and powerful and beautifully matched the hammering of steel against steel in the background. The echoing sounds reminded him of the heartbeat of a giant; an infinite entity as inexorable as time.

The man blinked against the sunlight, absently scratching his buttocks as he shifted his weight on the chair. A creak accompanied his movements.

He was a fat man, with short legs and short arms and a huge belly. His face was yellow and sweaty. His head, broad and misshaped, resembled a big potato, and his cheeks were two cascades of flesh that hung close to his neck. From his nostrils, a generous number of long, sturdy hairs came out.

The rest of his body was no different. Countless layers of

fat rested one over the other, like a peculiar Christmas tree made by a butcher with a despicable sense of humor.

Avalon breathed heavily while clogging up one nostril with his finger. His throat produced a weird sound, like the soft cry of a wild animal.

After a couple seconds, he spat out a gob of phlegm that joined the puddle of mucus and saliva a few inches from his feet.

He finally looked away from the city's skyline. The man grunted and breathed in one more time. It seemed as if he was about to spit again, but he changed his mind at the very last moment. Instead, he licked his hands and passed them slowly and carefully over his greasy hair.

He turned to the man who was watching him from behind, motionless and silent.

"An increase of those proportions in the northeast in such a short time makes no sense," Avalon said while rubbing his wet hands.

He grasped the table with both hands and pushed up his bottom. A long and intermittent noise burst from his body, changing tone several times before dying in a low splutter.

"It looks like I'll need another pair of pants, Hector."

The tall, lean man behind him had straight shoulders and a severe expression. He resembled a stiff surfboard that had never been used. His eyebrows formed a thin, dark line that marked the lower part of his wide and prominent forehead.

Hector frowned and cleared his throat. Ignoring the last comment, he simply focused on keeping his frown as taut as possible.

"Our analysis of the performances of the Somsak Khon Kaen confirms our suspicion, sir," he said, his hands clasped behind his back. "I checked the data half a dozen times."

"Half a dozen times?" Avalon whistled and slammed his hands on the table, blasting away some bowls. "Ah! And people say you have no sense of humor."

"A careful analysis seemed simply appropriate to me, sir," replied the man.

Avalon Moon shook his head and snorted. "Long Standing Mahaverik Curve?" he asked, rubbing his hand over his protruding belly.

"It has an exponential growth, as in the past three months. In the province of Khon Kaen alone, they have increased their profit by thirty percent. In other western provinces of the country, like Sakon Nakhon and Si Sa Ket, they managed a similar increase, despite all our countermeasures. Their resourcefulness is growing day by day."

Avalon's face paled further. The shadow of sarcasm that had spiced his voice a few moments before faded into a glooming face with no expression at all.

"And you say they're planning to expand in the north too?" he asked, after mulling it over for a few seconds.

"Yes, sir. They already have an established presence in Lampang Province," answered the assistant, his posture so rigid that it looked like someone had replaced his spine with a steel rod. "According to the logistics department, the Somsak Khon Kaen has also contacted some local landowners and farmers to secure part of their production of bamboo caterpillars. We know for a fact that they have increased their demand for insects from Laos and Burma. We suspect it is a move aimed at collecting and storing a considerable quantity of the product, to treat it and then sell it in other parts of Thailand and China."

"Crickets and weaver ants in the northeast, grasshoppers and giant water bugs in the east, and now an expansion in the market of bamboo caterpillars in the north,"

Avalon said, visibly irritated. "This is an attack on all fronts."

"As I have already shown you, sir, our market share continues to be dominant," Hector said, as if to emphasize something important. "Our advantage over their—"

"Spare me, will you?" Avalon raised a large, greasy finger. "I know a predator when I see one. We've made two mistakes. We've allowed an unknown sheep to join our flock, *and* we've just figured out that sheep is actually a fucking wolf. We underestimated this Somsak, took too many things for granted, shielding behind our damn statistics for far too long."

Avalon kept a finger pressed on the table, moving it slowly until it outlined an imaginary circle.

"These white muzzles came out of nowhere. *Nowhere*, and in a year they have done the impossible. Now, thanks to our stupidity, they control ten percent of the entire edible insect market of Southeast Asia."

"Fifteen, sir; fifteen percent of the market," Hector corrected him promptly.

"Shia!" cursed Avalon. "How did this happen? How?"

There was a moment of silence, interrupted only by the advance of the imperious herd of bulldozers, tractors, and Caterpillars orbiting nearby, intent on building parts of the city.

Avalon Moon slammed a hand on the table. "This Somsak Khon Kaen is a problem that must be solved. And we must solve it now!" He closed his hand in a fist. "This is my territory! I'd rather be eaten alive by a legion of army ants than allow this Yankee colony to dump their shit in my back yard."

Avalon spat on the ground again before turning to look into the assistant's eyes. "Make sure that the Q department finds out which farmers are supplying them with the product and which facilities they are using to process it. I also want to know how on earth they produced that amount of giant water bugs in such a short time? It doesn't make any sense. If we are to believe the reports, they have increased the production of that insect one hundred and fifty percent in four months. This is not possible, and the impossible is unacceptable! I want reliable data, not fairy tales. I want answers to these questions, satisfactory answers, and I want them now. Is that clear?"

"Yes, sir."

Avalon focused his attention on the table. On it, a dozen plates and bowls sat empty or half-empty. With a quick gesture of his arm, the fat man reached out for the only plate still full of food. For a moment, he considered its contents: a generous portion of fried grasshoppers, crickets, termites, and ants, all mixed into a paste-like crimson sauce. He sniffed loudly, then reached into the mixture of insects and tasted a couple, chewing with gusto. He shook his head slightly and added a little pepper before taking his fork and resuming his meal.

"Well, don't just stand there like a statue," Avalon said, swallowing hard. "What happened to our construction plan in Vietnam? You told me it was urgent that we speak of it. Well, speak."

Hector looked at the tablet he was holding. "Yes, sir." He hesitated for a few seconds, then said, "Unfortunately, it seems the local authorities are not inclined to give their consent to our project."

Avalon didn't stop eating, but grunted something at the assistant.

Hector went on. "In their preliminary report, they've raised several issues regarding our proposal. Among other things, the provincial authority cites the specifics of the plan, a lack of funds in the project, the negative impact on the environment, inadequate safety standards for the workers, negligible benefits for the local economy and for their workforce, a number of—"

Avalon closed his eyes and rubbed his temples. He interrupted the list, waving a hand full of red sauce.

"Translated, those vomit bags want a more substantial incentive. Am I reading between the lines here? Well?"

Hector shook his head. "Our...encouragement was not even considered, sir. Personally, I think they are trying to—"

"I know what they're trying to do," Avalon said, annoyed. "An excuse, like a predator, is easy to recognize." He bit the inside of his cheek. "I don't get it. They must have a damn good reason to keep us out of their territory. The question is: What is it? The reports showed a strong interest within the local community for our insects. They import more crickets and grasshoppers than Laos and Burma combined. They need the product. They want it. What game are they playing?"

Hector opened his mouth but closed it almost immediately. The question remained unanswered. Avalon resumed his meal.

He finished the last fried cricket and drained his glass of red wine, making a disgusting noise with his mouth.

The man snapped his fingers and raised his empty glass, and the young server who was waiting silently to his left moved quickly to fill it. When the glass was full, Avalon instructed him to clear the dishes and the empty bowls and to serve the next course.

The man licked his big lips slowly while exploring the vastness of his nostrils with his middle finger.

He watched the server clear, with professional grace, the last crumbs, clean the cutlery, and offer a new course.

"Nest of scorpions in soy sauce, vinegar, and raisins."

Avalon dismissed him by waving a hand.

Hector was evaluating the data on the tablet. His lips merged into a single horizontal line. "There's more regarding our plan in Vietnam, sir," he said in a low voice, as if he was afraid of being heard by somebody.

"I'm listening," Avalon said, chewing all the while.

The assistant went on. "It's a possibility that seems unlikely, but I did not feel comfortable excluding it from the report." Hector pointed to the data emitted by his device. "The true reason behind our problems in Vietnam may not depend on local administration policies, or at least not simply by them. An external factor could have caused it."

Avalon swallowed a mouthful, then wiped the trickle of dark sauce from the side of his mouth. "It's clear they don't want us messing around in their back yard. What external factors are you babbling about?"

Hector touched the tablet's screen. "The F department has sent a series of data. Individually, they don't seem to have any importance, and yet I suspect they explain what is really happening in Vietnam, if...well, if read in a certain way."

"I'm all ears," Avalon said.

"From the reports, the Somsak Khon Kaen is importing goods and establishing business relationships with all the edible insect marketplaces in the region, but they have not even remotely considered Vietnam."

"Proof that those pigs haven't the gift of ubiquity, it seems to me," said Avalon, triumphant. "Damn good news in this ocean of shit."

Hector shook his head. "Sir, the Somsak Khon Kaen has

been reported to be active in Malaysia, the Philippines, Indonesia, Burma, Laos, Cambodia, and even in Southern China—but not in Vietnam. No activity in that region. I'm not just talking about plans for contracts or contacts with the administration or the local workforce. Import, export, technical assistance, exchange of know-how, you name it. They've treated the region as a ghost area."

Avalon stopped suddenly, his fork midway between his plate and his open mouth. He let the information sink in. His neck stiffened as his brain elaborated on what the assistant had said.

"Let me see," he finally said, putting down his fork and moving his fingers impatiently.

Hector handed the tablet to his boss, who took it and studied the data.

"Their moves seem to suggest two possible explanations," Hector said while Avalon was reading. "Either they don't have the slightest trace of interest in the Vietnamese market, which doesn't seem to make much sense given their past behavior, or they are trying to—"

"They are trying not to get our attention," Avalon finished for him, clenching his jaw. "It would make sense if they were trying to expand into the east and, at the same time, they wanted to prevent us from entering the Vietnamese market."

"My same conclusion, sir."

Avalon continued to evaluate the data, eyes wide and bloodshot. "If that's true, the situation went south. Not only have they established a presence here, they are now looking to expand into a virgin area while trying to completely exclude us. But how on earth did they—"

"Your problem, gentlemen, is that you treat the Somsak as an obstacle rather than as an opportunity."

Both Avalon and Hector looked in the direction from which the voice had come.

The young server had crossed half of the balcony and sat down at the opposite end of the table, without either of them noticing it.

On the ground lay a tie, a jacket, a shirt, and a pair of shoes. Now—together with a simple canary-colored shirt and black trousers—he was wearing only a cocksure smile and an impudent expression.

Avalon looked him over from top to bottom.

The server appeared to be a completely different person, and yet he was the same one. The transformation had been so drastic that Avalon thought he was imagining it.

Avalon stared at the smiling young man. A part of his brain was still looking for the server.

The first one to recover from the surprise was Hector. "What are you doing?" he demanded with a tone somewhere between amazement and indignation.

"Saemangeum City is a view to be enjoyed while sitting, Mr. Hoberdan."

"What...what did you say?" hissed Hector, completely taken aback.

The young man shrugged. He leaned forward to pick up a bottle of water. Once the cap was off, he drank its contents.

"I'm calling security," Hector said, fiddling with his tablet.

Avalon frowned. The server was short and thin, with a sharp, tanned face. The almond-shaped eyes were amber and resembled two drops of dew embedded on a face with both Asian and Caucasian traits. A half-blood, thought Avalon; probably a cross between a Han and a Westerner.

When the server finished drinking, Avalon leaned toward him, pointing to the empty bottle.

"Can I get you more water? You seem quite thirsty, son."

"I'm fine, thanks."

"Orange juice, milk, hot chocolate?" continued to inquire Avalon, indicating the door of the balcony. "I can get them in a minute."

His server smiled a polite no.

Avalon planted his elbows on the table, crossed his fingers and rested his chin on them, staring at the young man without batting an eyelid. "Are you a nut, a charlatan, or someone who simply wants to get fired with style?"

The server grinned. "I'm all three things, and not one in particular."

"I want to know the reason for this charade, boy."

"Well, it's real simple: I'm here to advise you, Mr. Moon."

"You? Here to advise me? Am I missing something? I thought you were here to clean my table and serve the next course."

"That and make sure you become outrageously rich and powerful."

Avalon snorted. "This thing is going to end very, very bad for you. I don't like being teased, kid. You have the slightest idea who you're talking to?"

"Avalon Yolay Moon," the other replied, indicating the fat man. "Born in Singapore on March 31, 1985. Son of Jin-ho Moon and Anong Kasemsarn. Founder and president of Sanuk Edible Insects, Inc. Multimillionaire, workaholic, atheist, insectivore, and staunch supporter of the *six-legged livestock* movement. You consume only insects or products derived from them. You are a football and basketball lover, single, touchy, and extremely stubborn. You have a photographic memory and a questionable sense of humor." The boy paused and sniffed. "Not particularly fond of personal hygiene," he added. "Favorite color, brown. Favorite dish, scorpions grilled with barbecue sauce. You have two great passions: your company and your belly."

Avalon Moon ran a hand over his mouth. "Who the hell are you?"

"An interesting question that has multiple answers," the boy said, drumming his fingers on the table. "I'll be frank with you, Mr. Moon. My name is *Nobody*."

"Really?" Avalon said. "Well, I guess this simplifies things, doesn't it? Nobody will care if *Nobody*'s body will be found on the bed of the Dongjin River tonight."

Two women in emerald and gold uniforms appeared at the door. Hector pointed to the young server, still sitting peacefully, his legs on the table.

The guards nodded and walked briskly toward him.

"Tell me, Mr. Moon," the boy said, fiddling with the cap of the bottle, with little apparent regard for the two guards who were quickly approaching. "If someone puts what he claimed to be the winning lottery ticket in your hands, would you throw it away before or after making sure that it's not the winning one?"

Avalon raised an eyebrow. "Wait," he said, gesturing for the guards to step back.

"The Somsak Khon Kaen's new expansion in Vietnam is a matter of fact," said the boy, still fiddling with the bottle cap. "I'm here to tell you how to solve the problem and get an unexpected benefit from it at the same time."

"Let me get this straight," Avalon said. "Why in the world should I listen to a kid who, five minutes ago, was cleaning my table?"

"Mr. Moon, look at it this way. If I'm a farce, you'd have wasted ten minutes of your time. But if I'm not... Well, isn't this what makes the whole thing so interesting?"

The two guards looked at Avalon, waiting for instructions. He was unsure of what to do. The kid was definitely a hassle, but his manner sparked Avalon's curiosity. Furthermore, he intended to find out how the stranger knew so many things about him.

"Wait outside," Avalon said finally, signaling the door to the two women. The guards obeyed, leaving the balcony at once.

Hector started to say something, but Avalon interrupted him. "I want to hear what this nosy little punk has to say, before boxing him."

Hector nodded, although he didn't seem to approve.

"This conversation will continue on two conditions," clarified Avalon with an inflexible tone. "I want to know your name and the real reason for this sham."

The boy snorted, clearly annoyed, as if he had been asked to repeat a frustrating task for the umpteenth time.

"My name is a gift few people receive, Mr. Moon, and you did nothing to deserve it. However, if you really want to associate a series of letters to my face, *Omnilogos* will do for now."

"Omnilogos," Avalon repeated in a thoughtful voice, as if for the first time he had tasted an unfamiliar fruit. He turned to Hector.

The assistant was already fiddling with his tablet.

Ten seconds later, he raised his head. "According to DataMorph, it's a cyberio, sir."

Avalon closed his eyelids. "Should I know what the hell that's supposed to mean?"

Hector continued to read, "It's a term associated in the West with a group of terrorists in the cyberspace, such as The Brothers of Eternity and Animosity. It's not known whether it's a single individual or a group of individuals."

"Ta-Da!" said the boy, moving his hands in a theatrical

way. Then he looked at Hector. "Let me give you a piece of advice for your next research, Mr. Hoberdan. If you want real information, don't use that concentrate of media and governmental propaganda for your sources. Wikipedia is way better."

"You're a terrorist?" Avalon said, barely holding back a smile. The boy could not have been over sixteen years old.

"It's an unforgivable oversimplification," said the Omnilogos, "but I guess it explains why I don't get many cards at Christmas."

Avalon had nothing to say about that statement. It simply made no sense to him.

The boy held up two fingers. "As for the second question," he went on, "I think the answer is obvious. I doubt that Mr. Hoberdan here would have gladly set up an appointment with an unknown teenager. Am I right?"

"So you've taken the initiative and organized this show," Avalon said, narrowing his eyes. "And how did you enter my human resources department anyway?" He added, with a note of sarcasm in his voice, "*Omnilogos*."

"Does it really matter?"

A long silence followed. "No," Avalon growled. He turned to Hector. "Who's the head of HR?"

"Jiang Ping, sir," the assistant answered promptly.

"Right," Avalon said. "Transfer him to the leisure department."

Hector looked at his boss without answering. Eventually he said, "S-sir, there's no leisure department."

Avalon stared at him. "Do I have to spell out everything?"

Hector blinked. "I understand, sir," he said, touching his tablet. "Termination letter sent."

"How old are you, boy?" Avalon asked.

"I'm seventeen."

"Seventeen years old," Avalon echoed. "Well, Omnilogos, congratulations. Looks like your boldness managed to snatch ten minutes of my time. Use them well."

The Omnilogos' cheeky expression gave way to sheer determination. The sudden change surprised Avalon. The kid seemed to have aged ten years in ten seconds.

"The reason why I'm here, Mr. Moon, is because I know you." The Omnilogos looked at the plates filled with insects waiting on the table. "I know I'm in front of a special person who thinks outside the box and can concretize dreams. You are a man whose choices can shape the world. Five years ago, you invested in what most people believed was nothing but a joke: a chain of restaurants built around edible insects. Your goal was to sell a product considered taboo by half the world's population and profit from it. Thanks to your perseverance, you have created a whole new market and have turned a Thai custom into a widespread practice throughout Southeast Asia. You have created a business worth half a billion dollars that went beyond anyone's expectations. Now, five years after the beginning of that bet, no one is laughing and many eyes have turned with interest to you and what you're doing here in Asia."

Avalon stared in silence. That kid was obviously more than what his appearance suggested. Confident, enterprising, talkative, even erudite, the Omnilogos was a constant surprise, unpredictable, and impossible to ignore.

"I'm surprised, I admit it," Avalon said, raising his hands as though surrendering to the loquacity of the boy. "I was expecting a pedantic and insolent kid, not a pedantic and insolent kid who is also knowledgeable in the history of marketing. Now, what do you want me to do with your report about my past performance? You want to fill this chatterbox's place?" He pointed at Hector with a wave of his hand.

"What you did is no longer important," said the Omnilogos. "I'm interested in what you're going to do. That's why I'm here." He took a clean dish and put a fried cricket on it. "Five years ago, two-thirds of the inhabitants of this planet would have looked at this dish and wrinkled their nose. You, watching the same dish, saw a low-calorie, high concentration of amino acids, vitamin B12, riboflavin, vitamin A, and protein, incredibly easy to find, keep, process, store, and sell. All this by paying a ridiculously low price and getting in return ten times the money invested. Insects are one of the most underrated and misunderstood products of our time. They are incredibly efficient at converting plants into edible protein. Four grasshoppers provide as much calcium as contained in a glass of milk. One hundred grams of locusts contain more iron than beef and less than the equivalent amount of calories and fat. Insects produce less waste and greenhouse gases than traditional livestock. They need a limited amount of land and require less feed. If that wasn't enough, they are much more affordable for the environment, cost less in resources, and can generate many jobs."

The Omnilogos put the cricket in his mouth and chewed. "Did I mention that they are good?"

Avalon said nothing; he wanted to see where the boy was going with this speech.

"The creation of your Sanuk has shown the world that insects are a resource no one had really taken advantage of before," the Omnilogos went on. "And now, because of your actions, the edible insects market is about to change radically. Other businessmen have noticed that the time is ripe for investment in this sector, and soon enough, your leadership will be threatened. In fact, your leadership is challenged at this very moment, isn't it?"

"Is it?" Avalon frowned.

The Omnilogos pointed at Hector, while he kept looking Avalon straight in his eyes. "You bet. In time, you'll lose your leadership in this sector. The power of major multinationals will cast you away from the podium. You and your company will be reduced to an ordinary player without influence, forced to scrape the crumbs of what was once your own empire."

Avalon shifted in his chair. He didn't like the boy's words and tone. He didn't like them at all.

"So you're a marketing expert *and* a fortune teller?" the fat man said, rubbing his neck. "Your history lesson is interesting, I admit, but if your advice is to worry about a future that exists only in your head, then this conversation was a waste of my time. What do you want me to do with the predictions of a seventeen-year-old kid? You expect me to believe your words just because you put on this show and somehow managed to sneak in here?"

"No," the Omnilogos replied, leaning toward Avalon, "what I ask you to do is to think. Don't be fooled by my appearance. I'm asking you to focus on my message; the *message*, Mr. Moon."

"The message," Avalon repeated, losing patience. "There is no hidden message, plot, or conspiracy against my Sanuk. What you say is just plain nonsense. Have I lost some ground? Sure. Does that mean my business is doomed? Hell no. I'll bounce on my feet before you know it and crack some skulls on my way up, just as I always have."

"Come on," the Omnilogos said, rolling his eyes. "You're not stupid, Mr. Moon. You listened to Mr. Hoberdan's report and read the newspapers. Everyone knows what's happening."

"Enlighten me," said Avalon with a skeptical smile.

"Whether you like it or not, your hegemony of the edible insects market is disintegrating. Think about it! A new player who came out of nowhere has taken root in your territory. That competition took a tenth of your market in six months. More adaptable, aggressive, unpredictable, and confident than you ever thought possible, it seems to be always a step ahead of you. This player understands the product, understands the consumer and the market. He knows how to move the pieces on the chessboard and he's a couple moves away from declaring checkmate."

"You're talking about the Somsak Khon Kaen?" Avalon realized, gazing at the Omnilogos. "I don't understand what—"

"A small U.S. company is threatening your carefully calculated plan, tearing apart your control on the insects' market piece by piece. Foreigners—*white muzzles*, as you call them—have developed the ability to destroy everything you have worked for." The Omnilogos paused, the silence like a slap on Avalon's face. "Now listen to me," the boy resumed, leaning forward. "The Somsak Khon Kaen is only the beginning. Over the next five years, Southeast Asia will have half a dozen players, faster and more prepared than the Somsak Khon Kaen and ten times the size of your Sanuk. At that point, if you haven't been able to adapt, you'll find yourself completely disarmed. You'll be like a child playing at being a soldier against adults with nuclear weapons."

Avalon's brain laughed at the boy's statements; pretentious, rambling, without basis. Yet his heart beat faster. There was something ominous in the words of the Omnilogos, a feeling of inevitability that echoed in his sentences and entered Avalon's bones.

"You keep talking as if you had a damn crystal ball in front of you," Avalon said, snorting. "I clean my ass with your predictions, kid. I don't care what you think you know about my company. You're wrong."

"My statements are based on fact, Mr. Moon. If you have paid attention to what I said, it should be clear that I did my homework."

"So you're aware of information, news, data that we don't have? Evidence unknown to me and my company? Is that what you're trying to tell me?"

"I thought it was clear at this point."

Avalon reflected on that statement. "How do you know all this? I mean, you're babbling about this incoming war, the entry of new companies in the market and so on. I know nothing of all this crap." Avalon looked at his assistant. Hector shook his head, confirming he didn't have any evidence of what the boy had said.

"Listen, I can believe the story of the genius boy who wants to be noticed," continued Avalon. "I like your style and the way you put up this show, it was fun. But if you're talking about confidential information useful to me and my company, then this is the time to spit it out. Give me a reason to believe your story or get the hell out of here."

"All this is of little importance, Mr. Moon," said the Omnilogos. "Once again, pay attention to the message. Trust your instinct. What matters now is your response to this threat and your vision for the future."

"My response?" Avalon couldn't follow the Omnilogos, and this pissed him off a lot. "I'll give you my response right now. Hector." He started to get up. "Call the—"

"The Somsak Khon Kaen has proven to be dangerous for

your Sanuk. They've shown you they can beat you on your own territory. You're not facing a group of farmers that some of your men can scare, and you're not against a resourceless Thai businessman who will declare bankruptcy in six months. You're facing an aggressive and motivated foreign company. Their move in Vietnam is just the beginning. If you can't handle the situation fast, it will slip out of your hands. And believe me, you won't be able to handle it the way you want. The Somsak Khon Kaen is a new breed of enterprise and ingenuity, with an adaptable and unpredictable agenda. If you decide to start this war, I promise you it will be long and exhausting, and eventually you'll lose everything."

"Okay. I get it, I get it." Avalon threw his hands up. "You don't want to say how, don't want to say why, but you want to make us believe that you're three steps ahead of everyone else. You already know everything, right? You may as well put a mole as big as a house on your nose and put up your fortune teller tent. Or... No, wait! This is the magic moment when you suggest an alternative to avoid my inevitable defeat. This is the reason you're here, after all, to give me advice, right?"

"My advice is simple," said the Omnilogos. "Join forces with the Somsak Khon Kaen. It's the only way to avoid defeat."

"What... What did you say?"

"I'm talking about a merger, Mr. Moon. A merger between your Sanuk and the Somsak Khon Kaen is the only way to avoid oblivion."

"A merger?" Avalon remained awestruck for a few seconds. Then, as though emerging from a trance, he clapped his hands and giggled. "Ah! This is unbelievable! You're... Damn, you're a treasure chest of surprises, you little brat. Really! I can't believe half the bullshit you said, but you said it so well, I can't even move. Look! I have my ass glued to the chair. I like you. I love you! You are a hoot!"

"I'm just trying to help you, sir," the Omnilogos said. "That's all I'm here for."

Avalon wiped his mouth with the back of his hand. "Okay, okay, just for fun. Let's...let's play your little game. What makes you even think that the Somsak wants to have anything to do with me?"

"I know it for a fact, Mr. Moon."

"*How?*" barked Avalon, tired of the meaningless conversation.

The Omnilogos had an impassive face, a white mask with no expression.

"I know because I am the Somsak Khon Kaen," he said, his lips curling up to form a tiny smile.

A LONG SILENCE FOLLOWED THE OMNILOGOS' statement.

His last sentence hung in the air for seconds. No one dared to speak or move.

When Avalon resumed breathing, he burst out into raucous and uncontrollable laughter. He wiped his tears and sniffled a couple of times. He then tried to speak, but was interrupted by another round of laughter that he couldn't control. The tension that had been hovering in the air was now dead and buried.

"Hector, call the guards," Avalon said, red-faced, waving a hand in the direction of the entrance. "We're done with this farce."

Hector nodded and began to touch his tablet, but he was suddenly interrupted by the Omnilogos.

"And miss the look on your assistant's face when the secretariat of the Somsak Khon Kaen calls him? No way!"

"Really?" Avalon spat on the floor, then shook his head. "And when should this incredible turn of events happen?"

The Omnilogos began tapping a finger on the table. "In seven, six, five, four, three, two, one..."

Hector's tablet lit with a blue light. It emitted a rhythmic and repetitive ringing.

Avalon turned open-mouthed to his assistant, who returned a blank look.

When Hector touched the device, the sound stopped.

Avalon looked at the Omnilogos, who looked back at him.

"It's...it's the secretariat of the Somsak Khon Kaen, sir," said Hector.

"Go ahead," Avalon said, holding the boy's gaze. "What do they want?"

The atmosphere had again abruptly changed. It seemed as if someone had just put a bomb ready to detonate under the table.

"Their message simply says: *It's true*," reported Hector. "It doesn't say anything else."

"You will be contacted again, Mr. Moon," the Omnilogos said. "You face a choice that will determine the fate not only of the Sanuk and the Somsak, but of all those companies that will decide to enter this newborn market. With our combined forces, we can create an unstoppable covenant that no other company could counter. We could become the monopolist in this sector. And when the big names finally notice the cash cow, and the giant multinationals consider entering the stage, we'll be a long-established force, a powerhouse to be reckoned with."

Avalon wiped his forehead with the sleeve of his jacket

without taking his eyes off the Omnilogos. "Two plot twists in less than ten minutes," he said, struggling to process the Omnilogos' information. "Forget the tent and the crystal ball. You should consider a career on Broadway. You'd make a fortune."

Avalon ordered Hector to give him the tablet.

When he finished reading the message, he turned to regard the boy. "Do you have any other rabbits in your hat? I'd like to know if today is the day I die of a heart attack."

The Omnilogos opened his arms and showed his empty hands, as if he wanted to reassure him he wasn't dangerous. "I just have a couple more. Nothing lethal. For now, I ask you only to consider a healthy and profitable business proposition."

"You're talking about the merger?"

"I'm talking about a total fusion, to tell you the truth," the Omnilogos pointed out. "Your Sanuk will de facto absorb the Somsak Khon Kaen. The details have been transferred to your assistant."

Avalon looked at Hector, who responded with a quick motion of assent.

The fat man scratched his neck. It was still hard to believe that the kid was really who he claimed to be.

"This business proposal seems a gift," Avalon said, reading the data on the tablet. "I don't like gifts. They stink of rotten corpses. There's no such thing as a freebie in my world. Speak up. What are you really after?"

The Omnilogos laughed. For the very first time, the spontaneous and childlike sound reminded Avalon that he was talking to a teenager. This fact disquieted him much more than he cared to admit.

"You'll take full control of your rival, its resources, its technology, its contacts, and its staff," the Omnilogos said, pushing his hands deep in his pockets. "Everything that is the Somsak will be yours. I wish, however, that the key people who have made the Somsak Khon Kaen a force to be reckoned with become members of your board of directors, especially the researchers and the specialists in public relations, the two elements of which your Sanuk has great need."

Avalon frowned. "I expected conditions," he said. "This is another gift. I am sorry to point this out, kid, but you're still going to be one miracle short of sainthood."

The Omnilogos smirked. "The agreement will be arranged if you'll satisfy two non-negotiable conditions."

"Now we're talking," Avalon said. "Come on! Hit me!" He spread his arms theatrically.

"You'll expand the market of edible insects in Saemangeum City. I want this place to become the hub of your business empire."

Avalon's smile faded. "What? You mean here? In this city?"

"Exactly."

Avalon chortled. "What are you talking about, kid? This city is an empty shell. It has a population of hard hats, architects, and engineers. Who should I sell my bugs to, hmm? The fish?"

"Close your eyes, Mr. Moon. Imagine how this city will be fifteen years from now, when it will be populated by millions of people."

"I'm sorry," Avalon said, tapping his head. "I have a poor imagination."

The Omnilogos looked around, admiring the profile of some distant, unfinished skyscrapers. "It's true, after all," he said. "Saemangeum City is a gift few people understand."

Avalon ignored the last sentence. "Okay. Let me get this

straight. You want to sell insects to the Koreans. Is this what you want? This would be your first condition?"

"No, I don't want to sell to the Koreans. I want you to enter Saemangeum's market with your product. When the very first home is built—the first grocery store, the first school—I want you to be there, waiting with your product in hand and a wide smile on your face while selling it."

"Sorry to burst your bubble, kid, but I see you're quite weak in geography. Let me connect the dots for you. Saemangeum City *is* part of Korea. Why on earth do you speak as if they were two separate things?"

"Trust me, the two things may seem part of the same symphony now, but I assure you that this will not be the case for long."

"A poet." Avalon sighed.

The Omnilogos ignored him. "Think of Saemangeum City as a separate market, an independent city. It would make more sense if you'd use a bit of imagination, but I'm not asking you to do any of this. I'm simply offering you a possibility." The boy raised a finger, anticipating Avalon's comment. "This is not a discussion, Mr. Moon. This is a condition. Take it or leave it."

"I swear, kid, I don't get your stubbornness," Avalon insisted. "Today, tomorrow, a year from now; it makes no difference. Even if this damn city were a separate state with a population of ten million inhabitants on the verge of starvation, no one would buy my insects. Consider the geography of the place. Think of the culture and the traditions. I would have the same probability of selling crickets and ants to Saemangeumians as of selling the same stuff to the French or the Italians. These bastards will never eat insects. They have been trained to think they are disgusting."

The Omnilogos smiled. "Well, you would be surprised to

find out what an Italian will eat with just the right amount of tomato sauce on it."

"What?"

The Omnilogos shook his head. "Listen. We are witnessing the creation of the most advanced city that humanity has ever built. A city that doesn't rise from the backbone of a previous city, but a virgin, urban settlement that has been built in a brand-new province reclaimed from nature. This city is a blank sheet we can write on to our own liking, and the people who are smart enough to figure this out will work to shape it as they wish. Of one thing you can be sure. This city won't be what people expect it'll be. It will be a completely different breed: international, vertical, advanced, rich, and completely self-sustainable. I want the market of edible insects to play an important part in all this, Mr. Moon."

Avalon shrugged. "Even if it were heaven fallen on Earth, Saemangeum City is beyond my jurisdiction. Where would I find the resources to even dare do what you're asking? I don't even have the permits or the contacts to operate in this part of the world. You're suggesting a titanic investment based on a vision that could never come true."

The Omnilogos stretched an arm and pointed his finger toward the horizon. "Don't they call it capitalism for that reason, Mr. Moon?"

Avalon was not convinced. "The customer will have no interest in my product."

"They'll be interested if you make brave choices that men like you are called to make, choices that can undo simple individuals, or create legends."

Avalon grunted and settled back. "I feel like my head is about to explode. All this talking about the future got me a fucking headache. I need a sparkle of dust." He thrust his hand into his pants pocket and came out with a small vial filled with a peach-yellow powder. He jammed a pinch of the powder in his nostrils and sneezed five times in a row. When he touched his forehead, the headache was gone.

"Bless you," the Omnilogos said.

"After this *request* of yours, I'm afraid to hear the second one." Avalon wiped the yellowish snot with the palm of his hand. "What is it? Huh? You want me to solve world hunger? Reduce the ozone depletion?"

"I need you to put me in touch with Zhongnanhai."

Avalon dropped the vial with the powder, which shattered on the floor. "*What?*" he spat out, staring at the Omnilogos with bloodshot eyes.

"You heard me, Mr. Moon. I need to talk with your friend in the Chinese Politburo. Mr. Li, specifically. Mr. Chen too, if you can get past his security and give me ten minutes of his time."

Avalon's first impulse was to lie, to say that he didn't know what the boy was talking about, but he thought better of it. *I know you,* the Omnilogos had said before. Only now did Avalon realize the profound truth of those words. Perhaps, he thought, the Omnilogos was *really* the Omnilogos.

Avalon didn't deny having contact in the Chinese committee. His expression of surprise had already revealed everything there was to reveal.

He decided to play another card.

"In less than fifteen minutes, I found out that a teenager knows more about me than my mother," Avalon said dryly. "That story about the cyber-terrorist seems a lot more convincing now."

"You're a person with a lot of resources," the Omnilogos

said, "but you pay little attention to details, Mr. Moon. You're an open book that leaves many pages on display. Your company is a spitting image of its creator, and some people have learned to exploit this weakness. It's easy for me to know what you do and when you do it. Your problem is that you've never thought of being at war, so you've never learned how to aim and shoot. It's the problem of the biggest fish in the lake, isn't it? At a certain point, it becomes fat and lazy."

"So now you're saying that there's also a real mole in my organization?" Avalon felt his nostrils flare.

The Omnilogos smiled. "It took you some time. Do you feel enlightened now?"

"That explains why you're here."

"Nope, it doesn't. I'm here because I'm a damn good server."

Avalon closed his hands into fists. "Infiltration, deception, lies, probably extortion. Those are the best conditions to start a merger between companies, aren't they? Now that I think of it, what good would a merger do for our companies? We're already like the two buttocks of the same damn ass! I can't even figure out where the Sanuk begins, and the Somsak ends."

"Are you mad?"

"Mad? I'm choked, you little snot! I'd break your neck with my bare hands if you weren't so damn intriguing."

"I'm sure we'll become best friends, Mr. Moon. Can I call you Avalon?"

"No."

"That's fair enough. Well, do you agree to satisfy the two requests?"

"What? Are you serious? You don't really expect me to answer this question now, do you? I've just found out that my Sanuk is a sieve of information. I still need to decide whether to admire you or strangle you."

"Understandable. You've got twenty-four hours to decide." The Omnilogos rose from his chair.

"Hey! Where the hell are you going?"

"It is time for goodbyes, Mr. Moon. There's someone waiting for me outside. Gentlemen, this conversation is over."

Avalon glanced at Hector.

"The lobby doesn't report any car waiting outside, sir," said the assistant, studying his tablet.

"Who said anything about a car?" the Omnilogos replied, picking up his clothes.

"Wait a minute." Avalon staggered to his feet, swaying a little. "Assuming that I actually have a contact within the politburo, what of it? What good is that for you?"

"I need to deliver a gift," the Omnilogos replied, heading for the door.

Avalon blinked. "A gift? What gift?" he asked. "For whom?"

The Omnilogos opened the door. Before leaving the room, he looked behind him and said, "A gift to humankind."

7

GLADIA

VANCOUVER, KANATA CONVENTION CENTRE

2025

Gladia Egea knew she had lost even before she finished her last sentence.

She was nervous. If she could notice it, then the audience could too.

She took the glove off her hand and set it on the podium. The inquisitive eyes of the crowd followed her as she left the stage and returned to her seat.

The audience's applause was short. It sounded muffled.

It had been a mistake. She wasn't an animal bred to compete in an arena. And yet she had tried. The alternative would have been to let *him* win without a fight.

When Gladia was finally seated, she took a glass of water and drank the contents.

"Thank you, thank you, Dr. Egea, for your insight," the man sitting to her left was saying. "Now, our second guest is Douglas Woodside, speaking contrary to the motion of the day: *Space exploration is a necessary catalyst to the development of our civilization.* Woodside is quite a versatile man: explorer, journalist, and philanthropist. He is best known for founding LAND, which its members call the League for Human Development on Earth."

A three-dimensional reproduction of the symbol of the organization appeared, suspended above the huge room full of people.

"Right, Mr. Woodside," the commentator said, indicating the podium. "Let us hear what you have to say. You have ten minutes."

Douglas Woodside rose from his chair and greeted the audience with a raised arm. He was cheered by the majority, who applauded and called out his name. Once on stage, he put on the glove that Gladia had left on the podium and focused his attention on the audience. The hall was built on three levels and resembled a huge theater. It contained at least three thousand people.

Gladia, however, knew that the eyes that were studying his every movement were far more numerous. Dozens of cameras were broadcasting Woodside's reproduction to millions of homes around the world.

The Landist calmly sipped his water bottle. He made sure that the glove was turned on and cleared his throat.

"My friends, I must confess that after listening to Gladia's speech, I feel lost." Woodside glanced at Gladia. "The good woman came here, in front of us all, armed with evidence, statistics, numbers, facts, and surveys, displayed with passion and eloquence before our eyes. I admit it, my dear doctor. You've convinced me."

Woodside placed his wallet on the podium, so that everybody could see it. Eyes and cameras moved accordingly. "I don't need carpets," he continued, raising his voice, "my house is full of them, but, my friend Gladia, if you should happen to sell some when we're done, this is my credit card."

The audience burst into laughter. Woodside let a few moments pass, allowing the noise to slowly die. "Unfortunately, my friends," he resumed, "I have no numbers or data to show you. I have nothing to sell. I stand before you with a simple story. The story of Deng, a farmer I met in China some time ago." Woodside took a sip from the bottle and stretched out the silence. "Here's the story: After talking with him about family and politics, I also wanted to know the opinion that this gentleman—a representative of over three hundred million peasants who live in the Asian nation —had on the recent space station put into orbit by his government. This news, I'm sure you all know, has literally deluged the media all over the world for quite a while. So I asked Deng: 'What do you think of your accomplishment in outer space?' He looked at me for a few seconds before he asked, puzzled, 'What the heck is outer space?'"

Douglas Woodside moved his gloved hand, and at the center of the hall appeared the three-dimensional image of an object shaped like a walnut orbiting the Earth.

Woodside pointed at the object he had summoned.

"This *thing*, the function of which is not clear to anyone, has cost the Chinese government the equivalent of thirty billion dollars, and one Chinese out of five isn't even aware of its existence."

The audience was silent and attentive, eyes and cameras focused on the ruby-colored space station floating over their heads.

"But back to Deng and my story," continued Woodside. "A week ago, I returned to the village. I wanted to invite him and his family to be part of a documentary that I and some volunteers were shooting. Well, to my surprise, I discovered that Deng and half his fellow villagers were dead. A small non-profit involved in the area informed me that a recent chemical spill from an industrial plant had contaminated the drinking water supply in the whole region. As a result, one hundred and forty people have died from poisoning. Deng and his family were among them.

"I'm sure nobody in this room knows the least of what I'm talking about. And why should you anyway? The news is bad publicity. An inconvenient truth not meant for your ears. It's certainly not the latest fancy technological pride worth thirty billion dollars sent into orbit in full regalia."

Gladia Egea shifted in her chair. She didn't like where this was going.

Woodside lifted his chin and spread his arms. "In front of you all, I wish to represent those one hundred and forty ghosts and bring them as evidence against today's motion. You may wonder what the link is between this motion and a farmer in the southwest of China. Well, it might help you to know that a routine check of the old industrial plant would have identified the damage, alerted the authorities, and saved the village. This control would have cost the government the equivalent of one thousand five hundred dollars. Yes, you heard that right, fifteen hundred dollars that the bureaucrats in Beijing didn't spend because they considered the intervention impractical, unnecessary, and, I quote from the official response received by the spokesperson of the factory: 'uneconomic.'"

Woodside was interrupted by the growing murmur of the audience. He waited until the noise died down before continuing.

"Our history as a civilization results from a series of choices. I believe that what happened to Deng, his family, and the rest of the village, is evidence of a bad choice. Deng was a father and a husband, a tireless worker, an incurable optimist, and a friend. And now he's dead. And the blame is on us." Woodside pointed to the audience. "But don't you even think for a second that my story is an isolated case. Today on our planet, thousands of choices like this are made, and the vast majority of people don't even realize it. Today, the favorite sport of nations is the launch of expensive pieces of metal through the atmosphere with the sole purpose of being able to shout out from the rooftops, 'Me too, me too!' regardless of the real needs of the people living on this planet. Please, look..."

Woodside presented a series of three-dimensional images showing examples to support his position. As they were projected, the Landist commented on them briefly with sagacity.

There was the reproduction of a sparkling probe launched by NASA into the depths of the solar system, opposite to a young beggar at the entrance of a college pleading, "Please, pay for my instruction."

Then came a huge telescope that exhibited the ESA logo opposite the photo of a homeless man in front of the European Parliament showing the inscription: *Unemployed for twelve years*. It was followed by a short movie showing an army of Indian scientists surrounded by star maps, busy solving complicated calculations, while in a little street outside the building stood a group of naked children, malnourished and sick, sleeping abandoned and alone on a pile of garbage.

Woodside had staged the images to be disruptive. It was nothing less than an emotional bomb that was easy to empathize with.

The last image faded away while the Landist slipped off the glove and with icy eyes glared at the audience.

"Every minute, governments, private companies, and individuals spend millions of dollars on the so-called *space enterprise* with no real benefit to humanity. Resources that could be used to save lives are spent at this very moment on sending high-tech robots to rake sand and ice millions of miles away or to take colorful pictures of space objects that ceased to exist millions of years ago. Nobody can deny this truth! For decades, humanity has been wasting money, materials, facilities, ideas, and people on a hobby that has never brought and will never bring a real benefit to our civilization. Today's motion, its very existence, signifies the desire to change—to improve, to admit a mistake and move on. Today, before the entire world, you can help me make a difference, to take a stand, by voting a resounding *no* to this nonsense that is plaguing us all."

Woodside stepped down from the podium, surrounded by a shower of applause and an almost unanimous standing ovation. The Landist sipped from his water bottle as he walked back to sit a few feet away from Gladia.

"Thank you, thank you," the moderator interrupted, inviting everyone to sit down. "We have heard our two contenders. Now it's your turn, dear friends from the audience. You have a few minutes to think about questions to ask our two speakers. Meanwhile, I'll remind you how you voted before the debate began. I want to underline again that the motion of the day is: *Space exploration is a necessary catalyst to the development of our civilization.* Before the debate started, 1,200,109 people were in favor of the motion. Against the motion were 1,300,005 people. It's important to point out that 700,502 people were undecided at the time of the vote. Dr. Egea, Mr. Woodside, you'll have to convert this mass of abstentions to your point of view in order to win the debate."

Gladia glanced at Woodside. The Landist was smiling at her. She set her jaw grimly and looked away.

The commentator cleared his throat. "Shortly, we will ask our viewers at home and in the auditorium to vote a second time. We will then compare the results and determine a winner. All right, let's hear some questions." He looked at the audience and pointed to a man with both hands raised. "You! Yes, you, jumping on the chair. Here's someone who seems eager to ask his question. You can briefly introduce yourself."

From the audience, a tall, middle-aged man with sloping shoulders stood. "My name is John Bernardi," he said. "I work at the Jet Propulsion Laboratory in Pasadena. I wanted to ask Mr. Woodside if he realizes the nonsense he's been preaching to us. You, sir, talk of waste of resources, unnecessary research, of a *superfluous hobby* when referring to the achievements we have made as a civilization in space. I'm sure you don't have the slightest idea of the progress that we have inherited through the *Apollo* missions, from the Hubble Telescope, from the program of the Space Shuttle, the ISS, the—"

"Mr. Bernardi, we are losing you," the commentator interrupted, raising a hand. "Is there a question somewhere in your statement?"

The man nodded. "From what we've heard so far, people like you think that Queen Isabella made a mistake financing Columbus' expedition. You wanted a question? Here's the question: Why don't you go home and study some history?"

A portion of the audience applauded the intervention while the commentator nodded toward Woodside.

"I'd like to thank our friend from the JPL for his question," the Landist said. "Now, together, let's dwell on the admirable accomplishments that his space club buddies have really achieved. If I'm not mistaken, you've mentioned the *Apollo* program, the Hubble Telescope, the Space Shuttle, and the International Space Station. Well, let's analyze them closely. At its time, the *Apollo* program cost around 24 billion dollars, roughly 130 billion dollars today, adjusted for inflation. This was the largest commitment of resources ever made by a nation in peacetime. At its peak, the *Apollo* program employed around 400,000 people and required the support of 20,000 industrial firms and universities. I admit it." Woodside raised his hands, as if he was surrendering to someone. "I'd be a fool not to recognize that with all this money and manpower we got nearly 840 pounds of rock and lunar dust and we were finally able to solve the stone shortage devastating our planet."

The audience laughed for a full minute.

When the host regained control and the spectators quieted, Woodside resumed talking. "The Hubble Telescope has been the most expensive camera built in the history of humankind—and its usefulness is as obvious as its blurred photos. Over ten billion dollars were spent to know that Pluto has a fourth and a fifth satellite and that there are planets around stars other than our own. I'm sure that this has revolutionized the lives of the billion and a half people who live on less than three dollars a day." Whistles and shouts of approval were added to the laughter. The audience shouted and cheered.

Gladia opened her mouth and started saying something. The presenter glanced at her and shook his head. "You know the rules, Dr. Egea. In due time."

Gladia swallowed a curse and settled back on the chair.

"But let's move on, my friends!" Woodside said. "Let's

talk about the Space Shuttle. What a great deal! This wonderful piece of junk put a giant broken camera in space so that they could justify the cost to repair it. It also made the growth of some crystals in zero gravity possible and has allowed a group of scientists, trained for years at your expense, ladies and gentlemen, to take pictures of each other while pirouetting like tech-monkeys in zero gravity. And, oh yes! We can't fail to mention that this program cost the lives of fourteen people. I'm sure the families of the victims who are listening today will be happy to know that the corpses of their boys and girls have cost the U.S. government over two hundred and ten billion dollars, adjusted for inflation."

A burst of applause interrupted Woodside. Gladia snorted. She had never wanted to hit someone so hard in her entire life.

"Dear friends, maybe it's just me," Woodside said, raising his voice to be heard over the applause, "but I cannot call this an intelligent use of your tax dollars."

Someone in the audience whistled and others stood up and applauded.

"Okay, okay, people," interrupted the moderator, "let's move on to the next question."

"But I haven't finished yet, Your Honor." Woodside groaned, looking with a half-smile at the audience, who laughed again.

"I'm sure you'll have other opportunities to delight the audience," said the moderator. "Now, do we have a question for Dr. Egea? Yes, please, the lady in the fourth row with the chador. Yes, your question."

"Hello," the lady said. "I study solar physics and astronomy at the University of Tehran. I wanted to ask Doctor Egea: What do you think of the amount of funds that the U.S. government has granted NASA in this fiscal year? And what do you think about the role of private companies such as Far Horizon, Space World, and your SOL in what some people call the space industry of the next generation?"

Gladia cleared her throat. "Before I answer the questions, I wanted to point out to Mr. Woodside—and obviously our audience is educated enough to realize it—that the list he provided is not nearly as funny as a bad joke."

"Really?" Woodside asked, simulating surprise. "I don't know about you, my dear, but I heard a lot of people laughing."

"The question, Dr. Egea," the commentator reminded her.

Gladia shook her head as she looked at Woodside, undecided whether to answer the question, punch the Landist's smiling face, or do both at the same time.

"Fine," she said, trying to avoid looking at her opponent. "It is my opinion that the budget granted NASA today is just another bad joke..."

"Sure," Woodside stage-whispered with the clear intention to be heard by the public, his voice dripping with sarcasm. "They definitely need more money to produce pens that write in space."

The crowd let out another collective laugh.

"As far as I'm concerned," Gladia continued, overriding the audience's laughter, "I stand behind what I've always said about NASA and other governmental agencies around the world. Their role has been important in the past, but now it's over. The future of space exploration belongs to the private sector and to people who invested heavily in this endeavor. The SOL, for example, uses much of its budget in space research and sidereal technology. As you all know, the project 'Free Space' was the ultimate result of years of research and the joint effort of thousands of experts. The technology of degradable materials developed—"

Woodside interrupted her by clapping politely and nodding. "Seems to me that our audience is scarcely aware of the debt that humankind owes to your company, Gladia." The Landist moved his arms up and down, as if he wanted to incite the spectators in a football match. "I beg all present to thank Dr. Egea with a round of applause for once again sponsoring that magnificent vacuum cleaner that has removed the space paint above our heads."

Much of the public followed Woodside's invitation, politely applauding and thanking Gladia.

The woman chewed the inside of her cheek and gave Woodside an angry stare.

"Okay. Quiet, people. I said quiet." The commentator called for silence. "Mr. Woodside, I must ask you to refrain from personal comments when your opponent is talking."

"I will do my very best." Woodside bowed slightly.

"More questions," the commentator said. "Yes, you on the first balcony. You have a question for Mr. Woodside? All right, shoot."

"Sir, from what you've told us, it's clear you're not a big science fiction fan. I mean, have you ever caught your daughter watching *Star Trek*, or reading Asimov's books? What would you do in that case?"

Douglas Woodside rolled his eyes and stood up. "Are you kidding me? *Star Trek* is one of my favorite shows! I love it! As for Asimov, I gave my daughter the *Foundation* trilogy as a birthday present."

The audience, obviously confused, looked around, muttering.

"Excuse me," the moderator interrupted, "but doesn't this seem a bit of a contradiction to you, sir? I mean, these two sagas tell us about a humanity that lives and travels in space. In short, the exact opposite of what you're preaching."

Woodside sat down and turned to the moderator. "There is no contradiction at all. Let me ask you a question. If one day I wake up and decide that unicorns and hobbits are a good idea, do you think that spending the rest of my life to make one might be of some use for humankind? The answer is obvious, and people know these creatures are and will always remain fantasy; they can't possibly be created because they're just the outcome of imagination. *Imagination*, ladies and gentlemen." Woodside now looked at the audience. "There's nothing wrong with the imagination. The problem with our society is that someone one day got up and convinced the world that science fiction was a window to the future—something real rather than a fantasy that must be taken for what it is. Warp speed and time machines are marvelous inventions of the mind. The problem is that we've been trained to think that they're also possible. This mental operation is wrong and has a basic flaw. My LAND group and I are not opposing imagination, we are opposing people like *you*," he pointed to Gladia, "who are wasting men and resources to create hobbits and unicorns."

"Your problem is that you have the imagination of a toaster and no confidence in the ability of humankind," answered Gladia, staring back at the Landist and receiving a strong round of applause.

"And the problem with people like you is believing that robbing honest people will make some psychotic scientist's dreams come true," Woodside shot back, returning to focus on the audience. "Think about it! If I move a piece of wood and I say it's a magic wand capable of transforming a pear into an artichoke, everyone laughs. But if I am a guy dressed up in a white coat with a serious enough face announcing that in five years we will terraform Mars, I'm going to end up in the newspapers. Why? Because nobody taught us that there isn't any difference. Both are the fruit of our imagination. Nothing more, nothing less."

"All right, all right," the commentator cut the Landist off, and blocked the counter-response of Gladia with a raised hand. "Our next question is for Dr. Egea. Please, silence. Yes, you, ma'am. What is your question?"

A pregnant woman got up from her chair. "Dr. Egea, you have spoken about the need of the average family to conceive space exploration as a component of everyday life, something that fits into our typical day. I don't understand this. The funds from private and public entities in space exploration are, in my opinion, a waste of money. Let's say you have a family of five members and you must feed the children, pay for their education, provide medical care, and so on. If your finances are limited, as are the finances of all families, won't it be a waste of money to buy a jet and fly as a hobby?"

"I don't understand the analogy," Gladia said sourly, dismissing the question.

Woodside laughed heartily while a series of boos echoed through the room.

"Who's next?" said the moderator. "You in the first row. Yes, you, with the green jacket."

"Mr. Woodside, your movement has grown quite a lot in recent years. This is undeniable. Yet there are millions of people convinced that space exploration has been the advent of a new era for humankind, a unique opportunity, a new brilliant dream of audacity and hope. How can you deny the sincere passion born from the spirit of enterprise of some of our best minds?"

"My friend," said Woodside, "believe me, it hurts me to teleport you away from Disneyland, but I think an adult must give you some facts. Your wonderful space adventure was born from a squabble between two superpowers that were competing to see which of them could launch more dogs and monkeys into orbit." The Landist looked at the rest of the room and asked, frowning theatrically, "Good Lord, is there someone else here who believes in Santa Claus?"

The audience laughed as the moderator pointed to another spectator, who turned to Gladia.

"Dr. Egea, over the past seventy years, the use of vehicles such as cars, trains, ships, and airplanes has intensified formidably, and every year their efficiency increases and their cost decreases, allowing them to become more and more accessible to people. One example: seventy years ago, only a handful of people could afford the luxury of a plane ticket. Today, more than three billion travelers board an aircraft every year. In contrast, during the same period, less than a thousand people have gone into space, and the way in which we overcome the atmosphere's gravitational pull of Earth is more or less the same, an expensive method used by the rocket that carried the *Apollo 11* to the moon. What would it take, in your opinion, to make sure that space becomes more accessible to the common consumer?"

"Competitiveness, in one word," Gladia said. "This is the element that has always been missing and that has never allowed us to leap forward. Today it costs about ten thousand U.S. dollars to bring a pound of anything into orbit, and you can't possibly travel in space if you don't overcome Earth's gravitational field. In order to do this, we must reach a speed of seventeen thousand five hundred miles per hour, and as you have rightly pointed out, the only way we now do so is by using brute force—that is, an explosive chemical reaction using considerable amounts of fuel. We need to reduce the costs to leave Earth's orbit, and I believe that the only way to do that is by promoting a healthy and robust competition among public and private entities involved in the space industry."

"All right, people. Question time is over," ruled the moderator. "It's time to vote again. I remind the public voting from home that you only need to access the Cloud and give your input. The motion of the day is: *Space exploration is a necessary catalyst to the development of our civilization.*"

Gladia shifted uncomfortably in her chair. Minutes passed that felt like an eternity. Her hands were balled into white-knuckled fists as she spied Woodside chatting amiably with a couple of spectators in the front row, both of whom were laughing their hearts out, charmed in some inexplicable way by the Landist's words.

After a few minutes, the moderator started speaking again. "Dear friends in the auditorium and at home, voting is closed! Let me remind everyone that before this debate started, you voted the motion this way: 1,200,109 in favor, 1,300,005 against the motion, while 700,502 were undecided. Now for the final results. The number of people in favor of the motion has shifted from 1,200,109 to 502,223... Silence, please! Against the motion, we are now at 2,322,938. The undecided have dropped to 375,455. Looks like Mr. Woodside got quite a victory here. Congratulations to him. Thank you, people. Until the next time..."

Douglas Woodside quickly got up from his chair and strode forward toward Gladia, holding out his hand.

"That was a stimulating debate, wasn't it? We should do this more often."

Gladia dodged the outstretched hand. "You can do your

gloating somewhere else, Woodside," Gladia said through clenched teeth. "You think you won a race? You've proven nothing today. Nothing. Your fanaticism appeals only to frustrated, dissatisfied, and ignorant losers. There is a world of people with functioning brains out there, you realize that? Your movement is a meaningless smoke screen for willful ignorance."

"I'm not sure people feel the same, especially in recent times," said Woodside. "More and more are getting tired of your expensive hobby." He regarded her carefully. "Just look at yourself, Doctor. That's all it takes to see that things are changing."

"What's that supposed to mean?"

Woodside approached Gladia and whispered in a low voice, "You yourself no longer believe in what you say." He creased his lips into a smile, then took something from his pocket and handed it to Gladia. "LAND's doors are always open for people of your intelligence. You only need to clear your mind. When you can distinguish a *unicorn* from a *horse*, call me."

The Landist's hand was holding a business card. Gladia looked at it for a moment, then took the business card and tore it into pieces.

Gladia gathered her things and left the room without looking back.

ONCE OUT OF THE ELEVATOR, Gladia walked into a half-deserted corridor and within a few moments, she found herself outside the building.

The limo parked nearby opened a rear door when she touched its smooth surface.

Once inside the car, a mechanical female voice greeted her. "Welcome back, Dr. Egea."

"CP, today's schedule." Gladia closed her eyes, thankful that the cockpit was completely dark and no one could see how exhausted she was.

"13:45, business lunch with Mr. Gaspar O'Neil to discuss—"

"Clear it," said Gladia softly, rubbing her temples.

"16:30, opening speech at the semi-annual fundraising—"

"Clea— No, wait." Gladia grasped her neck with both hands. "Tell Orbit that the program has changed. I'll make the closing speech instead of the opening. Tell him I had... tell him I had a setback."

"Acknowledged. Transmitting the message... Message received. Continuing today's schedule. 21:00, beginning of the special event organized by the Terawatt Corporation at the Vancouver Convention Centre."

"Jesus." Gladia sighed. "You've got to be kidding. You sure it was today?"

"Affirmative. The event is scheduled for today, March 27, 2025, 21:00 pm PST."

"Christ. I need a drink."

Gladia opened the fridge to her right, looking for a bottle, but her hand caught nothing. She frowned and leaned over to check the inside of the refrigerator, only to discover that it was completely empty.

"I was wondering why on earth there was a Chianti Superiore inside that thing," said a male voice from somewhere in the cockpit.

Gladia spun and flattened against the door.

"CP, lights!" she screamed.

"I'm sorry, I cannot comply," the mechanical voice said.

"I mean," continued the figure shrouded by darkness, "you'd never drink a warm beer, right?"

"Who are you?"

"A big fan of yours."

Gladia tried to open the door. "CP! Open this fucking door!"

"I'm sorry," the voice repeated, with no nuances, "I cannot comply."

"Relax," the intruder said. "CP, lights."

A quartz-colored light brightened the cockpit and Gladia finally had the chance to see the stranger. He was a young man with amber eyes and a crew cut, wearing a simple pair of jeans and a rumpled shirt. He also wore a strange pendant, a cross between an eight and a snake coiled around itself. It occurred to her it might have been the symbol of infinity.

"Who the hell are you? What are you doing in my car?"

"Calm down. I don't mean to hurt you. You're safe."

"Said the hostage-taker in my car," Gladia replied sternly.

"Look, I'm a simple person with a business proposition for you."

"A business proposition," Gladia repeated, puzzled. "Couldn't you book a damn appointment?"

"And risk ending up like poor O'Neil? No thanks, this thing needs your full attention."

"I don't care who you are or what you want. I want to get out. Let me go! Now!"

"I'm sorry, but your CP car seems to believe we are surrounded by lethal doses of organophosphate. We're trapped." The stranger grinned while slowly sipping his Chianti.

Gladia didn't think twice. She threw herself against the door and tried to break through. She got nothing but pain.

Her kidnapper watched her in silence, doing nothing to stop her.

"Shit!" Gladia groaned, rubbing her sore shoulder. "Well, now what? Am I your hostage?"

"No, you're lucky. If you were a hostage, there would be weapons, screaming ladies, shady types, that sort of thing. Here it's just the two of us in the comfort of your private limo. I only ask to have a little chat with you."

"I would prefer the comfort of a public restaurant. If you really want to talk, we can do it outside."

"No, Dr. Egea. It doesn't work that way."

"Then I am your hostage, whoever the hell you are." Gladia leaned back in her seat. She regarded the stranger. He was probably around twenty. He didn't seem to have any weapons and didn't strike her as a dangerous person.

She didn't feel an immediate risk to her safety, so she rested her head on the seat and looked upward. "This day is getting worse by the minute." She snorted.

"If you're referring to today's debate, you're damn right." The stranger pointed an admonishing finger at her. "You could have done much better in there." He pointed to the building where she had debated with Woodside, then he went on, "I suppose that's not entirely your fault though. The outcome confirms one of my oldest beliefs: In a public debate, the sophist will beat the scientist hands down."

Gladia stiffened her back like a touchy cat and felt a sudden burst of energy. "What did you say?"

"Come on, Doctor. Don't look at me like that. Woodside humiliated you. We both know that."

"Excuse me?" Gladia stared at him. "You seize me in my car and then *lecture* me? What's next? Are you going to tell me what to eat for breakfast? Is everything included in this hostage package?"

The young man raised his hands. "Look, all I'm saying is that as your fan, I was expecting a better performance. That's all."

"So you're my fan, hmm? Well, I am very sorry to let you down. Can I go now?"

"First, we need to talk business."

"Right, your *business proposition*. Is this the moment you tell me what the hell you want from me?"

"Indeed." The young man smiled. "I followed your work and the way you manage your business, Doctor. What you did with the SOL in the past four years has been remarkable. Enough, in fact, to attract the attention of a guy like me looking for a partner."

"A partner for what?"

"For the development of an idea."

"Okay." Gladia took a deep breath. "Let's pretend I'm not a prisoner in my car and I'm not talking to my kidnapper. What exactly do you want from me?"

"Well, listening to what you said today, I think we want the same thing. That is, a fast, safe, and inexpensive way to sell the stars on the market."

Gladia arched an eyebrow. "Sell the stars on the market? What the hell does that mean?"

"At the risk of sounding a petulant smartass, didn't you say something on this line? 'We need to reduce the costs necessary to leave Earth's orbit, and I believe that the only way to do that is by promoting a healthy and robust competition among public and private entities involved in the space industry.'"

Gladia blinked. "My exact words," she admitted.

"Wiser words were never spoken," the young man said.

"A way to do what no one has done before: to make outer space the province of the common person." He handed Gladia a small, sapphire-colored object shaped like a pyramid.

When she turned it on by touching the tip of the pyramid, it soared into the air. From each of its sides, three-dimensional moving reproductions appeared. Gladia carefully studied the object. She had never seen a trigo-projector like this one. The images were incredibly sharp and stable, while the controls were simple and intuitive.

"I've never seen a trigoy like this," she admitted, concretizing her thoughts. "Who's the manufacturer?"

The boy grinned. "My sparkling hands," he replied.

"*You* made this?"

"Yes. But the image's resolution is not the point here. The reason I'm here, Doctor, is the *content*. Please, go ahead. Let me know what you think."

Gladia did as she was asked. She studied the images and the data that flowed back and forth, following her gestures.

After five minutes of silence, she forgot she was a prisoner in her car. She emerged from the reading as if she had left an important financial transaction open.

"Is this really what I think? I mean, building this...thing. It's not a joke?"

"I'm very serious."

"I've never seen anything like it. I mean, the design is... brilliant. Who do you work for? Who gave you this data?"

"Nobody," replied the young man, "and FYI, I'm self-employed."

"You work alone?"

"That's the meaning of the word *self-employed*. I don't work for other people, but I do work *with* other people. Special people, like you, Doctor. If I want to turn this mixture of equations and images into something concrete, I have to go to the next level—and that's why I need your help."

"My help?"

"I need the resources of your SOL to move the project forward. I need your technicians, engineers, laboratories, and your matrix."

Gladia looked at the stranger, but she didn't respond. She went back to studying the data projected by the trigoy.

"What do you say?" the young man asked. "Are you in?"

"In? What is that supposed to mean?"

"Oh, come on. I'm talking about the project you're looking at. Do you want to be part of it?"

"Of course not," Gladia replied, almost laughing. "I don't even know who the hell you are! You really believe I can make a decision like this on my own? Are you out of your goddamn mind? I answer to investors, shareholders, interest groups, not to mention—"

"Bullshit," the young man said. "I'm not stupid. I know how these things work, Doctor. You always have the first and last word, which is exactly what I need. I'm asking what you think, Gladia Egea. What do you think of those specs? Is this feasible?"

"Feasible? You mean this science fiction idea here?" She pointed to the projections that revolved around her. "I can't even begin to imagine how much a monstrosity like this would cost."

"Forget about money. Is the *idea* feasible?"

Gladia looked again at the projections, then to her kidnapper.

"What do you want me to say? In theory, an antimatter propulsion engine is feasible."

"Well, that might please *Star Trek* fans," the young man

said impatiently. "But what do you say of this?" He pointed to the trigoy.

"It has potential," Gladia said deliberately, slowly.

The other sighed with relief. "It's a start."

"A start?" Gladia laughed. "Am I missing something here? Do you really think that my opinion makes any difference?"

"Your opinion is the only one that matters to me, Doctor. It makes a world of difference."

"Okay. You've got my opinion. Now what?"

"Now we start to build," the young man answered, as if it were the most obvious thing in the world.

"Wha—?" Gladia looked at him with wide eyes. "Listen, I'm fed up with this whole game you're playing. I admit that this thing here"—she pointed to the trigoy—"is the best trigo-projector I've ever seen. I'm also willing to recognize that the data is good stuff for sci-fi junkies. What else do you want from me?"

"You said it's potentially feasible. That's more than enough for me."

"Enough for what?" Gladia snapped. "Cut the crap! Did you really believe that by forcing me to look at an equation and some images, you would get countersigned contract? You're delusional. I get dozens of proposals every single day. If I had to finance each, my SOL would have failed long ago."

"It's a question of money then?"

Gladia couldn't hold back a wry smile. "Isn't it always? Look, it doesn't matter what I think about your project, assuming it's really yours. If you want to submit this data to my experts, I have no problem. But it'll take time, compliance with a protocol, and you'll have to answer a lot of questions before you can even hope to—"

"I hate questions. They waste a lot of time," the young man said. "The calculations are accurate. Tech-wise, everything checks. However, I understand where you are coming from. I didn't give you any reason to trust me. Let's fix that. Let's say you receive an anonymous donation to preliminarily evaluate my data and determine whether or not this project is possible. What would you say to that?"

Gladia showed a contemptuous smile. "I'd say it'd have to be a very generous donation. Nothing you can afford anyway." She glanced at his worn jeans.

"CP," called the boy, patting a seat, "please update Dr. Egea on her current financial situation. Specify the activities related to her bank account in Andorra, considering only the last half hour."

"The bank account has received eight money transfers of unknown origin in the last twenty-eight minutes," said the mechanical voice.

"Really?" the boy asked, feigning astonishment. "Well, well. It seems your day just got brighter. CP, specify the total amount transferred."

"The total amount transferred is $3,291,980 USD."

Gladia actually gaped. Did she hear that right?

"Mmm. $3,291,980 is a curious amount." The young man folded his arms across his chest. "Maybe this figure contains some secret information, a coded message. Let's see. If we turn this number into a date, it turns out to be 3, 29, and 1980. Guess who was born on the 29th of March, 1980? That's right, it's you. Isn't it wonderful?"

"Seriously," Gladia said, looking nonplussed, "who the hell are you?"

"Another person bound to titles and names," said the unwanted occupant in her car. "All right, if you really need a label to attach to my face, you can call me Omnilogos. You want my real name, you'll have to earn it."

"Omnilogos?" Gladia repeated. Her brain felt slow and clumsy, but the word sounded familiar. "You mean *that* Omnilogos?"

"Today there are too many," he said, as though confessing a sin. "I was the first, but I have no power over the others who have taken my name. Crackers, hackers, rebel teenagers, dreamers, psychopaths, and virtual clowns— many have taken my name or joined my cause for similar or discordant reasons. None has my style." The Omnilogos smiled and looked up, as if recalling an old memory. When he looked again at Gladia, his expression changed radically; a transformation almost impossible to conceive. "I am a collector of hopes and peregrine truths, a shepherd of thoughts, ideas, projects, and dreams too important not to be realized. I'm an abstract concept that has no body, no smell, no boundaries, no shape, and no color. I am *the* Omnilogos."

It was as if someone had dropped Gladia into a pool filled with iced water. If what this guy said was true, she was sitting in front of a sort of living legend. The Omnilogos was a figure none really knew a damn thing about. People blamed the Omnilogos—that was believed to be an abstract concept—for crimes and praised it for outstanding discoveries such as the cure for osteosarcoma that had been downloaded to some of the major research institutions of the planet.

When the Nobel Assembly at the Karolinska Institute made public that they would award the Nobel Prize for medicine to anyone who proved to have created and spread that data, many waited for the Omnilogos to show up in Stockholm to receive the prize. It didn't happen.

Gladia roused from her thoughts when she noticed that the young man was staring at her.

"Heavens above," she said. "Kid, you just sparked my interest. You claim to be a terrorist wanted in three continents, not just a kidnapper with a knack for showmanship. Fine, let's say I believe that. Since we are diving in the realm of fantasy, let's say I also like the stuff I saw in your trigoy to the point I decide to support your project. Why me? Why make all the effort to organize this lovely chat?"

"You're the final piece of a puzzle started years ago, Doctor. I've always wanted to do this thing my way, with no compromise that would have limited my choices. Look, I could have given these schematics to the Pentagon or the Chinese PLA and I would have saved myself a lot of hard work, but my creation would have been crippled, corrupted, limited. I need visionaries, believers in the cause of space. People just like you, Doctor. Only then will I be sure that what comes out of those abstract projections is really what I wanted."

Gladia glanced at the trigoy and its data. The truth was that she didn't know what to say. Every second that passed, her curiosity and her uneasiness grew hand in hand. She needed to know more.

"According to this data," Gladia said, "your project involves other companies and corporations besides mine. Here I see the Paragon Corporation, Gaia, the I & I, and Archetype Unlimited."

"Exactly."

"The CEO of Gaia, Mark Strutzenberg, is a friend of mine," she said, smiling dryly. "If your idea is to rope in that old Kraut, you'll have a hard time. He is as stubborn as a mule about pretty much anything."

"Mark can be a real son of a bitch, that's true, but he knows a good deal when he sees one."

"You mean you know him?"

"I mean, we play chess when we don't tell dirty jokes. We have collaborated on several projects before. He has already said he will do his part."

Gladia pursed her lips, then stared at the Omnilogos intently. "Did the old fart keep pulling on his La Flor Dominicana as if he had a noose around his neck?"

"La Flor Dominicana?" the Omnilogos repeated, smiling thinly. "Mark would smoke dirt before even touching a Double Claro. His hands don't linger on anything that's not a Maduro or an Oscuro. But you know this better than I do, right?"

Gladia nodded. The Omnilogos knew Mark.

"Well, congratulations," Gladia said. "Having Mark on your team gives you some credibility, but you haven't convinced me yet. What about the I & I? I don't think it's really a company that you can rely upon too much these days. I've heard they're sailing through stormy water after the Joshua scandal."

"This is why they won't say no."

"I don't understand."

"I own the majority of their stock equity, and I have several contacts at the upper levels of their management. Let's just say that in the past, I made sure some unflattering information about the company filtered out when the right people were listening."

"You mean it'll be easier to blackmail them?"

"Blackmail them? No, of course we wouldn't do that. But I'm sure they'll have an open mind when they hear their biggest shareholder is promising to save them from doom."

"Well, kid, it seems you've done your homework." Gladia

read the next name on the list of companies. "And what is this Archetype Unlimited? I've never heard of it."

"That's because it doesn't exist yet."

"What do you mean, it doesn't exist yet?"

"That is exactly what I said."

"All right, forget it. What about Paragon? I don't think they have anything to do with what you're looking for. They definitely don't produce artifacts related to the aerospace industry. How could they? They're specialized in pharmaceutical products."

"They'll produce what I say."

"Why would they?"

"Because I am the Paragon Corporation."

Gladia was doing everything she could to appear in control of the situation, but the last ten minutes were just too much to digest. She was in the middle of a plan that had been hatched long before, whose dimensions were difficult to fathom.

If this guy was really what he claimed to be, and if he really had access to these kinds of resources, then the project he was proposing was not a farce. It was a real possibility. And this frightened her.

Gladia turned off the device and the little pyramid rested gently in her palm. She handed it over to the Omnilogos, who took it.

"How much will it cost?" Gladia asked, bracing herself for the answer.

"You want an estimate on what will be the single most expensive object in the history of humankind?"

"I want the truth."

"I haven't the faintest idea."

"So this is a gamble. If I decide to embark on this

venture, it will mean the largest commitment of resources that the SOL has ever made."

The Omnilogos nodded. "True, there are risks for your SOL and for all the people involved. Dr. Egea, you know risks are an essential part of any bet worthy of the name. Focus not on what your company might lose. Think of what humankind has to gain. Think about what *you* have to gain. Dare to dream. If you succeed in this endeavor, your name will be on people's mouths more often than good ol' Coca-Cola."

Gladia stared at the Omnilogos. She thought of the lost debate and of the public's reaction, followed by the bitter taste in her mouth when she was defeated. A sense of frustration was eating away at her gut. Then she recalled Douglas Woodside, his impeccable hairstyle, his handsome face, his square jaw, and his stupid toothy grin.

"Becoming more famous than a soda," Gladia finally said, unable to suppress a smile. She took an empty glass from a nearby shelf and handed it to the young man, pointing to the bottle of Chianti. "It's always been my dream."

8

DOUGLAS

NEW YORK CITY, LAND HEADQUARTERS

2028

Douglas Woodside took the trigoy from his pocket. From the other side of the oval table, three people looked at him; two men and a woman. Woodside waited for a few seconds, evaluating them one by one.

In the dim light of the room, the woman was the closest thing to a giant praying mantis. Her eyes, large and bulbous, were closer to her tiny ears than to her short and pointed nose. She was wearing a pair of rectangular glasses with thick lenses which amplified the ice-blue of her eyes. She had thin and protruding lips, sealed and curled in a strange smile. Her head was a nearly perfect triangle that began with a long, sharp chin and ended with a forehead covered by a helmet of shaped hair.

The short man to her left was decidedly less noticeable. With a flat face, a broad forehead, and small watery eyes, he resembled a stray dog. His neck was bent and his shoulders hunched, as if he wanted to hide from someone. The man's eyes darted from one side of the room to the other.

The last of the three seemed at ease, with his feet on the table and his fingers knitted behind his head. His dark beard, short and symmetrical, easily got lost on his black skin. The black hair and skin were paired well with his black suit. If it had not been for the white, opaque matter of his eyes and his silver tie, the man would have disappeared in the darkened room.

Woodside turned his gaze to the object in his hand, on which everybody's attention was focused. The Landist lit it with a gesture, letting it slip away from his fingers.

The trigoy spun on itself for a split second, then hovered in the air. It stopped about six feet from the floor.

The three-dimensional reproduction that appeared in front of them was both familiar and unwelcome at the same time.

A short person with dark hair and a sharp face was performing a deep bow.

"Good evening, everyone. My name is Wei Wang."

Woodside motioned near the trigoy to raise the volume and magnify Wei's image.

"My name will tell you nothing," Wei continued, touching his chest. "I am only a stranger who knocks on your door to advertise a product. I like to consider myself as the last link in a chain forged long ago by the needs that nourish humankind. A chain made of ideas that has moved and continues to move our civilization beyond the boundaries of explored knowledge. Like all the curious, brilliant, and arrogant people who have preceded me, it is my belief that I can offer you all something you need but that nobody else has ever given you."

Woodside fast-forwarded the projection for a few seconds. Wei appeared again, but in a completely different pose.

"The next step is to give flesh to the idea," Wei was saying, gesturing with his hands. "The inventor is working with a company that believes in his or her vision and that invests time and resources to develop, refine, and test it. In ninety-nine percent of the cases, the idea proves too volatile, fragile, and tenuous. What is the result? Well, the idea is overwhelmed by reality's hardship and sinks into oblivion. But in the one percent left, we find a world of possibilities hidden in uncharted territory, a challenge to be met."

Wei clasped his hands, throwing his arms up toward the ceiling of the room. Before their eyes, the reproduction of a very old car appeared.

"In that one percent rests the Model T, produced by Henry Ford in the early twentieth century, the first car cheap enough for the common middle-class American. It forever revolutionized the car industry, thanks to the introduction of the assembly line."

Wei paused, then moved his hands as he did earlier, and another reproduction appeared. It was a bitten apple.

"Steve Jobs, for those of you looking for a more recent example," Wei continued, pointing to the symbol. "His Macintosh in 1984 and the I-Phone in 2007 revolutionized the personal computer, telephone, and music industry."

Wei turned around, like an Olympic diver preparing for a two-and-a-half somersault. He folded his arms and formed an X. The symbol of the bitten apple and the car disappeared into thin air and the focus of the viewers returned to him.

"Two men with two companies changed the lives of hundreds of millions of people. I, like them, had an idea, and I have dedicated my life to making it real. But this idea is a bit different from all the others. First, it's different in its proportions. The two ideas of the past were each brought to life by a single company. On the other hand, I needed five multinationals just to make my creation feasible."

Woodside moved his hand again and sent the projection forward.

"Now imagine yourself finding two thousand dollars in a white envelope," Wei was saying, pointing to something. "I don't know about you, but I'd look around, pick up the envelope, and go on my own way with a smile on my face. After the fluke, I would start thinking about how to use the money. Today, there are several ways to spend two thousand dollars." Wei moved his fingers. A series of images followed one another as he spoke. "I can offer my buddies a dinner, I can buy groceries for three months, I can buy a non-stop plane ticket from Vancouver to New York, or maybe a stay in a luxury residence for my girlfriend and I. Two thousand dollars will not change my life, but it'll surely make my day."

Wei put his hands behind his back. "Now imagine a world where with this amount of money I can also buy a ticket to see our planet from the orbit of Earth itself. No, it's not a movie ticket, it's a ticket to get on one of these."

Woodside enlarged the object that Wei was showing. The Landist narrowed his eyes to see more clearly, as if he was trying to memorize every detail.

"Welcome aboard!" Wei joined thumb and index finger of both hands to form a virtual picture frame. An oval object with several grooves on the surface instantly appeared in the frame. It looked like a gigantic dragon egg.

"What you're seeing is a magnified image of Polaris, ready to begin its ascension. Polaris is...well, it's hard to explain. I can't make any comparison because it is the first of its kind. Let's just say that it would be fair to call it an orbital car, or rather, an orbital wagon. What is its destination? It travels to an observatory several thousand miles above the Earth's surface. What is its purpose? To open up to you the outstanding spectacle that is our planet."

Woodside fast-forwarded the projection once again. Polaris had disappeared. Wei was now sitting on a chair. A wide smile graced his face.

"Yes, I know. 'Science fiction' is certainly not the trend of the moment." Wei stood up and walked. "We live in a world where some people want to deny us the right to reach for the stars. I am talking about the so-called Landists and their followers. Well, I have a new concept for all of them: to *dare*. Here, in front of all the people of Earth, I declare I am a Hyperist, a person who aspires to the stars. I am a Hyperist and I'm damn proud of it. I am a person who raises his head and sees new possibilities for our species, obstacles to overcome, battles to win. I know that when I look up, I see my long-forgotten home. And I dare to think that one day I will reach it again. Stardust to stardust."

Wei clasped his hands and a sparkling powder that seemed made up of myriad multi-colored diamonds appeared in the room. The cloud of light slowly gathered in a few points until it started forming concrete shapes. They were letters. The tiny diamonds so assembled forged the words: *Stardust to Stardust*. It was a slogan and a declaration of war.

Woodside felt his heart beat faster. He clenched his jaw and fast-forwarded the projection one more time.

Polaris, the orbital wagon mentioned by Wei, was again the center of focus. This time, however, it was not alone. It seemed somehow linked to a very long cable on which the wagon was moving at an ever-increasing speed.

Wei was pointing to Polaris.

"After all," he was saying, "I'm talking about launching a satellite into a geostationary orbit and attaching it to a station in the Pacific Ocean with a 22,000-mile-long cable. This cable, ladies and gentlemen, will be just a few inches thick. On it will travel vehicles driven by inexhaustible energy capable of transporting people and material into Earth's orbit. All of this at the cost of a plane ticket. Most of you will be puzzled at this point, while others will probably be laughing. I understand you very well." The Hyperist scratched his forehead. "It's odd for me too, but not for the reason you're thinking. Some time ago, the writer Sir Arthur C. Clarke—the author of *2001: A Space Odyssey*—said that 'the space elevator will be built about fifty years after everyone stops laughing.' Well, my team and I stopped laughing a while ago, and we look forward to making science fiction your greatest adventure once again."

Woodside turned off the device and the three-dimensional image disappeared.

The mantis woman adjusted her glasses, moistening her lips with the tip of her tongue. The short man shifted uncomfortably in his chair, looking around as if he was desperate to find a window he could throw himself out of. The black man was an island of calm in a stormy sea. He toyed with his tie while keeping his feet on the table.

"Yesterday afternoon, any mammal linked to the Ether could see this fantastic commercial spot." Woodside spoke slowly, emphasizing each word. "Now, I want to know who the hell is this Wei Wang, and what the fuck is he talking about. Arvin?"

The short man jumped to his feet, as if the chair had been kicked out from under him. The flickering eyes were fixed on the data on his tablet.

"Wei Wang," squeaked Arvin, avoiding Woodside's blood-shot eyes, "born in Richmond, B.C., Canada, on January 1st, 2005. He moved three years later with his family to Orlando, Florida. His father, William, was a rope technician. His mother, Erika, was a housewife. Both died in a car accident when Wang was a child. After a short period in a children's home, a couple professors adopted him in Pasadena, where the boy remained until the age of thirteen." Arvin cleared his throat. There was silence in the room.

"I'm listening," said Woodside, inviting the other to go on.

"That's...ahem...all, sir," Arvin murmured, staring with scrupulous attention at his shoes. "I don't... We have no other information at the moment."

"That's all?" Woodside actually growled, grasping the edge of the table with both hands. An intricate web of veins emerged on his neck. "*This* is what you've been able to find out in twelve fucking hours on the most clicked person on the goddamn planet?"

Arvin looked at the mantis woman and the black man. His eyes seemed to beg for help. No one lifted a finger.

"S-sir," mumbled Arvin, short on words. His eyes were moving so fast that they seemed about to burst out of his head. "I—"

"You're fired!" Woodside bellowed.

Arvin squirmed. "Sir, that's... This Wang is a puzzle." His bulging eyes blinked. "There's no bank account registered in his name, no medical records, nothing in the database of any school. I did...I did what I could with the time given to me. I've got a group of people busy searching for any useful data related to Wang on the Ether and locally. I have men in Richmond, Orlando, and Pasadena as we speak."

"Right," Woodside said. "So you're running a cross-search of cyber and physical reports?"

"Yes, President."

Woodside evaluated his assistant carefully. "All right. I like it. You're hired again."

Arvin collapsed into his chair. He wiped his brow with a trembling hand and sighed.

"Tenoderia." Woodside turned to the woman. "Tell me this is the biggest, most shameless hype of the twenty-first century. That thing"—he pointed to the spot where Polaris had appeared shortly before—"is clearly impossible, isn't it?"

Tenoderia ran her slender fingers through her hair. She had long and well-groomed nails that ended with just a hint of scarlet-red nail polish.

"I'm afraid not," she replied, staring at the trigoy. "Thirty minutes after the speech, the five companies named by the subject released a joint statement confirming to the press what he said. A few hours ago, the named companies also issued generic schematics of some of the technologies introduced in the presentation. The subject—this Wei Wang—is not lying. I had little time to read the data, but the technologies he mentioned, the magnetic solar engine, the design of the device, and the super-intelligent material the cable is made of are all theoretically possible, according to the information they gave us."

"You mean this guy is really building a thing like that somewhere in the Pacific Ocean?"

"What I mean is that anyone who issued this information has a solid scientific basis that supports him and a technology ten years ahead of anything I've seen in the fields of robotics, biochemistry, mega-structures, nano engineering, and renewable energy. The only direct evidence of Polaris, the orbital carrier described by the subject, is that provided in the presentation."

"For Christ's sake." Woodside ran a hand over his forehead. "I was hoping for a good ol' 'you fell for it.'" The Landist turned toward the black man, imperturbable as ever with his feet put lazily on the table. "Komla! Jesus... Would you like a deckchair or do you prefer a damn mattress? Straighten up, man. At least pretend to be professional."

Komla pulled his feet down and off the table. "Trying to look the part, my friend," he said.

"You've got anything interesting for me?"

"This thing is on everyone's lips, Douglas," Komla said. "The birds tweet it, the dogs bark at it, and the cows—"

"Yeah, yeah," Woodside cut him off, raising a hand and closing his eyes in exasperation. "And the cats meow at it. Good God. Can you put two words straight without turning them into a goddam joke? I want to know what the buzz is on the *outside* of the zoo."

Komla leaned forward, placing both hands on the table. "Whoever designed this campaign is a genius. The timing of the news, the way it's been released, the channels used, and the information provided, all of this form a masterpiece of public relations. The mere fact that such a thing has remained secret for nearly three years is incredible. If only the echo of a sigh would have leaked out, we would have known it. However, until a few hours ago, no one knew a thing. I have a theory that explains how they kept this whole project a secret until yesterday. Douglas, I think that most of the people involved in the project didn't even know what they were working on."

"What the hell are you talking about?"

"Whoever oversaw this project has made sure that no information leaked out. Look, it's like making a movie by breaking down the script into separate parts. Every single actor is required to act in his or her scene, ensuring that he or she knows nothing about the general plot of the story. In the end, the director puts together the shots and gets his movie without the characters knowing anything about the script. As Tenoderia said, this space elevator is the sum of different components, but developed in areas related to each other. Consider this new super-material Wang describes in the presentation. It can be implemented in any field, but he used it as the backbone of his invention."

Woodside scratched his neck. He turned the pyramid-shaped object on and scanned the projection once again, stopping when Wei was using his fingers to evoke images, videos, and sounds. Woodside saw the presentation twice, then stopped the trigoy while Wei conjured the slogan, *Stardust to stardust*.

"Christ!" Woodside snapped, showing the projection to the rest of his crew. "Can you see any trigo-projector?"

"I don't think he's using one," Komla said, toying with his goatee.

That answer brought a bitter twist to Woodside's mouth. "Then how in hell can he play with those...*things*?"

"You mean the stuff he's using in the presentation?"

"Yes, Komla, that is what I mean. How can he evoke images out of thin air? Is he a fucking magician?"

"Could be," Arvin ventured, looking hypnotized by the way Wei moved his arms.

Woodside cursed. He turned to Tenoderia, a hint of hope in his eyes.

The woman shook her head. "He's not using a trigoy, that's obvious. He's not even using a source, or any other type of projector that we know."

"Then what the fuck is he using?"

"I don't know," Tenoderia said.

Woodside rewound the projection. He listened to the moment when Wei declared himself a Hyperist, then stopped the video.

"This story of the Hyperist... Does anyone know what he's talking about? What's a Hyperist anyway?"

"A person who aspires to the stars," Arvin answered promptly, quoting Wei.

Woodside threw him a withering look.

"Shortly after his speech," Komla said, indicating the projection, "some provinces of the Ether merged into a region called HYPER. The merger came about a bit too fast not to look like something organized. It could be linked to the concept of Hyperist inaugurated by Wang."

"HYPER?" repeated Woodside.

"Yes." Komla nodded. "It includes blogs, websites, social networks, and other units and utilities of cyberspace. Apparently, they all had one thing in common. You want to guess what it was?"

"Being opposed to the Landists," said Tenoderia.

"Bingo."

"How big is this HYPER?" Woodside asked.

"The last time I saw it this morning, it counted about 27,000 subscriptions, 110,000 users, and—"

"Forget it," Woodside said. "How many are there now?"

Tenoderia touched her glasses with a flick of the hand that spoke of old habit. Her eyes moved quickly up and down, as if scanning a list. When she finished reading, she took off her glasses, rubbed her eyes, and said nothing for a few seconds.

"Well?" Woodside asked, drumming his fingers on the table.

The woman put her glasses back on and straightened

her back. "Right now, three more regions of the Ether have merged under the effigy HYPER. The number of users and subscriptions is growing rapidly and—"

"Cut to the chase," Woodside broke off. "How many are there?"

Tenoderia inhaled sharply. "995,000 subscriptions, seven million users, sixty-four million accesses—"

Woodside stopped her with a raised arm. "Okay, I got it. Shit, it's worse than I thought. All right, folks, one thing at a time. Let's go back to that thing...that space elevator, or whatever it's called. I mean, what are we exactly talking about here? Is it even possible to build one? How does it work? Why have I never heard of it before?"

Tenoderia straightened her shirt. "The basic principle of a space elevator is quite simple. If you tie a string to a tennis ball and twirl the string above your head, it will remain taut and straight as long as the twirling motion is perpetuated. The Earth is spinning faster than your hand could ever manage, about 1,000 miles per hour. If you anchor an incredibly resistant ribbon or cable to the Earth's surface at the equator, and then attach the other end to a large enough mass—for example, a space station or a small asteroid—to keep it taut, you end up with a railroad track right into space. Once constructed and set up, wagons can ride it up and down via some sort of powered rails, or the ribbon itself could be the rail, with the wagon crawling up the cable with clamp-on wheels, thus easily delivering cargo into orbit without the use of expensive rockets."

"Wagons such as Polaris?" asked Komla, motioning toward the projection.

"Exactly," Tenoderia said. "With that type of carrier available, we could considerably reduce the cost of travel between Earth and space. The space elevator idea is theoretically simple to implement but with an important complication. The structural stress that the cable would have to bear would be immense. No existing material has the properties required to meet this need. At least...well, at least not until yesterday afternoon—"

"When that clown came up with his *fictionite* idea," Woodside finished for her while tapping his fingers on the table. "What do we know of this material that allegedly makes his space delivery nonsense possible?"

"Not much," Tenoderia admitted. "As I said, information is still being processed. This super-material should work like an extremely sophisticated artificial intelligence, capable of adapting to external physical and atmospheric conditions with the sole purpose of keeping itself both lightweight and incredibly resistant. Technically, the cable is made of special carbon nanotubes held together by a cybernetic system that is responsible for maintaining its stability, and, if necessary, of modifying its physical properties. This *fictionite*, as you called it, not only has the tensile strength needed to support the weight of this huge *bridge*, but can resist abrasion, adverse weather conditions, and cosmic and solar radiation without losing its basic properties, lightness, and strength. The cable also has a system of automatic maintenance. This means that if something were to ultimately damage or alter the chemical properties of the nanotubes, a specific program, similar to an anti-virus, would launch a diagnosis identifying the problem and solving it. Theoretically, this cable is almost indestructible."

Woodside sneered. "I don't give a rat's ass how technologically advanced this thing is or how many elephants it can support. We're not in Wonderland, for Christ's sake! Eventually, everything breaks. We're talking about an object longer than the circumference of the goddamn planet!

What happens if this monstrosity breaks and falls on our heads?"

"I don't have a satisfactory answer to that, sir," Tenoderia replied. "It would largely depend on the exact physical properties of the material used to build the cable—information we are not currently aware of. It would also depend on the location of the space elevator, the exact point where this supposed break would happen, and a multitude of other factors. It could be an isolated incident with few or no casualties or a global catastrophe."

"Mother of God." Woodside shook his head in disbelief. "Are you listening to yourself? Shit. I'm getting goosebumps. If this Wei Wang can actually do what he claims, we're facing the most dangerous psychotic megalomaniac of the century. This asshole is risking a disaster for the pleasure of a little advertising. It's fucked up, that's what it is! We need to throw everything we've got at him before this gets out of hand."

"Doug, listen to me," Komla said. "SOL and Gaia's shares rose by nine percent in the last five hours. People from all over the world are following the invitation launched by Wang, buying in bulk the *book the stars* package advertised in yesterday's presentation. Other companies are investigating the data regarding the technologies in the orbital elevator, to evaluate the opportunity to collaborate on the project or start one of their own. If Polaris has the potential we have seen and is already at an advanced stage of development, we are talking about the news of the century."

Woodside stared at him. "The news of the century? That thing? Are you shitting me?"

"I mean it, Doug. People are excited rather than scared. You need to understand that."

"A charlatan is trying to sell a load of shit to humankind. That's what I understand."

"Maybe," Komla said. "But try to put yourself in people's shoes. They want to know everything they can about the scoop of the moment. They want to speculate and to dream. Imagine snatching a huge candy bar from the hands of a hungry child, telling him he can't have it because it damages his teeth. Shouting out to the public that this thing is dangerous may not be the right move to make. If you want to go against Polaris, you'd better be well prepared. Let's wait till the child gets a bad stomachache."

Woodside studied him. "You got a plan?" he asked.

"That's what you pay me for, boss. To come up with plans."

"Come on then. Spit it."

Komla leaned on his chair. "Eventually, the excitement will fade and the common person will start asking what one usually asks when there is a huge infrastructure project like this one underway: 'What if something goes wrong?' Well, we'll be ready to answer that question, pointing out the flaws and dangers of the space elevator, flooding the media and the information channels with our version of the story. There are also other factors to consider before unleashing an offensive. This project has natural enemies. I guarantee you they just need an excuse to throw everything they've got at Wang."

Woodside narrowed his eyes. "I'm not following you."

"Think about it," Komla said. "How do you think companies like Kinoper, BTF, or Extros Mobility will react when they realize that along with tourism and space exploration, the main purpose of Polaris is to promote the use of renewable energy? If Wang is right about the potential of his invention, in less than a decade the CEOs of these companies will have to get a real job."

Woodside looked at his collaborators for a long moment, then he settled back on his chair and sighed. "I hear you," he finally said. "God is my witness. I don't have a damn clue how to—"

The President of LAND was interrupted by Tenoderia, who suddenly raised her hand.

"What is it?" he asked.

"We're getting new output from the Ether," she said, her eyes dancing behind her glasses. After a few moments, Tenoderia looked at Woodside with an unreadable expression.

"What's wrong?" asked Woodside.

"The XCTV has just made it known that a satellite of unspecified characteristics will be launched in a week from the Xichang Space Launch Center in China." Tenoderia adjusted her glasses and kept on reading. "The launch was requested by the I & I and has just been approved by the government."

"The I & I," Arvin said. "Wasn't that one of the five companies named by Wang?"

"Good Lord, it's already started," Komla murmured, disbelief in his voice. "Wang is doing it for real."

Woodside jumped up from his chair and began pacing. "We have to keep up, be focused on what to do and how to do it. Okay, listen up. Time is of the essence." He pointed to Arvin. "You've got twenty-four hours to get your hands on something useful. I don't care how you do it, but I want to know everything about this Wang. Everything! When you bring me his underpants, I hope for you they're full of shit. Is that clear?"

"Y-yes, sir."

It was Tenoderia's turn.

"Analyze Wang's data," Woodside ordered. "Analyze it well. Find me reasons why Polaris should never be built. If you don't find any, do more analyzing. There's something important that we're not getting in all this, I can feel it, and this space elevator just can't be the miraculous invention that charlatan is advertising."

"Will do," said Tenoderia.

Woodside put a hand on Komla's shoulder. "Work your magic, my friend. Act on people's doubts and hesitations. Mobilize any contact you have. As soon as you get useful info from Tenoderia, give it to anyone who can put it to good use."

Komla gave him a thumbs up. "You got it, boss."

"As for me," Woodside went on, "if there's a reason LAND exists, it's to prevent this kind of madness from happening. This *Hyperist* has no idea of the ocean of shit he's going to drown in. I swear it on my mother's grave: Polaris will never rise."

9

CANTARA

WASHINGTON D.C., HYPER HEADQUARTERS

2029

Gladia Egea pointed out the images projected by the trigoy to the man gnawing at his cigar.

"Woodside and his lackeys couldn't have possibly chosen a better time to spread their message on the Ether." Gladia touched the back of her neck. "There are people who already speak of burning the headquarters of the Gaia, the SOL, and the I & I to the ground to prevent the launch."

Mark Strutzenberg breathed noisily. After a while, a jet of smoke came from his nostrils, for a few seconds obscuring his broad face. The man absently scratched his platinum-colored beard. "Well, can't say the Landists don't have a sense of humor, eh?" he murmured, staring at the pictures. The tip of his cigar exploded for a second of bright orange light while the man inhaled nicotine and exhaled the smoke from his mouth. He bit his lower lip and continued talking. "Douglas crawled out of his hole and decided to use his nuclear weapons."

The co-founder of the SOL gave Mark an annoyed look, not amused by the metaphor he used to describe the situation. Then she asked, "What's on your mind, old man? I can see your brain is working."

"Just wondering what happened to our PR guy, the one that made Polaris' stunt a success." Mark glanced at her. "One day he was on the team and then he wasn't."

Gladia shrugged. "No idea. He's just gone. Don't know why. I didn't ask."

"Right," Mark said, sighing.

"Anyway, this leaves us little room to maneuver," Gladia said while still staring at the trigoy's data. "We're running out of time. The Planetary Court's decision is scheduled for next Friday."

Mark grunted at that statement. He stared at the flux of information with more than simple attention; the vertical line that furrowed his brow spoke of nervousness. "Well, this doesn't help a bit, that's for sure," he said. "The members of the Court contrary to the launch were waiting for something like this to happen. Those motherfuckers are going to do everything they can to stop Polaris." After a pause, the man added, "As if we didn't have enough shit to deal with. Have you got Shimao's report?" He looked at Gladia with an expression that left little room for interpretation.

Gladia nodded gravely. "Yeah, read it a dozen times. Bad news never comes alone. Shimao, Trudeau, and Nazarov are doing what they can with the time and resources they've got," she said, trying not to sound resigned. "I'm confident they'll be able to solve Infinity's structural problems, but we can't ask them for miracles. Woodside's allegations will turn them into the favorite topic of the etheric grapevine and we can't do much to prevent that."

Mark gnawed at his cigar. "What does our young man think of Douglas' move?"

Gladia put both hands on her hips and looked away from Mark. "Wei knows nothing about what's happening, and I made damn sure it stays that way."

Mark jerked his head toward Gladia so suddenly that his cigar almost darted from his mouth. "*What?*" he blurted.

"Wei has enough on his hands right now," she said, shifting her weight from one foot to the other. "He doesn't have time to spare in order to take care of this. Don't look at me like that, old man. You know I'm right. Also, I've already thought about how to deal with Woodside. We don't need Wei to babysit us. We can deal with this ourselves."

For a long time, Mark looked at the projections surrounding the trigoy. Then he went back to study Gladia's expression. "I pray to God that you know what you're doing, my friend." He waved a hand, inviting her to keep talking. "What's the plan?"

"We have to catch up. Quickly," Gladia said. "In order to do that, we need to resort to exceptional measures."

"*How* exceptional?" Mark asked, two deep greenish shadows besieging his eyes. A piece of ash broke away from his cigar and fell to the ground. Neither of them noticed it.

"Enough to involve someone who can turn the situation around and give us some space," Gladia said. "This is a battle that has moved faster than we ever thought possible from the talk shows to the public opinion. Until the last moment, Woodside has made us believe he was an idiot, hungry for applause, just to give us *this* gift at the last minute. He took us completely by surprise." Gladia pointed to the trigoy's projections with a slow movement of her head. "We underestimated that sophist and now we're paying the consequences. We need someone who can rescue us from this situation and who, at the same time, can put enough pressure on the Planetary Court to save Polaris and the Infinity control center."

Mark looked at Gladia with an expression that betrayed skepticism. "Let's hear it. Who do you have in mind for the job?"

Gladia waited an outrageously long time. Finally, she said, "Does the name *Cantara* ring a bell?"

Mark's jaw twitched. "Cantara Handal? The Black Widow of the Ether?" The man spat out the name as if the words were made of acid. He stepped back without even realizing it. "You're kidding me, right? That woman would dismember her daughter for a few dozen subscriptions to her region!"

"She *would* have dismembered her daughter," remarked Gladia. "That's the problem. Looks like Cantara has abandoned her Ether-related business, confining herself to some kind of isolation from the media, so to speak."

"Confined," Mark repeated, frowning. "You mean she retired? At her age?"

"As far as I know, you can't retire from a job like hers. All I know is that Cantara has suspended her involvement on the Ether, delegating her business to someone else. Now all she does is give private lessons to a bunch of teenagers."

"She went from world famous etherion to babysitter?" Mark grunted. "This story reeks of dirty underwear. Who talked you into involving her in this mess?"

"I spoke with Gregor and the Board of Propaganda at the public relations department," Gladia said. "According to the smart folks, bringing Cantara to our side would work wonders for us. We are losing this media war, Mark. It makes sense to get one of the most influential etherions on the planet to stand on our side. I'm planning to talk to her tomorrow."

"The public relations folks have suggested this? Are they so desperate? I don't see how the solution to our problems could be that...that...*woman*."

"Despite her withdrawal, Cantara continues to have a strong presence on the Ether and a significant impact on the slice of public opinion that has remained neutral until now," Gladia explained. "There's a shitload of people who listen to what she says and trust her judgment. Not to mention the special relationships she has with many of the most influential etherions on the planet and folks all over entertainment land. Cantara is a real treasure trove of resources."

Mark did not seem convinced. "Even if that's the case, why should you be the one to talk to her?"

"Public relations discovered that Cantara shows respect for enterprising female figures with an attitude: 'women with balls,' I think is the phrase Gregor used." Gladia smiled a little.

Mark's face suddenly relaxed. "Modesty aside, of course," he said, pointing to his colleague with his cigar.

"Whatever the case might be," Gladia said, "Gregor stressed that Cantara seems to respect my position because she knows my personal history well."

Mark nodded. "In short, you intrigue her."

"That's what the brains think. This makes me the Hyperist with the best chance of getting her on our side."

Mark glanced at the trigo-projector and pointed to the images. "You mean she could be *our* atomic bomb?"

"Something like that."

Mark slowly breathed in and crossed his arms. He

seemed to wait for Gladia to say something else, but she remained silent. "So, what's the plan?" he asked after a moment. "How are you going to convince her to help us?"

A smile flashed across Gladia's face. "I've studied her psychophysical profile. Cantara shows a propensity to be involved in something bigger than herself, in projects where one person can make a difference. This behavior of hers is unique, something I can bend to our advantage."

"I don't get it," Mark said, shaking his head. "How is this helpful?"

"I'm going to make her an offer she can't refuse," Gladia said, smirking at the puzzled man.

Mark's frowned deepened. "Does this *offer* include a gun and the threat of brains scattered over a contract?"

"No." Gladia shook her head. "Let's just say I'll show her something that will give her lots to think about. The fear of missing out will do the rest."

"That's it?" Mark twisted his beard in frustration. "That's all I get? You want me to die of curiosity?"

"You seem agitated, old Kraut." Gladia pointed to his cigar. "Breathe. Light another one of your bazookas and relax. We wouldn't want your blood pressure skyrocketing, would we? Trust me, you have nothing to worry about."

Mark snorted. "This is your way of keeping me out of the party? Nice try, but I will not sit on my hands. If Douglas has decided to bombard us, I could buy you a few extra days with—"

"No, Mark," Gladia interrupted him. "I want you to stay put."

"But—"

"Listen. The last thing we need now is to throw fuel on the fire. I am the coordinator of the Polaris project. I get to decide what we do, and how we do it. I'm sorry, my friend. I'm going in, you're staying out. That's my final word."

Mark's mouth twitched. "You sure about this?"

"I am positive."

Mark sighed. "I don't know. I have a bad feeling about this whole thing." He pressed the burning end of his cigar in the ashtray and put an end to the stream of smoke that had flooded the room with its exotic aroma.

"Mark, you've got a bad feeling about *everything*," Gladia said as she turned the trigoy off.

"Statistically speaking, this proves me right fifty percent of the time."

Gladia pocketed the device and started toward the door. "Well, my old friend," she said before leaving the room, "let's pray that this time you're dead wrong."

CANTARA HANDAL LOOKED at the seven students in a semicircle around her and crossed her arms. "Well?" she asked, her eyes lingering on each of them. "Does anyone have any idea?"

The students looked at one another for a few seconds. Then seven arms shot up almost at the same time.

Cantara smiled. She looked to her right. "Angelica," she said, nodding toward the girl and inviting her to speak.

Angelica was tall and lean, with almond-shaped eyes partially hidden by the glare of light reflected by her glasses. She looked at the trigo-projection in front of them.

"I don't think... I believe..." Angelica paused for a second, thinking carefully to her next words. "I think that the four units we're examining have no mutual affinity. They'll probably never reach the merging process. Judging by the preliminary analysis, they'll disappear in the coming weeks. We shouldn't waste any more time studying them. It's a poor use of resources that could be better used in other ways."

"You are right and wrong," said Cantara, clasping her hands behind her back and evaluating the young girl. The students followed their teacher with their eyes as she approached the trigo-projection, which was showing charts, numbers, and images. Cantara pointed to the data with a nod.

"Forget everything you think you know about their past performances. Concentrate instead on their Baussial curve. Judging by their etheric reciprocity, the four units have much more in common than it may seem from the simple preliminary analysis. Angelica, remind me of something: What do I always say about the merging process?"

"In the merging process, the first impression is always the wrong one."

Cantara waved a hand. A new three-dimensional graph appeared in front of them. "Correct," she said. "Now, let's focus on your second mistake. The units will *not* disappear in the short to medium term." Cantara moved her index finger and highlighted some parts of the graph. "True, their activity hasn't grown much in the past few days, but this doesn't mean that the units are about to shrink or disappear. If you consider the column of interactivity, you can clearly see that the number of subscriptions has now stabilized to over five hundred per day. See here and here? They are no longer trying to expand; they are trying to solidify and hold their ground. In a nutshell, they're striving to balance each other, even if it means that they must sacrifice their size and the number of subscriptions. It's a clever move. Whoever the architects are, it's clear they're looking at the broad picture. Their aim is to eliminate inconsistencies and find a common ground on which to develop."

Cantara turned slowly, her back now facing the class, and headed toward the desk. Once in front of the table, she picked up a steaming cup and gingerly drank the contents. The unmistakable fragrance of green tea relaxed her senses. For a few seconds, there was no other sound but the woman's slow sipping.

Meanwhile, behind her, some students were nodding as they revisited the graph explained by Cantara. A couple of them moved their hands quickly to add notes into their own trigoy in the form of words, images, and sounds.

Cantara put her cup down and swallowed. She raised her head, straightened her back, and looked in front of her.

The circular-shaped mirror on the wall of the room caught her attention. Cantara Handal was a tall, slim woman, with thin arms and long legs. Her slender body made her seem a rare cross between a model and an ice-skating dancer.

Her beautiful eyes were a triumph of green streaked with silver-gray. Her whole face was crowned with a heavy mask of makeup that stretched toward the temples and almost reached the ears, giving her the look of an Egyptian queen.

There were many who might argue that Cantara was one of the most attractive public figures on the planet, and that she could have been even more beautiful if it had not been for her completely shaved head. No one knew why Cantara had banished the hair from her life. It was one of the mysteries that added to the many others that surrounded her, such as the meaning of the pendant, shaped like an hourglass, that she always wore as though it were a wedding ring.

Her sensual but dangerous appearance, her known predilection for dark and green colors, along with her reputation as a ruthless etherion had earned her the nickname the *Black Widow of the Ether*.

Cantara looked away from the mirror and turned around again. She glanced at Angelica, a satisfied smile lighting up her face. "However," the teacher said, "you're right in saying that devoting attention to this imminent merger is a waste of resources. Whatever will arise out of it, it's still too early to make predictions about its usefulness for our region. Better to wait for future developments while keeping our eyes open."

Angelica nodded. "Yes, Madame," she said.

Cantara clapped her hands, then spread her arms, as if to welcome the whole class. "Very well. Now, let's analyze last week's assignment." The woman extended an arm toward the trigo-projector and her open hand attracted the object. Cantara pocketed the trigoy and looked back at one of her students. "Sebastian, remind the class of your assignment."

Sebastian, a boy with short-cropped hair and an expression that suggested stark seriousness, stood up. "Yes, Madame," the boy said, lifting his chin. "You requested we consider the following phrase: *Now and then: From the conservative Internet to the everlasting Ether*."

"Awesome," Cantara said. "Let's start with your work, Sebastian. Illustrate for the class your analysis. Begin with your sources, then continue with the synopsis and close with your own conclusions. You have five minutes, beginning now."

Cantara turned her thumb up, and a countdown appeared in the middle of the class.

Sebastian looked at the numbers in red hanging over

their heads. He cleared his throat and took his trigoy from his pocket. When he tossed it into the air, the little pyramid-shaped object positioned itself at the exact center of the room. Pictures and letters swirled around the trigo-projector.

"For my research," Sebastian began, putting his hands in his pockets and nodding to the data, "I consulted several sources and interviewed half a dozen people involved in the media and specialized in Ether-related sectors. In my thesis, I consider the evolution from the Internet to the modern Ether as a gradual transition from one type of worldwide computer network to a virtual community of people connected directly to each other via one or several regions of the cyberspace. In my analysis—"

"Your eyes, Sebastian. Look your audience in the *eyes*." Cantara pointed to the other students with a green-enam-eled nail.

Sebastian paused for a second, then shifted his gaze to the rest of the students. His cheeks took on a tinge of red as he resumed talking.

Cantara continued sipping the contents of her cup as she nodded occasionally at what Sebastian was saying. When the countdown signaled just over one minute left, Cantara raised her hand and squeezed it into a fist.

"All right, Sebastian. Could you express your final thoughts?"

Sebastian glanced at the remaining time. He looked back at the rest of the class. "In my opinion, the transforma-tion undergone over time from this global system of inter-connection between devices has reached a stage where the control has shifted from a physical device to the organic consciousness of individuals who today are directly connected to the Ether. This type of evolution from the technology to the organic will open the possibility to process and to share in the future virtual world not only images, colors, and smells, but also feelings and emotions. The Ether may soon become the catalyst for a whole new way to define the very meaning of virtual and real interrelation and, in time, to merge the two concepts."

Sebastian sat down. The room remained quiet for a few seconds.

Cantara took a couple steps toward the students. She stopped a few inches from Sebastian.

"I can't give you more than a Delta in posture and exposition," she said, looking steadily at the student. "Sebastian, you need to learn to look into the eyes of your audience and to stop hiding your hands. Just clasp them behind your back if you can't hold back the tremor. This gives you a better posture and elegance. In a public debate, these qualities of presentation could make the difference between victory and defeat."

Cantara read embarrassment and frustration on the boy's face, but not resignation. She left her words hanging in the air and then continued, her face slightly more relaxed. "You deserve, however, a Gamma for the approach you used to analyze the subject. You did a great job in reviewing the sources and your conclusion is plausible, given the premise of your argument. But sometimes you have to risk something to give more originality to your work. You must understand that standing on the shoulders of giants is not always a good idea. Learn to trust your instincts and remember that you're telling a story—a *story*, Sebastian. You can better sell your point of view if you show the audience a calculated range of emotions, rather than a simple list of data and statistics."

Cantara walked away from the boy. "All right, Asha," she

said, turning to the girl next to Angelica. "Show us what you've got. You have five minutes from now."

It was with well-concealed pride that Cantara listened for the next twenty-five minutes to intelligent, witty, and never predictable expositions.

Her pupils had made progress by leaps and bounds, but the life they had chosen for themselves was not simple. In order to be an etherion—a shepherd of the public opinion —sacrifice and unparalleled mental effort would be required of them. It was a constant challenge to expand their own awareness and skill, in a competition with other aspiring etherions contending for professional standing and public acceptance as opinion leaders. Only a handful of them would ultimately be successful, and an insignificant percentage of this fraction would make a real difference. In a world like theirs, failure and success might be two equally dangerous sides of the same coin.

"Let's think about this point for a moment," Cantara said, indicating the last student who had just finished speaking. "Lucius' hypothesis is quite interesting, isn't it? To consider what once was known as the *network* no longer as a simple virtual hangout where you can connect and exchange information, but as a chessboard on which countless pieces are arranged and controlled by different players who collide against each other. The contenders in this match are therefore committed to doing everything to checkmate their opponents. Now let's try to push this concept further. Can some of you tell me what the important implication of Lucius' exposition is, if taken to the extreme? What would happen if the Ether really became a huge battlefield?"

The hand of James Ark, the boy at the far left of the semicircle of students, was the only one to rise.

Cantara turned toward the skinny, short boy dressed all in black, with the usual dark glasses hiding his eyes.

"James," Cantara called, inviting the student to speak.

"It means that the Ether can be conquered," he said.

Cantara looked away from the pupil. She nodded toward the class. "It means that the Ether can be conquered," she repeated, pointing to James. "It means that the Ether could become a battleground in which those who conquer and stabilize more regions under a single hegemony have an unprecedented control over—"

A beep coming from her arm interrupted her. Cantara took some time to understand what it was. Then she touched her wrist and said in a clearly irritated tone, "What is it, Ebony? I asked not to be disturbed."

"I'm sorry, Madame. Your appointment with Dr. Egea is scheduled in fifteen minutes."

Cantara glanced at the time. She frowned. "Right." The etherion sighed. "Well, time's up. You can go. James, we haven't had time to hear your exposition. Leave your file in my In-Stat. I'll have a look at it tomorrow."

James transferred his file into the input station with two quick movements of his hand. The input station glowed with a scarlet light to emphasize a new file not yet read.

The students quickly gathered their things and left the room. Cantara waited until the door was closed.

"Control," she said when she was alone, addressing the ceiling. "Return to the office configuration."

The room came alive.

The chairs and the seven input stations arranged in a semicircle in the center of the room were absorbed by the floor, while the large desk was disassembled and reshaped in a more compact and elegant version. Two armchairs and two tables emerged where the input stations had been, and a minibar appeared where a few seconds before there had been empty space.

The room completed the new configuration just in time before a voice announced the lengthy title of Gladia Egea: co-founder of the SOL, second vertex of the Hexahedron, and the coordinator of the Polaris project.

Cantara stepped toward her guest and shook her hand, then pointed to one of the armchairs.

"Gladia Egea, it is an honor," the Madame said, smiling warmly. "Would you like some tea or coffee?"

"Hot water with lemon wedges, thanks," Gladia said as she sat down.

Cantara walked to the small minibar. She returned a few seconds later with two steaming cups and a glass filled with lemon wedges.

When both were seated, Cantara looked at the other woman, evaluating her carefully. She took a sip from her drink, then placed her cup on the nearby table. "I am confused," Cantara began, frowning. "I heard that Wei Wang personally harasses the people that he needs. All day I've been expecting him to jump out of my wardrobe or to ambush me in some clever way. But no, I deserve only the visit of his second in command." She nodded to Gladia, then concluded with a slight tinge of sarcasm, "Well? Should I be offended?"

"Madame Handal—" Gladia began.

"Cantara, please," the etherion said. "Let's leave the formalities at the door."

Gladia nodded. "Cantara, I will be very frank. The First Hyperist knows nothing of this visit, and even less about..." She paused, as if to find the most appropriate word, then continued, "...about the *information* disclosed by Woodside and his followers. I have seen to it that he remains unaware of all this."

Cantara stared at her guest. "*Unaware?* How is this even possible? The news has been out for over twenty-four hours. My table knows of what we're talking about! Is Wang still on our planet or has he ascended prematurely to the stars?"

Gladia smiled thinly. "The First Hyperist is engaged in a matter that requires all of his attention. I decided not to distract him with the rumors that are raging on the Ether."

"Rumors," Cantara repeated, as if the phrase had been poorly worded. "That's a huge understatement. I wouldn't describe Woodside's counter-offensive as *rumors*. It's more of a well-aimed punch in the face that puts an end to the boxing match. My dear doctor, these *rumors* are the reason Polaris will never rise."

Cantara sipped her tea, scanning Gladia's face, looking for any hint she could use to divine her feelings. She just found a stark mask of flesh displaying nothing but patience and grace. The etherion smiled inwardly. Good. Gladia Egea knew how the game was played.

"That being said," Cantara continued while touching the rim of her cup with her thumb, "it's clear that the Landists are eating you guys alive. I don't see how an intelligent person like you can ignore this fact."

"That Woodside's allegations have raised some interest among the public and in some members of the Planetary Court is undeniable," Gladia said, "but I wouldn't jump to conclusions. You know what they say: 'Listen to everything, believe nothing.' I don't see how a person as *cautious* as you can ignore a saying like that."

The last sentence lingered in the air for a few seconds.

"Touché," Cantara said, nodding toward her guest. "You have a point, Doctor."

"And that's exactly why I'm here," Gladia said.

"You get straight to the point." Cantara crossed her legs, never taking her eyes off her guest. "The kind of woman I prefer. Allow me to be as frank as you were. I'm sure you have heard rumors of my early retirement. I am enjoying this time away from the annoying background noises of everyday life, trying to instill common sense into young minds that are not yet completely corrupted by society. I have no intention of entering into the game again, let alone into *this* kind of game. I'm sorry you came all this way for a cup of hot water and a few slices of lemon."

Gladia shifted in her chair. "May I ask you why? I mean, I'm curious. There are advantages and disadvantages in the backing the Hyperist movement..."

"Because I'm too good at recognizing a lost cause," Cantara said.

"A lost cause." Gladia took a piece of lemon and squeezed it over her cup. "This matter is far from being the end of the Polaris project."

"Is that so?" Cantara waved a hand dismissively. "Woodside has given the Planetary Court a damn good reason to put an end to your space picnic. It doesn't matter if the projections and calculations of his experts are reliable or not. Now that the public opinion *believes* they are, you're screwed."

Gladia said something, but Cantara raised a hand, interrupting her. "As if that were not enough, my dear, the Ether is packed with not so encouraging news about the construction of the Infinity control center itself. News concerning complications in the design of your space elevator, about the growing difficulties to mass produce the intelligent hyperfilament that must support your prodigious creation, and other technical difficulties that not even your best brains seem to understand. Half of your mythical Hexahedron is busy trying to solve structural problems that you guys hadn't even foreseen at the beginning of Polaris' construction."

"For a retired woman," Gladia said, "you're fairly up to date on the... What did you call them? Oh yes! *Annoying background noises.*"

Cantara shrugged. "Nonsense," she replied, smacking her lips after sipping some tea. "I'm just a woman who keeps her ear to the ground and who loves elaborating on conjectures. And my conjectures tell me that other problems and complications will arise soon and that the departure of Polaris will be an increasingly complex and unpleasant business to handle for you Hyperists. Now tell me, my dear, did you keep the genius boy unaware of *this* too?"

Gladia stared at Cantara. "The First Hyperist is well aware of our progress and is more than confident that his team will solve any complications."

The Madame let out a giggle. "Sure," she said, as she took a napkin and passed it over her lips, "this can be the encouraging chorus that you guys repeat to each other, but the people that keep both feet on the ground don't seem to feel the same way, and I'm not referring only to Landists. My dear Gladia, there are things that simply can't be done, regardless of will, power, or money."

"I disagree," Gladia said. "Anything can be done if there's enough will."

"Oh come on, Doctor! Let's try at least to behave like adults. I admit, what you want to do might seem simple: to drop something toward Earth from a satellite hovering just above the equator. A child could grasp the concept. And yet —and I'm sure you'll agree with me—we both know that in an experiment like this, *simple* is a very complicated word.

Let's put this into perspective. If you try to take a shortcut, you waste more energy. If you try to slow down, you speed up. If you aim for one direction, you go in the opposite. No one before has ever tried to drive a probe attached to a forty-thousand-kilometer-long cable, and for a good reason."

Gladia didn't hide her surprise. "I didn't know you were an expert in aerodynamics."

"I'm not, but my consultant in orbital transportation is paid handsomely to be in my place, and he tells me that your Polaris project has several flaws, many of which can't be overcome, not with our current technologies at least. Maybe in fifty years your space elevator *could* be feasible, but today it's a little less ridiculous than the idea of flying pigs."

"The space elevator has no flaw, mathematically and technically speaking." Gladia straightened her back. "In theory, there is nothing to prevent it from happening."

Cantara studied her fingernails with a playful smile. "See, my nail polish costs five times the equivalent that you find on the average hypermarket and in *theory* it should last for a month, should be completely odorless, always remain shiny, and not contain any trace of chemicals. In *practice*, the color fades after a week and there is something in this formula that causes me a slight itching. As if that were not enough, sometimes I could swear I smell a distinct odor of tar while applying it. What do you think all this means?"

"It means you need a new nail polish," Gladia replied dryly.

"I agree," Cantara said. "It also means that you should never trust what a label says, or what's written in a psychophysical profile." She pointed to Gladia with her cup. "In *theory*, the woman sitting in front of me is smart, driven, and gifted with a critical and analytical mind. And yet, I stare at a person who drinks the words of a twenty-four-year-old megalomaniac with a dangerously inflated ego."

Gladia rested both hands on her knees, but did not reply.

The Madame set her cup on the table. "Technically, my dear, this is when you fall on your knees and start begging me to save your Hyperists from total annihilation."

"No," Gladia said, crossing her arms over her chest. "I think this is when I invite you to witness a story that will make you believe in miracles."

"Gladia," Cantara said, slightly moving her shoulders. "Of all the things I thought you were, I didn't expect *believer* was part of the list." A pause, then she asked sarcastically, "Let's see. Does this story begin about two thousand years ago, in a remote province of the Roman Empire?"

Gladia smiled. "No. It's a story that began a few years ago and that is still in progress. And I'm offering you the chance to be part of it and to shape the world around you as you've never done before."

Cantara blinked. "I beg your pardon?"

Gladia rose from the chair and motioned for Cantara to follow her. "How would you like to make a difference?"

CANTARA ALMOST COULDN'T BELIEVE that she was actually there.

Curiosity and a sense of adventure might have been two of the main reasons why Gladia had convinced her to board SOL's jet, but she thought there was something more than that.

Little did it matter now that she was sitting there, in a room shrouded by pitch-black darkness that reminded her so much of a huge movie theater. She was almost expecting that someone would approach and offer her a bag of popcorn.

The only difference between this place and the replica of a cinema was the peculiar spherical shape of the room and the countless bluish lights that covered the walls and the ceiling like a giant phosphorescent plant. There was also a solitary raised platform in the middle of the vast space that had no apparent reason for being there. Cantara had no idea what the purpose of the place was and Gladia had revealed little.

Almost without realizing it, she watched, for the hundredth time, the veins of bluish light that snaked to the sides of the room, the only source of light in a space otherwise shrouded in darkness. The place, the Madame soon realized, instilled in her a sense of anticipation and wonder, as if she were in a huge cathedral where a secret religious function was about to start.

"So *this* would be the place where miracles happen?" Cantara asked, breaking a silence that had lasted several minutes.

Gladia, sitting to her left, was staring at the distant platform. "No," the Hyperist answered, keeping her voice down, as if to respect the sacred silence of the place. "This is the place where miracles are *created*."

Cantara skeptically studied the other woman, but did not reply to that statement.

The Madame recalled the events that had led her to this strange place. The fact that she was in a restricted area didn't surprise her so much. HYPER headquarters was a spartan structure, simple and very unwelcoming. The only sections she saw while passing from one checkpoint to the next had revealed a small army of security drones, dozens of

244   MICHELE AMITRANI

armed men, and very few smiles. She suspected that Gladia
Egea had to call on quite a few favors to give her the privi-
lege of sitting in this very chair.

After all, the Madame thought, if she had agreed to
come all that way to end up here, it was only because Gladia
had convinced her that the event she was about to witness
would be something unique and exceptional.

She really hoped that the trip had been worth the
trouble.

Just as she was about to ask another question, the
already dim light of the room went out and total darkness
enveloped the surrounding environment. Cantara lost sight
of the platform at the center of the enormous spherical
space, the only point of reference in a temple of silence.

It was as if something had suddenly sucked away all the
energy in the room.

The Madame looked around and her eyes caught sight
of a figure moving in the darkness near the platform.

A subdued light glowed somewhere above their heads,
and Cantara could finally see the figure that had appeared
out of nowhere. When she recognized him, her eyes widened.

Before them, a few dozen yards away, was Wei Wang. He
was wearing black running shorts and nothing else.

Cantara blinked. She rubbed her eyes vigorously, but
Wei Wang continued to stay where he was. His pale skin,
barely illuminated by the dim light, made him look like a
ghostly presence.

Cantara whirled toward Gladia, who didn't seem
surprised by the sudden appearance. The Madame forgot
what she wanted to ask and looked again at the First Hyperist. The light was getting progressively more intense. Now
she could see Wei's body.

Her first impression, she realized, was disappointment. Wei Wang was short—much shorter than he appeared in the media. Yet Cantara was surprised to discover how much his body, albeit minute, was defined and muscular, not very different from that of a Greek statue.

From that distance, it wasn't easy to see every detail, such as the expression on his face, but other than that, the boy's identity was unmistakable. Cantara could not believe that she was a stone's throw away from the most famous and controversial person on the planet.

Her thoughts were suddenly interrupted when the First Hyperist spoke.

"EVE," Wei called out, addressing the ceiling. "Open the file: *Spacefaring Civilization*."

A solitary note reverberated in the enormous room.

"Close your eyes," Gladia said suddenly.

Cantara didn't understand what the other woman meant. "What do you mea—"

She never finished the question. With no other warning, a cobalt-blue light exploded in the huge room and Cantara was forced to protect her face with her arm to avoid being blinded.

When her eyes adjusted to the brightness, she realized that a gigantic shape loomed in the center of the room.

It was a circle... *No*, Cantara thought after a few seconds of silent amazement, it was a *sphere*...a huge blue sphere interspersed with portions of white, green, and brown; portions with a very familiar shape.

Cantara found that she was staring at Europe a few moments before the Old Continent rotated out of her sight, revealing the American continent, followed by the Pacific Ocean, Asia, and Europe once more. It was an incredibly faithful reproduction of the planet Earth that revolved before her eyes.

Cantara glanced around, looking for the source of the titanic multidimensional projection, but couldn't see any trigo-projector in the area near them. Her mind was spinning. It was impossible to conceive that an image so impressive had appeared out of nowhere in the space of a split second.

The reproduction of the Earth was so detailed, so realistic, that Cantara felt like an astronaut staring at her own planet from several hundred kilometers above the ground.

Cantara's eyes slowly moved from the giant sphere—which rotated above their heads—to the infinitely smaller Wei Wang, who was stretching his arms and legs, like an Olympic swimmer preparing for a competition.

She wondered if the boy knew that in that moment someone was spying on him. She and Gladia were wrapped in an area of darkness that seemed immune to the light coming from the reproduction of the Earth.

The Madame turned back to Gladia, who was smiling, her eyes shining with a light that had nothing to do with the glow coming from the crystal-clear reproduction of the planet.

"Remember to breathe," Gladia whispered.

Cantara was about to answer, but she was forced to stop when Wei started speaking again.

"EVE," the First Hyperist called. "Load the most recent file. Summary and overview."

A mechanical voice with a feminine tone replied to Wei's request. "In the file you've selected," the voice said, "we are at the end of the year 2041. In this scenario, there are no significant threats to the Master Project, and the dangerous variable has been eliminated or prevented successfully by your past actions."

"All right then, buckle up," Wei said. "Let's leap into the future. Determine when the next major threat to the Master Project will occur."

Cantara didn't understand what was going on. She glanced at Gladia, but the only answer she got was a pointed finger that invited her to keep watching.

"Processing terminated," EVE announced.

The reproduction of planet Earth vanished and reappeared a second later. Cantara didn't notice any major difference between the previous planet and the one that rotated now before her eyes—except for some small forms that were orbiting above Oceania. She leaned forward and squinted. The forms were too small and too far apart to be distinguished from the background.

"This is the beginning of the year 2047," EVE said. "The emerging space economy is revealing some chronic problems that are due primarily to an inability to increase the volume of orbital traffic while maintaining reasonable protection standards in the transportation of goods and people. Polaris can no longer adequately meet the growing demand for transport. Private companies providing orbital shuttles must comply with strict safeguard requirements that prevent them from substantially increasing the tonnage of their vehicles or testing new propulsion systems. Three incidents occurred in five years, in which thirteen victims were reported. Laws and regulations that prohibit the expansion of human transport in orbit will be approved. Similar regulations will affect the transport of goods. As a result, the GXP of the space economy will enter a recession for the first time in history. The projections show that the GXP will also decrease in the coming years, threatening the expansion of so-called astral tourism, orbital trade, the astral industry, and the entire space economy."

Wei nodded while assimilating EVE's report. After a few seconds of silence, the First Hyperist moved his body in a slow and sinuous way, reminding Cantara of the movements of a dancer who follows the rhythm of an alien music. The *dance* generated a series of characteristic blue data—graphics, numbers, images, and such—that began appearing out of thin air. The data orbited around Wei's head. He spent a couple of minutes studying them.

Eventually the young man sighed and made the data disappear with a quick jerk of his index finger. He turned to look at the ceiling with a thoughtful expression.

"The most important cause of the GXP contraction seems to be a new series of strict orbital transportation regulations," he assessed. "My understanding is that the new Planetary Court created them following the three accidents you were mentioning."

"That is correct," EVE replied.

Wei seemed to think for a while. Then he formed an X crossing his arms—and the movement of the Earth instantly froze. Once again, the Madame spent a few seconds searching for the source of the multi-dimensional reproduction of the planet, but with no luck. It was as though Wei controlled that show of lights and shapes with the power of his thought.

The young man began enlarging the area over Oceania, where Cantara had seen tiny forms. As the visual scale expanded, the Madame realized that the forms were actually structures that orbited many hundreds of miles above Earth. They appeared to be just a bunch of silver-grey shapes.

"EVE," Wei suddenly said, "which was the company with the highest spatial turnover reported in 2046?"

"Titan Asteros Corporation," the voice replied at once.

"What is the most significant source of its income?"

"Titan Asteros Corporation obtains forty-five percent of its revenue from the construction of orbital astrals, twenty-five percent from astral tourism, seven percent from the production of—"

"Okay, got it," Wei cut EVE off. "Who are its major clients?"

"Are you referring to its customers or its contractors?"

"Both," Wei explained. "I'm referring to anyone whose work depends on performing a service or for the construction of an astral."

"Titan Asteros Corporation provides services mainly to private agencies and private citizens. Do you want a detailed list?"

"No." Wei seemed disappointed. He made a half-twirl with his body and raised both arms in unison. The silver-colored shapes disappeared instantly, replaced by another area of Earth's orbit, apparently free of any forms.

The First Hyperist produced other data, these, too, shaded in a characteristic blue color. After having studied them for a few seconds, he asked, "EVE, which space companies do the US, the EUROCON, and China use most?"

"Are you referring to military or civilian companies?"

"Both."

"In this case, these three political entities are served mostly by a union of corporations called Astrocorp. This union comprises eleven companies specialized in different sectors of the space economy and of astral technology."

"Provide a list of the services they offer."

"Astral tourism, orbital transportation, manufacture of military and civilian equipment, refinement of—"

"I understand." Wei crossed his arms and repeatedly tapped his foot on the floor. He seemed lost in his thoughts for several minutes. After a while, he read a new string of data. "EVE," he asked while still scanning the information, "how many of the disputes that the Planetary Court is expected to settle this year are classified as *important*?"

"Three thousand and eighty-eight," EVE answered.

"Well," Wei said, suddenly stopping the tapping of his foot. He straightened his back and shoulders, then continued. "Maybe we can put more pressure on their shoulders."

Wei became busy evoking data and evaluating a huge amount of information.

Cantara noticed that the omnipresent voice—the one called EVE—not only provided information, but also described the events that occurred following the decisions that Wei made from time to time. That simulation of a possible future—or whatever else it was—reminded her of an extremely complex real-time strategy game that changed and adapted depending on Wei's choices. EVE created the scenario which, if completed in an appropriate manner, allowed advancement to the next level. Wei had to figure out what the problem was and use the information and resources he had to solve it, thus fulfilling the mission objective.

Cantara witnessed the latest decision of Wei completed with an elegant dancing movement of his body.

EVE's evaluation of Wei's choices was swift. "Wei, my analysis shows that four of the eleven companies that constitute Astrocorp have established a block of all orbital activities. The block looks like a form of protest against the regulations of the Planetary Court concerning orbital transportation."

"You can call it a *strike*, EVE. And I'm not done yet." Wei moved his arms again and described an imaginary square with his hands. "EVE, activate a three-day time ellipse."

EVE carried out the order and Cantara saw the reproduction of planet Earth becoming opaque for a split second before returning exactly as it was before.

At that point EVE said, "Time ellipse confirmed," then it commented on the result of Wei's actions. "Three days after the decision of the four companies, Blue Galacta, Asteroid Dominion, Farpoint Alfa, Sinospace, JAXA Earth, Terracorp, and Equinox also have suspended or drastically limited their presence on or below orbit. Astrocorp as a whole seems to have blocked any form of space activity. It appears that your...*strike* is contagious."

"How are the US, the EUROCON, and China handling this strike?" Wei asked.

"The three political entities have asked Astrocorp to justify this unexpected strike. The cessation of all Astrocorp orbital activities could cause a substantial loss of income for the US, the EUROCON, and China. In the worst-case scenario, their economies could contract. A legal dispute is about to begin between the two parties."

"Yeah," Wei said. "It's going to get bloody. The big players will start a pissing contest, but they have no idea just how big the real prey is. Have the eleven corporations forming Astrocorp responded with a joint statement to the pressures of the US, the EUROCON, and China?"

"They have," EVE confirmed. "Astrocorp publicly declared its inability to complete its work and remain faithful to its contracts due to the current rules governing the orbital transportation."

"Sweet." Wei put the blue data tables aside—those which he had used up to that point—and began completely different research with new data characterized by a bright white color. Wei spent some time evaluating the new information.

If this simulation really worked like a real-time strategy game, Cantara imagined that those different colors signaled different resources Wei could use to fulfill his goal. Hers was just a speculation, but the simulation's rules seemed quite simple to understand. The Madame continued to watch events unfold, finding herself much more interested than she wanted to admit in the elaborate show of light and shapes. At the same time, she reminded herself she must not let the flashy spectacle obscure her judgment. She couldn't risk being ruled by the impressions of the moment. The advice she gave to her students worked as a rule of thumb: *The first impression is always the wrong one.*

Wei spoke again. "EVE, what does the slice of public opinion not politically involved think of the space economy?"

"Your question is beyond the scope of this scenario," EVE noted, as if the question made no sense.

Wei rephrased the question. "According to the Ether and traditional media, what seems to be the opinion that the planetary population, not declared Hyperist or Landist, holds toward the space economy? What do the *neutralists* think?"

"The subject is too recent to generate consistent data," EVE answered. "However, from the information available on the Ether, most of the public classified as neutralist consider the space economy as an interesting new element with potential. A recent survey determined that seventy-five percent of respondents that define themselves neutralists would take an astral holiday if they had the money to afford it."

Wei nodded, then evoked new images and charts while shaping the simulation.

EVE evaluated Wei's decisions and the use of his resources. "You have started on the Ether a campaign of protest against the regulations regarding orbital transportation."

"You bet," Wei said, his hands dancing as he evoked, triaged, and deployed new resources. It seemed to Cantara that the greater the amount of information EVE fed to Wei, the faster his processing speed needed to be in order to match the scenario. Consequently, even the movements of his body had to keep pace with the increasing speed of the simulation. Soon, the body of the Hyperist began to shimmer with a sheen of sweat. The Madame understood why Wei had chosen to be almost completely naked. Clothes were disregarded as a form of obstruction that could limit his movements and affect his performance.

As time went by, and with the increasing difficulty of the scenario, Cantara noticed that Wei was showing the first symptoms of fatigue. The young man was clearly affected, mentally and physically, by the increasing pace of the simulation. His breathing became more rapid and irregular, and he seemed to spend more time assimilating the volume of data that orbited around his body. At that time, dozens of charts, graphs, and reports demanded his attention.

Wei wiped away the sweat beading his forehead. "I want a two-week time ellipse."

"Confirmed," EVE said. The planet became opaque for the second time. "We are now two weeks into the future."

Wei held his breath. "How many of the disputes are now classified important by the Planetary Court?"

"Five thousand two hundred sixty-six and growing," EVE answered. "Most of them are caused by Astrocorp's strike, by the protests coming from the EUROCON, the US, and China, and by a growing movement in public opinion favorable to the relaxation of the orbital transportation regulations."

The First Hyperist now seemed excited. "Give me another week-long time ellipse," he said. "Report."

EVE carried out the order and continued with its report. "Wei, the Planetary Court is undergoing multiple pressures from the world of business, media, and politics to relax the constraints on the orbital transportation. EUROCON, the United States, China, and eighty-six other political entities are voting in order to remove different decision-making powers from the Planetary Court regarding the space economy. Strong pressure from public opinion is also favoring a heated debate, in traditional media and on the Ether, concerning the need to establish new safeguards without limiting the orbital transportation of goods and people."

"Give me another time ellipse," Wei said, breathing heavily while studying his data. "I need five more days. Report."

EVE answered promptly. "It is expected that the Planetary Court will make a new decision regarding the orbital transportation shortly." A pause lasted a few seconds, then EVE continued. "The vote has just ended. Seventy-five percent of the members are now in favor of the new regulations. Moreover, the day after the vote, the Planetary Court undergoes a substantial downsizing of its powers in orbital and space-related business."

Wei breathed through his teeth, then asked, "Can you generate a report on the performance of the space economy two quarters after the new regulations?"

"Affirmative," EVE responded. "The GXP of the space economy will grow slowly but steadily over the next two quarters. Polaris will be modified to carry double the tonnage compared to the past. The modernization of the space elevator will be completed by 2052. In addition, thanks to the relaxation of the rules on orbital transport, new companies will spring up. The supply of services will be able to appropriately meet the demand."

Wei took a bottle of water from the floor and finished half of the contents in a few gulps. "EVE," he said while wiping his mouth, "illustrate the consequences of the victory of Astrocorp over the Planetary Court."

"Astrocorp will see its membership grow considerably. Twenty-nine corporations and companies involved in the astral industry, tourism, and commerce will become part of the union. In 2049, Astrocorp will officially change its name to Stellar Guild. Titan Asteros Corporation will join the Guild in the following year. Wei, this scenario no longer presents significant threats to the Master Project, and the dangerous variables have been eliminated or successfully prevented by your past actions."

Wei raised his fist to the air triumphantly. "EVE, save the file: *Spacefaring Civilization*."

"Confirmed. The file has been saved."

Cantara could barely digest what she had seen. Confusion, disbelief, suspicion, and amazement were fermenting inside her, battling to gain the upper hand. She turned to study Gladia's expression and was surprised to find the woman sitting on the edge of her chair, as she absently nibbled her thumb. Gladia whispered something inaudible, eyes fixed on Wei, who stood at the center of the room.

"What was that?" Cantara asked.

"He never managed to get past this scenario before," Gladia whispered.

"I don't understand. What do you mean?"

"He was never able to reach this point. Now he's in a completely uncharted territory."

Cantara returned her attention toward the First Hyperist, who was wiping his face with a towel. When he spoke, his voice was low and raspy. "Right, EVE. Let's move forward. Determine when the next major threat to the Master Project will occur."

Again, the planet disappeared and abruptly reappeared in the blink of an eye.

Cantara carefully studied the new multi-dimensional projection. This time she could see a greater number of geometric shapes spread on Earth's orbit. Their number had doubled in comparison to the previous simulation.

"Processing terminated," EVE informed Wei. "We are now at the end of the year 2058. In this scenario, there are multiple threats to the Master Project."

Wei was rubbing his arms, evidently trying to soothe his muscles. He breathed in and out for a few seconds, then said, "Describe the three major threats in order of severity."

"First threat: a growing tension between the US and China due to a territorial dispute in Southeast Asia, which is deteriorating rapidly. It is expected to degenerate into a full-scale armed conflict in the short term. All diplomatic relations between the two powers ceased a month ago. Both nations are conducting repeated military exercises on the borders of their respective spheres of influence. Some attempts made by the Planetary Court and other supranational entities to mediate the growing tension don't seem to have any effect."

There was a brief pause, then EVE continued. "Second

threat: the construction of a second space elevator, christened *Sirius,* began about a year ago. Its completion would dramatically increase orbital traffic, allowing the construction of triple the number of astrals in half the time currently required. This second structure is the result of a joint effort between several nations participating in the Commercial Covenant. The construction of Sirius has already consumed the equivalent of one-ninth of the world GDP and is proving to be more complex than expected. Some nations are abandoning their involvement in the project because of rising costs. In addition, a protest movement originated from public opinion begins to question the usefulness of this infrastructure and the huge resources needed for its completion."

Cantara saw Wei nodding briskly. There was something different in his posture. He seemed more tense; his eyes stared blankly toward the ceiling.

"Third threat: a new group of Landist extremists known as the Children of the Sun has grown in recent years, perpetrating several successful terrorist attacks at some of the major corporations involved in the space economy. The construction of Sirius has increased the influence of this movement. In a recent statement, the Asian section of the Children of the Sun says they are preparing an attack against Sirius itself, should its construction continue."

Wei opened his arms and legs and planted his feet on the ground, as if he were preparing to stop an avalanche with his bare hands. Abruptly, dozens of data of different colors exploded around him. The First Hyperist began as quickly as possible to become familiar with the new simulation. It was clear to Cantara that the difficulty of the scenario had grown.

It soon became obvious that Wei was unable to assimilate the enormous volume of information as quickly as he did before.

"EVE," Wei said, shaking his head, "I need more time to figure out a line of action. Anything you can give me? I could use a breather right about now."

The automated voice was not inclined to satisfy his request. "Wei, you have exhausted your supply of temporal stasis two scenarios ago. The simulation must proceed according to the rules established by the program."

Wei cursed. He evoked double the amount of data and began laboring on it.

"Wei," EVE interrupted him, breaking a silence that had lasted less than a minute, "the tension between China and the United States has worsened as a result of military exercises conducted by the Chinese fleet in the Gulf of Alaska."

"Shit!" Wei blurted out, making the data disappear. He began to move his body. Cantara could not help but notice that something had changed in his movements. Wei had undeniably lost the grace he possessed in the previous scenario.

"Wei," EVE called, while the young man was busy reading a new string of information, "your attempt to involve Canada in the negotiations between the two powers seems to have partially affected the scenario. The US government has agreed to meet the Chinese if they cease to deploy their fleet on US waters. The politburo agreed. Official delegations of both powers are expected to meet in three days in Vancouver."

Wei allowed himself to relax for a moment. He summoned the data and tried to catch up with the new developments but was interrupted again by EVE's update.

"Wei, the terrorist group known as the Children of the Sun has successfully completed an attack on an astral refinery owed by Equinox. Result: nine victims, damages totaling fifty-nine million bancars. The news is broadcasted everywhere. Two other attacks are announced against other companies forming part of the Stellar Guild."

With a nearly superhuman effort, Wei summoned around him a cloud of information of a dozen different colors.

Yet this time it seemed there was simply too much to handle. Cantara saw him shaking his head more than once while trying to keep up with the increasing complexity of the scenario.

"Wei," EVE said, "your latest action resulted in the destruction of the Asian section of the terrorist movement, but the Children of the Sun operate as separate and independent cells. Your counter-offensive does not seem to have destabilized the operational capacity of the movement as a whole. EUROCON, African, American, and Arabic sections of the Children of the Sun announced actions against multiple installations related to the astral industry." There was a pause no longer than a minute while Wei was assimilating data in order to shape new events, then EVE resumed talking. "Wei, the terrorist group has successfully carried out an attack on the Half-Way station of Polaris. Seven passengers were stranded twenty-five thousand kilometers from the ground. The Infinity control center has been contaminated by a gas of unknown origin. Infinity is being evacuated at this moment. Meanwhile, the group has declared that it intends to carry out an attack against Sirius."

Wei was clearly at the limit of his strength. As he faced the unravelling of the events with increasingly slow and imprecise actions, the First Hyperist said, "EVE! I'm using my etherions to give birth to a movement in the public opinion to put pressure on the Commercial Covenant to temporarily stop the construction of Sirius. Are there any consequences?"

"Wei," EVE said with an unyielding tone, "the use of your etheric resources will not affect the construction of Sirius. In addition, the Secretary of the Commercial Covenant has publicly stated, and I quote, '*We will not bow to terrorist threats of any kind. The work on the construction of Sirius will continue as planned.*' The statement was released on the Ether. The terrorist group has responded by intensifying its attacks on the headquarters of the Stellar Guild and the Commercial Covenant. Four attacks have been carried out successfully so far. One hundred and thirteen deaths, about two hundred injured. Damages for a total of four hundred and nine million bancars resulting in—"

"Damn it!" Wei shouted, interrupting EVE's report. "Listen, I want to use an emergency resolution of the Planetary Court to suspend the construction of Sirius while—"

"Wei." It was EVE's turn to interrupt him. "The Planetary Court doesn't have any power over this matter. Your maneuver in the scenario set in 2047 has drastically reduced its involvement in space economy-related affairs. Your actions do not appear to affect the intensifying chaotic situation. The degeneration of the system is reaching a critical point. The status of equilibrium is shifting away."

"The hell it is!" Wei was besieged by images, graphics, and numbers. No matter how fast he made decisions, it seemed that for every situation he solved there were three others popping out of nowhere.

"Wei, the negotiations between China and the United States have failed. An accident between the fifth US fleet and the aircraft carrier *Deng Xiaoping* has just provoked a localized conflict between the two powers two hundred miles from the Gulf of Alaska."

"No," Wei said through clenched teeth, moving hands and arms, sweat covering every inch of his body. "Not now!"

EVE continued, insistent and relentless as a jackhammer. "The conflict between the US and China has escalated into war." This statement was followed by a few minutes of silence that seemed to last for hours. Then EVE continued to update Wei on the evolving situation. "After several clashes between the two fleets off the American coast, Mexico and Canada declared their neutrality. The Planetary Court and other peacekeeping forces don't seem to be able to stop the conflict. The estimated loss of life as a result of the hostilities is now rising to six thousand and six units and the number is growing rapidly. The damage to the economies..."

Wei did not pay attention to the rest of the report and tried a desperate countermeasure to turn the tables. EVE evaluated his action, then ruled, "The Planetary Court and other major peacekeeping forces cannot stop the conflict even with the heavy sanctions approved by the majority of the nations of the world. The President of the United States authorizes the use of nuclear weapons."

Cantara felt Gladia hold her breath. She seemed completely absorbed by the events.

"The first atomic bomb has been dropped for demonstration purposes about five hundred miles from Shanghai, in the East China Sea," EVE said.

A dome spawning a shining white light suddenly appeared in the area named by EVE. Cantara and Gladia gasped in unison. Again Cantara was surprised by the quality and detail of the projection. The simulation had clearly ceased for her to be such. Now her brain seemed to classify the images she was seeing as a window on the future, something no less real than the room she was in.

EVE's voice roused her from her thoughts. "The Chinese politburo retaliated against the US two days after the attack, dropping three nuclear devices in the Sonora Desert in Arizona. To this moment, the conflict has caused fifty thousand three hundred and twenty-two casualties."

The situation seemed to get worse by the second.

Cantara listened to the calm and quiet voice of EVE which, with merciless efficiency, brought news of death and destruction upon them.

"Wei, the world GDP and the GXP of the space economy are collapsing. It is estimated that both will lose around ten percent in the next quarter. It is also estimated that fifty-five million people will become unemployed in the same period. Crime and social unrest are increasing, especially in areas affected by the conflict. The Children of the Sun attributed the outbreak of the conflict to the exorbitant costs required to complete the space elevator Sirius. The public is witnessing the collapse of manufacturing and their standard of living. Martial law has been declared in one hundred and seventeen capitals of the world..."

"EVE! Stop the construction of the second space elevator! I'm using all that I have left of my—"

"Wei, the construction has already been suspended for lack of funds and manpower." The ubiquitous voice silenced him. "The Commercial Covenant has ceased to exist. Other attacks are perpetrated against companies and institutions related to the astral industry. The authorities are unable to isolate the growing extremist groups." EVE continued down the list, overlaying one piece of information over the other. Cantara could only catch glimpses of information among the flood of news of disasters that followed one after the other like an unstoppable domino effect.

"...It is estimated that the world GDP will fall another fifteen points in the next quarter... The standard of living is decreasing exponentially... Half a million deaths caused by the conflict... The explosion of an epidemic...collapse... loss...unrest...poverty...war..."

Wei Wang collapsed, exhausted. The young man was gasping for air and coughing, his hands on the floor, his body shaking uncontrollably, hit by waves of spasms. He appeared to struggle to breathe. His muscles, tense and tested by the enormous effort, no longer seemed able to support his weight.

The First Hyperist tried to say something, but neither Cantara nor Gladia nor EVE were able to hear it. Wei fell first on his knees, then on his back, eyes closed and arms wrapped around his body in a desperate attempt to stop the spasms.

"What's the matter with him?" Cantara asked, staring at Wei. "Why is he shaking?"

Gladia did not answer. She just looked at Wei with an expression that Cantara thought was equal part sadness and helplessness.

Meanwhile Wei lay motionless on the floor. He was no longer trembling, but was barely breathing. EVE continued to update him with a matter-of-fact tone.

Then, after what felt like an eternity, the First Hyperist raised a solitary hand. To Cantara that gesture resembled a white flag waved in front of an enemy.

"All right, EVE," Wei murmured, in a voice so low that Cantara struggled to hear, "I lost. Close...close the file: *Spacefaring Civilization*."

EVE executed the order and the colossal Earth suddenly vanished. For the second time the room fell into pitch-black darkness.

Everything around was still and silent. Only then did Cantara realize she had both arms wrapped around her knees. She shook her head, trying to regain her composure, but the knuckles of her hands were still white and numb.

After a few moments, the familiar blue light returned to the room.

Cantara glanced around. She was trying to process a wide range of information while inspecting the room. The planet Earth, the multicolored data, and Wei Wang had disappeared as if they had never existed. Even EVE's voice had deserted the hall.

"Where...where is he?" Cantara asked in a halting voice. "Where is Wang?"

Gladia tipped her head to the side and gazed at Cantara. "He's probably gone to take a shower and eat something. He'll sleep for a few hours and then start all over again."

"All over again..." the Madame trailed off, blinking. "To start *what* all over again, exactly? What was all of that about?" She motioned to the platform on which, a few minutes before, the Earth's reproduction was revolving.

A tired smile flashed on Gladia's face. "That," she said, "is difficult to explain. I call it *Wei's bet.*"

"Wei's bet?"

"Nobody really knows what he's up to," Gladia said. "Not even us, the members of the Hexahedron, his inner circle. We only know that for the last few months Wei has confined himself here, doing...well, probably doing what he does best."

Cantara pressed her lips into a fine line. "And what would that be?"

"Trying to make a difference," Gladia answered, as if it were the most obvious thing in the world.

"I don't..." Cantara didn't finish the sentence. She didn't

even know how to continue it. *Wei's bet* seemed to her the best way to define what she had seen. But was it really a bet? And even if that was the case, why was the busiest person on the planet spending his time doing this? And most importantly, why had Gladia Egea wanted to show her the process?

Then a thought struck her like a bolt; one question that arose spontaneously after watching the simulation. Cantara carefully studied Gladia's face and asked, "What happens in this simulation if Polaris is not built?" She pointed to the platform in the center of the room. "Wang must have explored this eventuality, given the nature of the simulation. He calls this simulation *Spacefaring Civilization*, doesn't he? It seems that all...*this* started from the fact that Polaris has been built and that it is operational."

Gladia's eyes were blank and distant, clouded by thoughts. "Yes," she said slowly. "I saw that eventuality occur."

"Well?" Cantara pressed her. "What happens if Polaris never rises?"

Gladia's mouth twitched. "In *that* scenario," she said, "our civilization continues to develop some technologies that greatly enhance Ether's control over humankind. We close in on ourselves and never develop a space economy of significant size. We become increasingly dependent on the virtual world and on its related services." Gladia paused. She rubbed her hands on her pants and looked away from Cantara. Then she continued, staring at the floor.

"In the year 2069, humans live fifty-nine percent of their lives on the Ether, surrounded by automatic mechanisms that pump life into their bodies. In 2111, the human race is a complex mechanism of automated and artificial interconnections. We live our whole lives in a world carefully planned to meet our needs. At some point, however, something happens. In the year 2133, a deficiency in the Ether that EVE calls the *Singularity* begins to attack the delicate mechanism that keeps this complex artificial world together. There are neither engineers nor experts left to fix the problem and the sentinel programs designed by humanity to protect our virtual sleep fail to solve this discrepancy. Eight hundred and twenty-nine million lives, all that's left of our species, cease to exist in a heartbeat on March 31st, 2134, at five-thirty in the afternoon, Greenwich time, when the Singularity irreversibly compromises the system."

Gladia's eyes were closed, her hands clasped, an unreadable expression on her face. Eventually, she looked at the Madame again and concluded, "The human race dies out lying in bed."

Cantara swallowed hard. Even though she understood that she had witnessed a simulation, the result of a program's calculations, even though a part of her brain was laughing at those apocalyptic statements, a sense of urgency and inevitability began to invade her body.

"That's not the end of it," Gladia resumed. "The Singularity is not merely related to the building of Polaris. It's a constant in every single scenario Wei ran, like a shadow clinging to the very fate of humankind. It will happen at some point, no matter what we try to do to stop it, unless we develop a way to render the Singularity effect less severe."

"Less severe? How?"

"By becoming a spacefaring civilization," Gladia said. "By spreading far and wide, increasing our chances of survival by diversifying our genetic and technological output."

Cantara bit her lip. She stared at Gladia for several moments before realizing she had held her breath.

She had seen nothing but a game, Cantara reminded herself, repeating that phrase as a mantra while she recalled the hours spent watching Wei Wang shape the future of the human civilization. Just a game. But was it really just that?

Was *Wei's bet* really a way to make a difference?

"What did I see?" Cantara asked, without noticing that the question was in fact addressed to herself.

Gladia crossed her arms. "Over the years, I've learned that trying to define Wei's actions and intentions would be like hitting a bullet with another bullet while you are tied up, upside down, on the back of a running horse. What did you see? You've seen a vision of a future that could be, a shadow cast on a wall, a column of smoke in the darkness. You saw a dream. You can call it whatever you like. One description is as worthy as the next. None has any value, and all of them have the meaning that you choose to give them."

"A dream," Cantara echoed, looking at the empty platform with scorn. "This is why you came to me? Because you want my help to realize the boy's fantasies? Because you really think that his dream will become reality?" She snorted. "I'm disappointed, Gladia. You didn't strike me as a blind, idealistic fool. Until now."

Gladia's smile was all in her eyes. "I used to call myself a realist and regarded facts and numbers as the principle elements of truth. Then I met Wei and everything changed. I've known him for five years, and if there's one thing I realized over this time, it's that he has a gift for turning his dreams into reality. I look at you and I look at Wei and I see two sides of the same coin, two people who are satisfied only when they shape the world around them, when they can make a difference. And what I'm proposing now, Cantara, is just that: to make a difference."

"There you go again with that sentence: *To make a difference*." Cantara sneered. "How do you propose to do that? By building castles in the clouds?"

Gladia stared at the etherion, then she burst out laughing.

Cantara blinked. "What's so funny?"

"Gilbert Keith Chesterton," Gladia managed to say while wiping her eyes with the backs of her hands.

"What's that?" Cantara frowned.

"Gilbert Keith Chesterton," Gladia repeated, straightening her back. "A British writer Wei would have loved to meet, I guess. You reminded me of something he said: 'There are no rules of architecture for a castle in the clouds.' Don't you find it funny and enlightening at the same time? What better answer to your question?"

Cantara found Gladia's words totally senseless. Was the Hyperist just making fun of her?

"This is ridiculous," she blurted, rising from her chair. "Are we talking about fairy tales and chimeras, about fairies and mermaids? Don't you have any real answers to my questions? Or are you just completely nuts? I mean, do you seriously believe that Wei Wang is planning the future? Here? *Now?*"

"No." Gladia shook her head. She smiled. "I believe that Wei Wang is not merely planning the future, but the future of the future."

CANTARA COULDN'T SLEEP that night.

No matter from what angle she analyzed Polaris' media

debacle, the Planetary Court was going to exercise a veto against the space elevator's project. It was as inevitable as death and taxes.

Douglas Woodside had done an excellent job in making everyone believe that he had lost the battle against the Hyperists when in fact he was simply preparing his counterattack.

The days of Wei Wang and his project were numbered.

Cantara sighed, frustrated, as she shifted uncomfortably in her bed. This knowledge had not bothered her twenty-four hours before. Now she was losing sleep over it.

What had changed after witnessing *Wei's bet*? Why did she feel as if she had left unfinished business in that room, an important task that had to be accomplished?

She couldn't deny it. Something had clicked inside her. Yet, no matter how hard she tried, she couldn't pin down the feeling. It was like a premonition that flashed on the border of her consciousness and lasted for a few heartbeats before disappearing, swallowed up into darkness.

After turning again and again in her bed, Cantara decided she might as well get up and start her day a few hours before schedule. She sat on the bed, put on a crimson-colored robe, and headed for the bathroom.

After freshening up, she walked through a dimly lit corridor and opened the door of her office. She immediately noticed that the input station at the end of the room was glowing. Cantara approached the object warily. She frowned and cocked her head, surprised. Then suddenly she remembered James' homework.

It seemed as if a year had passed since her last lecture.

She waved a hand to access the file. Cantara sat in one of the armchairs and sighed. *I might as well start from here*, she thought.

Cantara read the title: *The War of the Ether*. She could not suppress a smile. It was a presumptuous and catchy title, typical of James.

She evaluated the student's work and, as she went on, found herself fascinated by its content. The homework was not only original, engaging, and well written, it was also accurate. She paused for a few minutes on one of the last sentences and read it aloud: "Sometimes the final victory cannot be obtained without a calculated number of losses. A strategic retreat can sometimes be the best alternative to avoid total defeat."

That sentence made her think for a few minutes. She stared at the words. It did not sound like the deliberations of an aspiring etherion. It was more like the declaration of a general who is preparing for battle. James' entire approach was fascinating. Cantara read the last sentence again. She felt there was something important hidden in that simple sequence of words, some implication that escaped her, like a word on the tip of her tongue that she could not quite remember but she felt she must know.

Then the awareness hit her like a bucket of icy water dropped on her head.

The etherion jumped up from her chair. She looked around, then quickly reached toward her desk and put her wrist on the communication panel.

Cantara Handal suddenly knew exactly how to make a difference.

THE MADAME STUDIED the emblem of the Hyperists—a silver-colored infinity symbol—hovering several feet above the ground, in the exact center of the room. There were no wires or support to justify its position, no visible trigo-projector explaining its silvery sheen. The symbol of the HYPER was hanging in the air seemingly without any plausible explanation, defying with impunity both gravity and common sense.

"So? What's your answer?"

Gladia's question did not catch her off guard. She had expected it since she entered that room.

"My answer is a clear *no,* my dear," Cantara said, looking at Gladia without blinking. "I'm going to continue to enjoy my retirement."

Gladia started to speak but Cantara cut her off.

"Save your breath, Doctor. My decision is final."

Gladia frowned. "You came all the way to tell me this personally? A simple call would have done—"

"Moreover," interrupted Cantara, raising a finger to silence the Hyperist, "the Planetary Court will decide *against* the construction of Polaris. It's as sure as hellfire."

Gladia managed to look puzzled and outraged at the same time. "What's this?" she said, her nostrils flaring. "Your attempt at pissing me off? If you came to waste my time with—"

"I'm not done yet," the Madame went on inexorably. "In a few weeks there will be another decision of the Planetary Court concerning the construction of the Infinity control center and the launch of Polaris. Once again, Woodside and his Landists will bury you alive."

Gladia raised her arm in the direction of the door. "Get the hell out of—"

"Still," Cantara resumed talking, "I promise you that the third time, the Planetary Court will approve the Polaris project and give you the green light."

"The *third* time?" Gladia's eyes widened. "Are you

kidding? The Planetary Court has never ruled three times on the same dispute."

"It will do so for this case. It will set a precedent."

"Right," Gladia said, skeptical. "And how would you know all this?"

"Rumors," Cantara said, carefully studying her long nails.

"Rumors?" echoed Gladia, a closed-lipped smile flashing on her face. "Are you going to elaborate on that?"

"Rumors in the right hallways," Cantara explained. "That's all I've got for you right now."

"Just like that?" Gladia looked at the etherion with a flat gaze. "Cantara Handal snaps her fingers and all the stars are suddenly aligned?"

"Darling, you have no idea what happens when I pull the rug from under the right person's feet or call in a favor. Let me do the heavy lifting. You just sit back and relax."

"Let me get this straight. I should trust you on your say-so? Without knowing what you're going to do?"

"Do you have any other choice?"

Gladia pursed her lips. "I don't like it."

"I didn't say it was going to be pleasant." Cantara leaned back, a distant smile on her face. "Listen, this Friday the Planetary Court will reject *de jure* the construction of the Infinity complex and won't give permission to the departure of Polaris, but *de facto* the Hyperists will be able to continue their plans. Think of it as a planned setback to prevent total defeat."

Gladia curled the side of her mouth. "You're talking in plain legalese. I didn't know you were an expert in planetary lawmaking."

"I'm not," Cantara said, "but my consultant in Corporate Lawmaking and International Legislation—"

"Is paid handsomely to be in your place," filled in Gladia. "Yeah, I should have expected that kind of answer. You're saying the fate of Polaris depends on these *rumors* you're talking about and your word?"

"The *presumption* of my word," Cantara pointed out, her fingers loosely clasped in her lap. "I would deny to anyone that we have had this nice conversation."

"All right," Gladia said. "Let's get to the part where you ask me something in return."

Cantara blinked; she looked abashed. "I might be doing this out of my kindness."

Gladia snorted. "I might sooner believe the idea of a talking toaster. I wasn't born yesterday, Madame. There is no such thing as a free lunch."

Cantara smiled. "True that."

"So, what do you want?"

"You mean besides the gratitude of one of the most influential women on the planet?" The Madame flashed a smile at Gladia.

"Yeah, besides that," Gladia said, answering with a small nod. "What do you need to make your *rumors* come true?"

"Well." Cantara smoothed the front of her shirt. "I thought of yesterday's show. You picked up my interest, my dear. I have decided there is something you have that might come in handy."

Gladia crossed her arms. "Yes?"

Cantara was unnaturally still. "I want EVE and I want the simulation program used by Wang."

For a good thirty seconds, even the echo of a noise deserted the room. Then Gladia shouted, "What?"

"I've thought about a possible alternative application of that program," Cantara said. "See, I can adapt EVE to my needs, I can turn it into something capable of making my lessons more interesting and engaging. It would give my students an edge. It's an opportunity I can't pass up."

Gladia tilted her head to the side. "You're not joking," she said. "You really want EVE."

"It's non-negotiable. Take it or leave it."

"You'd pull your weight to get Polaris a second chance to have a program that increases the performance of your students? Is this really what you want?"

"My students are incredibly gifted, Gladia. Some of them have what it takes to become real engines capable of shaping the future public opinion, to be truly remarkable founders of trends, linchpins, and builders of cultural empires. However, the industry in which we move changes at the speed of light, and it's a minefield that has claimed more than one life. I want my kids to have the best chance I can offer them when they go out there, trying to make a difference in the real world. Wang's program will help me do just that."

"So you'd use EVE to forge the best etherions of the world?"

"What I want is none of your business." Cantara's voice was steel. "Now pay attention, because I won't repeat this again. You have thirty seconds to give me an answer." Then, looking at Gladia with eyes that shone like polished emeralds, she added, "Today is *your* turn to make a difference, Gladia Egea, co-founder of the SOL, second vertex of the Hexahedron, and coordinator of the Polaris project."

Cantara stood up and waved a hand. A rush of scarlet light appeared in front of the symbol of infinity.

Gladia studied the trigoy as it projected a countdown.

Thirty seconds.

Gladia looked at the numbers and then to Cantara. She took a step back, almost without realizing it.

Twenty-nine seconds.

"I want EVE and the simulator used by your genius boy," ordered the Black Widow of the Ether, quirking an eyebrow as she smiled. "Give me these two things, Gladia, and I assure you that Polaris will rise. Give me what I want, and I promise Wei Wang will continue to build unchallenged his castles in the clouds."

10

ERIK

DÜSSELDORF, PRIVATE RESIDENCE OF SOFIA
DERINGER

2030

"Sonnie, is it time yet?" Erik asked, absently chewing his gum. The boy was lying on the couch, his eyes glued to the images projected by the telegoy.

"The launch is scheduled in one hour, thirty minutes, and twenty seconds."

"That long? I'm bored!"

Erik sat up. Annoyed, he stared at the transparent visor of the autotron that was serving him a tuna sandwich and a glass of milk. The autotron was the most recent expensive prototype his mother was working on. It was expected to go into mass production in two months and, as usual, his mother had decided to use her son as a tester.

Sonnie was physically thinner than its predecessors, somehow more basic. It was the first of a completely new generation of Pentanidus.

When his mother assigned the autotron to him, Erik

immediately noticed that the sinskin—the autotron's covering—had been removed, replaced by a simpler translucent carbonglass. When the child touched Sonnie's smooth, hard surface for the first time, he'd asked why this autotron had no skin.

His mother had replied that the average consumer was a capricious beast. Apparently, people did not want an autotron that looked like a human.

"Whole-grain bread, tuna, and tomatoes with partially skimmed milk," Sonnie said, holding the tray.

"Not hungry."

"Erik, I received precise instructions regarding the fourth meal of the day."

"I said I don't want it!"

"Refusal to comply with a direct instruction is non-acceptable behavior. Mrs. Deringer ordered to call the number 667 883 98854 in case of non-compliance."

"What? Mom told you to call Uncle Ramor if I didn't want her smelly—"

"Connection established," Sonnie said. "Standing by and waiting for an answer."

"Hey, hey, *hey!*" Erik moved his hands in front of the autotron's visor. "Okay, you won. I'll eat it."

The boy spat out the chewing gum and shoved the sandwich in his mouth. "I'hm heatin'," he mumbled. "Chan't ya shee?"

"Call aborted," the autotron said finally, taking the empty glass and dish and going back to the kitchen.

Erik wiped his mouth and watched Sonnie go away. He snorted. This time his mother had created a real monster. With previous models, he had always been able to find a way to do what he wanted, but with this new Pentanidus, things were different. Smarter, faster, more adaptable,

Sonnie was a completely new class of autotron designed and built specifically to supervise the offspring of humankind.

His mother was expecting to sell quite a few of them.

Erik looked back at the giant platform in the middle of the ocean that had been displayed on the telegoy for the past three days, without interruption.

The platform was actually a giant mega-structure packed with bridges, walls, and towers. To the child, that colossus resembled an imposing silver fortress; an artificial monolith that inspired a kind of awe. The Hyperists decided to name this enormous structure *Infinity*.

Erik focused on the highest tower of the mega-structure, from which the cable of the space elevator aspired to the vastness of space.

The commentator on the telegoy interrupted his thoughts. "All systems are on standby and waiting for the impending launch," the man was saying, flushed with excitement. "Polaris is ready to..."

Erik moved his hand and the commentator's face was replaced by another man in a suit with an even more excited look.

"After yesterday's press conference, where Wei Wang answered questions regarding the safety and reliability of Polaris..."

Erik flicked his wrist and another channel was displayed.

"...Huge groups of Landists poured into the main squares of dozens of different cities to protest against the upcoming launch, while the headquarters of SOL, Gaia, and I & I were assaulted and damaged. Numerous clashes between Landists and Hyperists have left several dozen wounded on the street, some of them in serious..."

Sonnie returned from the kitchen and examined the spreadsheet left earlier on the table by Erik.

"You have answered ninety-six percent of the questions correctly. Your performance does not require any action on my part. I'm sending the data to Mrs. Deringer."

The autotron barely left Erik time to look away from the face of the commentator.

"Your result has been acknowledged by Mrs. Deringer." Then the autotron froze on the spot. Its visor flashed with a green light. "Incoming action from the recipient," Sonnie announced. "Sofia Deringer has established remote control of my systems. Please stand by while she initiates a live connection..."

On the autotron's visor appeared Sofia Deringer's face.

"Honey, I'll be late again today," said Erik's mother. Her blonde, tangled hair looked unwashed and there were two greenish grooves under her eyes.

"Again?" Erik muttered. "But you said—"

"I know, cupcake, but Professor Kurosawa and I have some stuff to fix. How's Sonnie?"

"It's a nightmare, Mom! Please turn it off."

His mother nodded. "Excellent," she said, smiling. "So it's doing its job."

"Please don't sell this kind on the market," Erik pleaded, joining hands.

"Why shouldn't I?"

"It'll kill thousands of innocent children from boredom."

"No it won't. This is the point, isn't it? With autotrons like Sonnie, mothers like me can sleep soundly. By the way, are you getting ready for nighty-night?"

"But, Mom," Erik protested, indicating the telegoy. "They're broadcasting the departure of—"

"Lights go out at nine o'clock, Erik. Not a second later."

"But—"

"No buts. You gotta wake up early tomorrow. Sonnie knows it."

Erik cursed under his breath.

"Now give me a kiss."

The boy grimaced. He knew his mother had complete control over Sonnie's systems. If she wanted a kiss, she was going to get one, whether he liked it or not.

"Do I have to?" Erik complained. "It's cold."

His mother turned Sonnie's head and leaned toward him, waiting.

Erik snorted and reluctantly brushed the autotron's visor with his lips.

"Love you."

Erik said good-bye to his mother. Sonnie's visor was turned off and went transparent again.

At that moment, Sonnie regained control over its system.

SONNIE DETERMINED that Mrs. Deringer had severed her control over the autotron's mobile functions. Sonnie moved its right arm and stood upright while running a system diagnostic.

...Central system online...

...Database clear of service loops...

...Operational functions in normal range...

...Systemic energy flux established...

...Proceeding with Erik Deringer's supervisory activity...

Sonnie stood at the child's side, waiting.

He watched Erik wipe his lips with the back of his hand while looking at the images projected by the telegoy.

The channel was showing a variety of cities as they prepared to celebrate the upcoming launch.

"Wow! Look how many people are packed in there! Sonnie, what place is that?"

The autotron stared at the projection. "Beijing, Tiananmen Square," the autotron replied.

"How many are there? I've never seen so many people in one place."

"The authorities estimate a total of three million two hundred thousand people."

"What about this place over here? How many are there?"

"That is Saemangeum City, U-complex. There are almost three hundred thousand people."

"And this one?"

"Rio de Janeiro, Copacabana, about one million seven hundred thousand people."

"Looks like they're really having fun, right?"

Sonnie looked at the boy, but didn't answer.

Erik changed the channel and this time a familiar face appeared. The commentator was saying, "After twice successfully stopping the launch, and refusing to give up at less than an hour from countdown, Douglas Woodside is currently busy with his supporters in a violent campaign against Wei Wang and his space elevator."

"Sonnie, how long before Polaris takes off?" asked Erik.

"Fifty-three minutes, thirteen seconds."

"Then this time he's screwed," said the boy, grinning. "He's not going to stop the launch."

The boy gave each channel he'd seen its own separate projection so that he could watch all of the events happening at once. There were now five videos, each showing a different live event happening at that moment: the mega-structure surrounded by the ocean, two commentators excitedly talking about Polaris, the audience from half a dozen cities crowded in as many squares, and Douglas Woodside busy haranguing his public.

Erik focused on Woodside, who was describing in great detail the danger of the space elevator.

"Sonnie, what's the probability that Polaris' cable breaks?"

"Detailed information on the composition of the cable has not been made public," the autotron said. "For this reason, I can't give a satisfactory answer to your question. The cable has a tested tensile strength of around 200 giga-pascal and a multi-purpose AI that maintains unaltered the physical properties of the material. The probability that such a cable may be damaged is extremely small."

"How long will it take to get Polaris to its destination?"

"Ideally, keeping the cruise speed constant and assuming that altitude, temperature, and humidity are what the Infinity control center forecasted, Polaris should reach its destination in one day, two hours, eight minutes, and ten seconds. Problems with the equipment, the module, and adverse weather conditions may, however, require different types of interventions on the speed of the vehicle, thus increasing the total duration of the ascension."

Erik pursed his lips. "What is it carrying exactly? No one is saying that."

"Wei Wang and the board of directors of the project Space Zero have kept Polaris' cargo secret. Several dozen independent agencies and NGOs, however, have assessed the content, considering it harmless. Each inspector was required to sign a binding contract that forbade them from disclosing the exact nature of the cargo."

The boy nodded, but did so with a tightness in his expression that spoke of uncertainty. He listened to Woodside talking, then asked Sonnie, "So there can't be any weapons inside it, right?"

"According to several statements made by the inspectors, Polaris is carrying a non-organic object of negligible economic value, negligible weight, and negligible mass, devoid of any electronic component."

"Oh come on! It's impossible no one knows anything! I mean, how many people have inspected that cargo?"

"Three hundred forty-five."

"And no one let out even a whisper?"

Sonnie turned its visor toward Erik. "There are rumors. Most of them speak of a metal key. Wei Wang himself announced that it would have been a unique object, structurally compact, with a simple, symbolic value."

"Okay, I got it," the boy said while waving a hand and making Woodside's image disappear.

Erik kept asking questions for another forty minutes and Sonnie replied to each by drawing from its database.

The boy suddenly stopped speaking and whirled around when the commentator said, "Only five minutes before Polaris' ascension from Infinity!"

"You hear that? It's almost time, Sonnie!"

Polaris, an oval-shaped vehicle, was slowly climbing the majestic tower. It was connected to a cable that apparently had no end, like a bridge thousands of miles long linking Earth to the universe.

"Three minutes remaining!" the commentator was saying with growing excitement. "The system is being powered up at this very moment and the cable responds to the signals from the Infinity control center. Polaris is ready to go, waiting for the thrust that will mark the beginning of the first stage called *the five minutes of terror*."

"Erik," Sonnie said, turning toward the boy, "do I start playing the tune you have requested for the event?"

"Geez! I almost forgot," said the boy, clapping his hands. "Well said, Sonnie! Yes, give us some atmosphere. Rock and Roll!"

At exactly one minute from the launch, Sonnie positioned itself at the center of the room and its electronic amplifiers exploded with rhythmic music, intense and full of energy.

"Less than fifty seconds to the launch, ladies and gentlemen! The airspace around the structure is clear."

The autotron continued to blast the music, the commentator's words barely audible over the loud music.

"We have a go from the control center. The start of the automatic countdown begins now!"

"Yes!" Erik cheered.

"Twenty seconds! Polaris is fully energized! The AI on board now has complete control of the functions of the carrier."

Erik waved his hands frantically. "Go, go, go!"

"Fifteen...twelve...ten, nine, eight, seven, six, five, four..."

"We're almost there, Sonnie!"

"Polaris comes to life! It rises. Accelerates. Continues the vertical ascent. No signs of structural failure. We're getting the preliminary data from the control center and...everything is going according to plan. Polaris has almost reached—"

"Look at it go!" Erik cried out, standing up and bouncing on the couch. "Yes! Go, go, *go!*"

Sonnie looked at the boy, then turned toward the images of Polaris, which was moving fast and gradually increasing its speed.

The journalist commenting on Polaris' ascension had a

purplish face and bulging eyes. The autotron calculated thirteen percent chance of a heart attack.

Sonnie moved its visor and focused on the images of people celebrating in London, on the Molotov cocktails thrown by demonstrators in Washington and Moscow, and on the violent clashes between Hyperists and Landists in dozens of different cities despite the intervention of the police.

The autotron turned back to look at Erik waving his arms in the air, dancing on the couch, and following Polaris' unstoppable rise while blowing a long, loud whistle.

Sonnie noticed that the boy's heartbeat sped up, that his breathing was irregular, and that his pupils were dilated. These were all disturbing but not life-threatening parameters, the autotron decided in a few nanoseconds, classifying the abnormal physical state as *euphoric human behavior*. It crossed out the pending decision to call an ambulance, but at the same time stopped the music and the television broadcasts.

"What the hell?" Erik shouted. "Why did you do that?"

"Erik, I have classified your current behavior as moderately dangerous. Also, your bio-values are out of scale. Please bring your physical parameters back within acceptable levels."

"You sonofa... Turn it back on. Now!"

"I have not registered a significant change in your bio-values. Please stand by."

Erik let out a frustrated shout. He stared at Sonnie, let out a sigh, and then sat down with his arms crossed.

"Fluctuating but acceptable bio-values."

"Good. Could you *please* turn it back on?"

"I'm powering up the telegoy."

The images returned to brighten the room.

"What about the music?" Erik asked.

"The song has been considered by my analysis to be the main cause of your distress. The playing of the song has been interrupted to ensure your safety."

Erik raised his middle finger. Sonnie didn't seem to grasp the meaning of the gesture.

"Let's now go live with the Infinity control center," the commentator was saying with the image of Polaris behind him. "Now that the five minutes of terror have passed, Wei Wang is now expected in the press room to comment on the performance of the launch and answer questions."

There was a moment of silence, someone moved behind the journalist, and the camera went out of focus for a few seconds.

"The door is opening," the commentator said, his forehead glistening with sweat. "Yes, there he is! Wei Wang is greeted with applause and a general standing ovation."

Erik made all the other projections disappear and focused only on the image of Wei, followed by five people who he recognized as Wei's closest partners, the members of the Hexahedron. Mark Strutzenberg, Gaia's CEO, strode forward with a cigar in his mouth, while Gladia Egea, Wei's right arm, walked alongside him. They were followed by Patrick Trudeau, Chief Engineer of I & I; Isaac Nazarov, the founder of Archetype Unlimited; and Toshio Shimao, head researcher at the Paragon Corporation.

Sonnie focused on Wei Wang. The Hyperist looked wearied. He was breathing very slowly and his face was skeletal and almost blue. His eyes were besieged by dark shadows, his hair was tousled, and the muscles in his neck were tense. Wang smiled and waved his hand, but he didn't seem to realize where he was or what he was doing.

The autotron estimated that the First Hyperist must be

suffering from malnutrition, sleep deprivation, and high levels of stress.

The commentator in the meantime was describing the triumphal march of Wei and his colleagues.

Only after a few minutes did Sonnie notice the glow that surrounded the stage where Wang and the other five Hyperists were about to sit. It enlarged the image and leaned forward. It was a force field: a Lambda Trust Mark III, the best defense field available on the market. The organizers of the event had clearly taken the safety of the members of the Hexahedron very seriously.

When the crowd was finally seated, the commentator disappeared, substituted by the image of Wei Wang, who was introduced by a mechanical voice as "visionary mind, the First Hyperist, the creator of Polaris, and the director of the project Space Zero."

A silence full of excitement permeated the room packed with people.

"To write history is a wonderful experience," Wei began, smiling at his audience. "It gives you a very special perspective on the world around you and helps you understand one very important thing: impossible is only a possibility that has not yet been discovered."

A standing ovation from the public prevented Wei from continuing his speech. Twice he tried to resume talking and twice was interrupted by whistles and applause.

Erik imitated the audience by clapping and cheering wildly. Then he looked at the autotron, staring at him in silence. The boy sat down with a sigh.

It all happened in a matter of seconds.

A sudden explosion erupted from within the room, throwing half of the audience to the ground. Almost immediately it was followed by a wave of multicolored light.

Erik gasped, one trembling hand over his mouth.

Sonnie saw the majority of the audience screaming and throwing themselves on the ground, or rushing to the emergency exits in disorder, pushing and stumbling over other people. The room transformed into a chaos of screams, bodies, and noises that overlapped, making it impossible to distinguish one from the other. Security drones came out from their slots in the walls and dozens of men in black and silver uniforms moved quickly, shouting orders and warnings to each other.

Sonnie saw Wei Wang turning his head slowly, his face devoid of emotion. His eyes were fixed on a specific point in front of him.

It was in that moment of panic and confusion that the autotron heard the second explosion.

Wei Wang was thrown away from the chair by an unknown force. Sonnie couldn't see what hit him. The First Hyperist struck the wall of the stage. He fell, first on his knees, his hands stiff at his sides, and then to the pavement, slumped back like a lifeless mannequin.

Wang remained motionless.

Sonnie registered the voice of the commentator among the cacophony of terror.

"God and Heaven! I think...I think they are shooting at them..." A pause, followed by cries for help, and two other explosions tore through the room. "They're still shooting! Strutzenberg and Shimao...both hit by...I don't know what it was. I can't...I can't see..."

The commentator disappeared from the screen. In his stead appeared a close-up shot showing Wei Wang with eyes wide open. The video changed, the visual backed up a bit, and showed his immediate surroundings: Wang was lying on the pavement, with Gladia Egea weeping at his side.

A security man picked her up and carried her away before another explosion occurred.

A crowd of people invaded the stage, moving frantically, shouting and shoving other people.

"Oh no," Erik whispered. "Please don't ..."

The cameras recorded Wang being hurriedly transported out on a stretcher.

Sonnie analyzed the images without commenting on them. "Erik," the autotron called after a few minutes. The boy was shivering in silence, eyes wild. "The cessation of all activities is scheduled in sixty seconds. I must ask you to get ready for bed and—"

"What?" Erik blinked, his eyes shining with tears. "Do you even know what just happened? I'm not going to bed. Forget it!"

Sonnie interrupted the broadcast and dimmed the lights of the room.

"Wha—? Sonnie, turn it back on. Now! I want to know what happened to Wei!"

In an instant Sonnie constructed an answer to give the boy.

"Wei Wang died four minutes ago."

11

ARIUL

FLORIDA, CAPE CANAVERAL

7 days later

The sky was covered with thick, dark clouds the color of dirty water, motionless in the inexorable vastness.

Gladia Egea opened the urn. She looked at it, undecided, as if she didn't remember what she should do with it. She closed it and felt her heart beat wildly. Slowly she opened the urn a second time.

The wind ruffled her hair. The salty air had a strange smell; stark but pleasant. It was like being in the middle of a garden made of seaweeds and shells, salt and sand.

Gladia looked at the contents: Light grey ashes, all that was left of Wei Wang.

Reluctantly, the woman threw the ashes into the air.

They disappeared in the blink of an eye, collected by a gust of wind.

Gladia closed the urn and sat down on the sand.

The ocean was calm, an immensely wide and still table, like a sheet of glass enclosing an endless world within the world.

Somewhere not far away in that corner of Florida was the Kennedy Space Center, the outpost from which humankind had sent its messengers, daring to challenge the infinite and the unknown, aspiring to the stars.

Long-forgotten past.

Now the place was little more than a tourist attraction.

Wei had told her that that place constituted one of his first memories. There, Wei and his father had admired the powerful engines of the *Atlantis*, the last Space Shuttle to leave Earth.

Gladia reached into the sand and began to dig. It was pleasant to feel the grains between her fingers and under her nails, almost therapeutic.

A few minutes later, her hand emerged, clutching a mixture of yellow and white sand.

Looking at it, the memory of that strange morning overcame her. She closed her eyes and recalled the smell of bacon and pancakes.

She smiled.

"Damn it," she had said when the sugar bowl rolled and spilled its contents on the table.

Her hand had been full of white grains; a pearl-colored sand.

"Leave it," Wei had said, grabbing the small container before it fell off the table.

"Christ. I'm so sleepy I can't keep my eyes open," Gladia had complained, shaking the last grains of sugar off her hand.

"Another napkin?" Wei had handed her one.

She had waved it away. "Just tell me why the hell you dragged me here in the middle of the night."

"I need your opinion."

"Here?" She had looked around wide-eyed. A server was bringing sausages and scrambled eggs to a customer a couple tables away. The room had smelled like maple syrup. "What's wrong with the lab?"

"The laboratory stinks of work. Now shut up and close your eyes."

"What?"

"Close your eyes."

"You want me to fall asleep on the spot?"

"Just do it."

Gladia had snorted, closing her eyes reluctantly.

"Imagine you are in front of a door," Wei had said. "It's locked, but you have the key to open it. As you get closer you realize there is a chain with a padlock that keeps you from opening it. You listening?"

"Hmm."

"Good. How do you get in?"

"Mother of God. Wei, did you wake me up at four in the morning for a fucking mind game?"

"Stay with me." Wei had snapped a finger. "Closed door, chain locked. You got it?"

Gladia had yawned. "Yeah... Augh... I got the picture."

"Then answer. How do you get in?"

"I guess I need to open the damn lock."

"Exactly. Now let's pretend that a Good Samaritan passing by opens it for you."

"A Good Samaritan?"

"Yeah, a Good Samaritan. What happens then?"

Gladia had sighed. "The goddamn door opens and I can finally go to sleep."

"No. The door won't open. Have you been listening? The door is still closed. You have to use the key to open it."

"Okay," she had said, propping her cheek with her hand and yawning again. "Before I open the door with the damn key"—she'd pointed to a nearby table—"do I at least win a pancake?"

"Think about what we're doing," Wei had continued, his eyes alight. "Polaris is the Good Samaritan who opens the lock, but it must be humanity that decides to open the door. Entering the room is not a consequence of the action of the Good Samaritan, but of *your* action. It's a consequence of your willingness to find out what's inside the room."

Wei had rummaged in his pockets and come out with an open padlock. He had placed it on the table.

"What's this?" Gladia had asked, frowning.

"Polaris' cargo," Wei had replied as if it were the most obvious thing in the world.

Gladia let the sand slip through her fingers. The memory faded away. She breathed in the ocean air and closed her eyes.

The timeless whisper of the ocean was calling her.

She stood up and took off her shoes, walking closer to the water. It was cold and colorless, as Wei's skin had been before going on stage. The skin of a man who was slowly wasting away...

Other images flashed before her eyes: old, painful memories she had forced away and that now were surfacing, bringing with them the bitter tang of sorrow.

"Wei, you don't have to do it. Mark and I can handle it. Don't be stupid."

"Listen to her, boy," Mark had chimed in eagerly, chewing on his cigar. "You look like shit."

"Mom, Dad," Wei had said with an impatient snort, "I'm as healthy as a crab…"

"…in a goddamn California roll." Mark had actually glared at the young man.

"Wei, look at you, for God's sake!" Gladia was shaking, speaking through the teeth with forced restraint. "You can't even stand up. You fell twice in the last forty-eight hours. Think we'd forget that? You're exhausted!"

"I didn't fall," Wei had protested. "I was just sniffing the floor while resting my eyes. Don't you ever do that? It's fun. You should try."

Gladia had thrown her hands up. "Some people are immune to good advice."

Mark Strutzenberg had planted a big, fat finger on Wei's chest. "Listen to the doctor, genius. You look like a twice-dead corpse."

Gladia had opened her mouth to add something else, but Wei had waved a hand dismissively. "Don't worry." He had grinned. "I'll be fine."

And he was gone without another word.

Gladia had both feet in the ocean now, and was slowly getting used to the cold water. She was breathing heavily, fighting back the tears.

She knelt down to plunge her hands into the water. Once, twice, three times. She looked at them in silence.

No matter how many times she washed them, her hands continued to emerge soaked in blood.

It was Wei's blood, while around them other explosions were tearing the room apart, followed by screams, curses, and cries for help.

But the rest wasn't important. For her there were only those almond-shaped eyes staring at her. Once they had been lightened with a unique sparkle, now they were blank and half-closed. The hand she was holding was white and cold.

There had been blood in and out of Wei's broken body.

Two lips had moved. A word had been spoken. Gladia had put Wei's hand on her chest.

When the security guard had pushed her away, bringing her to safety, Wei's hand had fallen to the floor with a thud, his lips still.

Gladia wiped her eyes and shuddered.

She turned, got out of the water, and started running. At some point she tripped on a stone and fell on the beach. For a few minutes she did nothing but breathe, replaying Wei's death over and over again.

Every time she discovered something new she could have done to prevent his death.

One way to save him.

One way to avoid the death of his dream.

A beep on her arm shook her from her thoughts.

She sat up, arms wrapped around her knees, forehead resting on her arms. She drew her breath and released it before answering. "What is it?"

"Time's up. We've got to go."

Gladia didn't answer.

The voice continued, unyielding. "Don't make me say it twice."

Gladia pretended not to hear. She closed her eyes and waited for the world to stop spinning around her.

She waited in vain.

When she finally got up, Gladia had run out of tears.

The car was waiting on the side of the road, exactly where she had left it.

A tall man dressed in a white suit was waiting with his hands clasped behind his back.

"Get in," he said, his eyes scanning around.

Gladia cleared her throat and swallowed hard. She removed the last layer of sand from her foot and got into the car.

The man on guard peered around one last time. He moved his wrist toward his mouth. "Alpha to Commodore," he said. "We're leaving."

"Copy that, Alpha. We've got you on the screens."

The bodyguard got into the car and closed the door.

"That was the stupidest thing you could have done. There, I said it."

Gladia shifted in her seat. "I heard you the first time, Leon," she said, her fingernails biting into her palms. "Get over it."

"This is dangerous. Do you understand what's at stake here? You're brushing off my warnings like they're some kind of—"

"It was his last wish, for Christ's sake."

"Your safety—"

"Not my problem," Gladia said stiffly. "It's your job to keep me alive."

The bodyguard rubbed the back of his neck. "Well, you're making it a hell of a lot harder than it should be."

"Sorry for the inconvenience I've caused. It's something I had to do. End of discussion."

Leon stared out the window, chewing on his lips.

Gladia felt sick. Wei's pale face continued to flash before her eyes. His lips were opening and closing. He was uttering a word...

Leon interrupted her thoughts. "While you were..." His

words drifted off. The man glanced at her and continued in a neutral tone. "While you were doing your thing, I received updates."

"Okay." Gladia cleared her throat. "What's the word? Anything new about Nazarov and Trudeau?"

Leon shook his head. "Our PIs and the police still believe that they are two separate cases of suicide. They've found no evidence to confirm—"

"Of course they've found no evidence," Gladia snapped. "If I wanted to kill the brain and the legs of Polaris, I wouldn't leave a trail of shit behind me. Can't they put two and two together? Jesus Christ, what kind of people are running this show?"

"Need a handkerchief?"

"I need some goddamn answers. What about Shimao and Strutzenberg's autopsies?"

Leon raised a hand. His face became an expressionless mask.

"Yes, Commodore," he said, talking on his wrist. "Confirmed, ten twenty-two at the rendezvous."

Leon gave some instructions to the driver, who nodded and increased the speed of the car.

The bodyguard turned toward Gladia. "You were saying?"

"I was asking about Shimao and Strutzenberg. Do we know what killed them?"

"Yes," Leon said, tugging at his ginger-colored beard. "All tests have confirmed the earlier results. We know they died almost immediately. Same way Wang did."

"Almost immediate collapse of the internal organs," Gladia said, running a hand through her hair. "We still have no idea what kind of weapon did that?"

Leon's laugh was bitter. "We haven't the faintest. We

don't even know how the hell the terrorists brought those weapons inside Infinity. The PIs and the authorities are so clueless that someone is throwing the name *organic weapon* into the mix. That'll make things more entertaining for the press, I guess."

"Organic weapon?" Gladia narrowed her eyes. "What the hell is that supposed to mean?"

"I don't know." Leon shrugged. "I wasn't given any specifics, but looking at the security recording, it seems that the terrorists shot with...well, using their own bodies."

"Using their bodies?" Gladia blinked. "I don't even know how to respond to that."

"Neither do I. If we had a corpse, we could learn more, but..." Leon trailed off meaningfully.

"Right." Gladia let out a heavy sigh. According to eyewitnesses and the recording of the cameras, the terrorist's bodies had liquefied when the security was about to overwhelm them. Another mystery none had been able to solve.

Leon's brows drew closer, his face tightened. "When and *if* we find out how they brought those weapons into the room, we'll have to figure out how on earth they penetrated the force field. It was a goddamned Lampda Trust protecting you, Wang, and the others. I can't even begin to imagine what could penetrate that thing."

"So it's confirmed? It wasn't disabled?"

"Nope. It was up and running. Their damn weapons went through it like hot blades through butter."

"Their weapons." Gladia went quiet for a moment, then glanced at Leon. "Do we know anything more about these people?"

"The main track continues to suggest an extremist Landist faction."

"That's it?"

Leon offered a curt nod.

Gladia clasped her hands behind her neck. "You're saying we don't know anything more about these fuckers after a week of digging around?"

Leon crossed his arms. "We're only sure of one thing."

"What is that?"

"These are dangerous people—someone damn well organized we have never had to deal with before. They could be anything. A new group of cyberio, technorists as we've never seen in the past, unsatisfied Landists, the four goddamned Horsemen of the Apocalypse—"

"Leon." Gladia pinched the bridge of her nose as she closed her eyes. "Spare me. Will you?"

"It's true, we have no clue. They're ghosts in the darkness. These guys were able to kill three people in the most heavily guarded building on the planet. They probably killed Nazarov and Trudeau too, making it look like suicide. I wouldn't want to fuck with them. *You* wouldn't want to fuck with them, which brings me back to square one. Your safety."

"Please don't start that again."

"Listen." Leon leaned toward her, his eyes as hard as stones. "Five of the six people most directly involved in the Polaris project are dead. Dead! You hear me? That makes you the only member of the Hexahedron still breathing. Now, you might not care about your well-being, but the Hyperist movement depends on you, now more than ever. You need to put on your big-girl pants and fill Wang's spot."

Gladia snorted. "Don't fuck with me, Leon. I'm not Wei."

"Goddamn right you're not, but you're the next best thing. It'll have to do."

Leon stopped talking all of a sudden.

"What?" Gladia tilted her head and stared at the bodyguard.

"Quiet," Leon hushed her. "Alpha to Commodore. Alpha to Commodore. Do you read me?"

"Sir," said the car's driver. "We've just lost contact with Commod—"

"Tell me something I don't know, genius," Leon cut him off. "I don't like this. Speed up and try to—"

An explosion cut off his words.

The car was hit by a violent shockwave. The driver lost control of the vehicle for a few seconds and nearly ended up off the road.

Another explosion occurred.

Gladia put her hands over her ears and closed her eyes.

The car was tossed from side to side.

"Take off! NOW!"

Leon's scream was the last thing she heard before the third explosion hit the car like a giant hammer from the sky.

Gladia lost her hearing while her body surged against the seat belt. Then the car flew into the air. It flipped twice before falling to the ground.

A sharp pain at the base of her stomach and on her back coursed through her body, then something struck Gladia on the head. Everything became gray and indistinct. Her eyelids slowly closed and she lost consciousness.

When she opened her eyes again, the world was a strange collection of blurred images, with no sounds and no smells.

She couldn't feel her arms and her legs. She didn't even remember who she was, but she understood that she was moving. Gladia was searching for the door.

She had to get out. Get away. She had to keep breathing.

She never found the door handle, but the door was opened anyway...from the outside.

A hand dragged her away from the back seat.

She couldn't see very well.

Was someone laughing?

Gladia tried to focus on the figure, the human shape before her. That was the only thing she was able to recognize. It was so close... So close.

Her brain stored the image but couldn't understand or identify it. She must have hit her head harder that she thought.

She blinked, tried to see again.

There was an incredibly tall autotron looking at her with two bright red eyes. A voice inside her brain gave her confirmation that that couldn't possibly be true. Autotrons don't smile.

It was a face she had never seen before. An iron-colored face.

Her strength was deserting her. She realized that the raised arm of her assailant was changing, becoming something else. Then she heard another laugh.

What a strange dream, Gladia thought, fascinated by the hazy outline of the figure that loomed before her.

A sudden sound came from her left, followed by a flash of light. She closed her eyes for a second. The light was too strong, too piercing.

When she opened her eyes, she saw the assailant's arm move away from her face and point somewhere else.

Her eyelids closed once more. She heard noises. Perhaps it was another explosion. Her hearing was coming back, but her vision was weakening.

Her attacker was now on his knees, apparently

exhausted. His face was half flesh, half blood. He wasn't smiling anymore.

Then another noise came from somewhere on her right and the man's body was thrown out of sight.

Bright spots swam across her field of vision. Her eyes were failing her.

Gladia realized that she could no longer breathe but her stubborn heart continued beating.

She forced herself to keep her eyes open, but saw only light; a blinding light, and a hand.

Was she seeing stars in front of her?

Her eyelids closed and she slipped away from the world of sounds and senses.

All that remained was a bunch of confused feelings and memories.

Her mind recalled Wei's last moments.

The Omnilogos' lips had moved. He had whispered a name.

Darkness took over her.

GLADIA COUGHED.

It was dark all around.

She opened her eyes but still didn't see anything.

Something seemed to be hammering on her right temple from inside her skull.

"Welcome back from Wonderland, princess."

The voice made her jump. More than a voice, it sounded like a distant echo. Was she still asleep? Or was she awake?

She couldn't remember anything.

"My...my eyes." She croaked. She could feel her dry throat as she swallowed hard.

"Yes. A real pain in the ass," said the distant echo. "I'm afraid your sight won't be back for a couple days at least. Nothing permanent, don't worry. We'll get you up and about in no time."

The echo was gone. The voice was slowly becoming clearer and more understandable.

"How're you feeling?" the voice asked.

"I...I don't know. Am I still dreaming?"

"No, you're not, sweetheart. This is as real as it gets."

Her sense of smell also was coming back. And in that moment, she would have gladly done without it.

She smelled a strong, unpleasant stench wafting around her. It seemed like a mixture of sweat and dirty underwear.

"What...what is this stink?"

"Stink?" the voice repeated. "I don't smell anything."

I, thought Gladia. Only now did she realize that she wasn't talking to herself. There was someone else with her.

"Who are you?"

"An acquired friend, thanks to my relationship with Wei." Gladia heard the stranger snort. "I was his partner; a special one, like you. A member of his exclusive circle of people meant to change the world." The man laughed bitterly, snorted again. "Our superhero trusted me enough to reveal to me his secret identity. I suppose you know what I'm talking about, hmm?"

The Omnilogos, thought Gladia. The man was talking about Wei and his secret. So he knew?

Wei once confided in her that only a handful of people were aware of that detail.

He never said who the others were.

"A tragic loss," the stranger complained, but he didn't seem distressed, or even sorry. His voice was calm and even, and Gladia could imagine him grinning while talking. "The man is dead," the stranger resumed, "but his ideas persist. And they are stronger than ever. It's the martyrs' legacy."

Gladia frowned. "The martyrs' legacy?"

"Of course," the stranger said. "Stardust to stardust, and all that. Wei was a showman, and a goddamn good one at that. It's easy to kill a man, but an idea... Well, ideas are like a bunch of cockroaches. They hide in the most unthinkable spots, breed faster than rabbits, and develop resistance to the worst kind of pesticides. You just can't get rid of them."

Gladia was still trying to decide if it was a dream or reality. If it wasn't a dream, where was she? Why couldn't she see? Why couldn't she remember anything past...

Then a wave of emotions hit her. She remembered everything that had happened. Wei's ashes, the ocean, Leon and the car. She remembered the attack, and the face of the monster who'd try to kill her.

Her head almost split in two. "God." She gasped, tried to move her arm but realized that something was attached to her wrist. "We...we've been attacked. I..." She tried to get up, failed, tried again, and then she felt a hand resting on her shoulder.

"Relax, princess." The stranger pushed her back down on the bed. "You're safe now. I promise."

"There was another man with me and the driver," Gladia said. "What happened to him?" She clenched her jaw as she waited for the answer.

The man cleared his throat. "I'm afraid the driver and Mr. Politis did not survive the attack." There was a shuffling of feet, then the stranger's voice became more distinct, as if leaning closer to her. "You've been incredibly lucky. Let me stress the word *incredibly* here. I'm not one to believe in miracles, but if there is a God, you must be in his good graces."

Gladia decided that this was an awful nightmare. She couldn't bring herself to believe that someone else had died. Leon was right. She had killed him.

All she wanted to do now was sink into darkness, drift back to sleep where there was nothing but empty void.

Her head began to ache, her temples throbbed, and a wave of nausea hit her like a brick. She could barely keep from throwing up.

"You've got to understand that—"

"No." Gladia raised a hand to interrupt him. "Leave me alone. Please. I'm tired. I just want to sleep."

The man made a strange noise with his throat, something similar to a low grunt, then he said, "Oh, you're going to. You're going to sleep and nothing I said will matter to you. This war has already killed you in more ways than a bullet can. I'm not going to let you die twice."

"War?" she heard herself asking despite her tiredness. "What war?"

The voice was quiet for a long time. "Albert Einstein said he didn't know how the Third World War would be fought," the stranger said, paused, then continued talking. "I've got the answer: In silence. And it's already begun, though few people know it."

Gladia couldn't make sense of the stranger's words. Her head was pounding so fiercely it was hard to keep things straight.

"It's sad and ridiculous, isn't it?" the voice continued, inexorable. "But also horribly true. Last week's corpses just show how much this cold war got a hell of a lot hotter. Anyone could be the next one parked in a coffin." The man sighed, his voice somehow wearier than it was before. "Polaris was one of Wei's projects. He had many."

Gladia was weak and exhausted, but her brain was

processing that information. Wei had *many* projects? What projects?

"The boy knew what was coming and took his precautions. Our little friend was overly cautious by nature. He liked to put his eggs in more than one basket, as well as the people who were involved in them. He didn't trust anyone —*especially* the people he trusted." The man chuckled, but his words had a sharp edge about them that made Gladia's skin crawl. "A strange soothsayer, our Omnilogos was, wouldn't you agree? Think about the two of us. I don't know a damn thing about your Polaris, except what I've seen with the rest of the public. And you, my dear, don't know the first thing about the project he's entrusted me with."

Gladia hated the man for his persistence and his undesired presence. But she was a woman whose job was to hunt down answers, and the voice seemed to give her some really interesting ones.

Curiosity got the better of her. "What project?" Gladia asked.

The man shifted in his seat. "The Ariul project," he said.

A flash exploded in the darkness. Gladia saw Wei's lips move, utter a name. It was as if someone had slapped her face.

"Ariul." Gladia was quivering. She tried to get up. "*Ariul*."

"Hmm. You know what I'm talking about?" The voice sounded surprised.

"It's the last word he said, during the terrorist attack. He looked at me in the eyes and said, 'Ariul.'"

"Did he?" The voice no longer seemed surprised. Now it sounded almost pleased, amused even. "That is strange. Well, I guess we'll never find out why."

"I tried...I tried for days to find out what that meant. But there are too many people with that name. I haven't been able to figure out... To find..." Gladia paused. She felt her strength fading away, but forced herself to remain vigilant. She had to know. She had to understand.

"Who's Ariul?"

"Not who," the man corrected her. "*What* is Ariul?"

"I don't understand."

"Ariul isn't the name of a person. It's a compound word in Korean. It means *City of Water*."

"City of Water?" Gladia repeated. No bell rang in her head.

"Few call it that now," the voice continued. "You see, the name was invented to make it easier to pronounce for you white muzz...for Westerners. Today the city is known by another name."

"Which name?" Gladia was shaking now. She felt on the verge of passing out.

She heard a noise coming from somewhere above her head. It sounded like a fast beeping. Then came a scratching sound on her left, like a chair moving. The man got up from his chair, it seemed.

"Your bio-values are unstable, my dear. I'm afraid I've overly taken advantage of your strength. I apologize. I only wanted to make sure that there were no permanent damages. Now you need to rest."

"The name. I want to know what the name means."

The man was silent for an outrageously long time, then he said with something resembling regret, "It won't make any difference for you to know, sweetie."

He touched her cheek. He had stubby and sweaty fingers.

She heard him leave her.

A door opened.

"Please," Gladia said. "I need to know."

The man was still in the room; Gladia could hear his heavy breathing. "I guess you do," he said after an eternity.

"Tell me," Gladia said. "Please."

There was a brief silence, then the man who knew the real identity of the Omnilogos said, "Saemangeum City. That's the meaning of the name. That is what's behind the Ariul project." Another pause, as long as the eternity of the cosmos, then the voice concluded, "And right now, princess, you find yourself in it."

EPILOGUE

PASADENA, FALLSIDE MEMORIAL PARK

The cemetery was covered by a heavy blanket of fog.

The moon, a silver scythe against the pitch black of the sky, was trying to fight its way through a thick layer of clouds.

The place was quiet and cold. The profiles of the objects were vague, almost indistinguishable. Noises and sounds came from the high trees all around.

An owl opened and closed its wings as it perched on a large branch. The head of the bird snapped to the right and to the left. It cocked its head on one side, with an inquisitive look, while watching the world below its claws.

The bird studied the lone figure in the night.

The stranger was cloaked in a long coat and a hood that hid his face almost entirely. He was staring at a tombstone with a strange shape.

The solid stone seemed to be an extension of the night itself. As black as ink, it had thin, scarlet-red veins running through it. The base was a cylinder that slowly tapered upward and then widened again just before the end, forming a sculpture with various points projecting out in all directions. They were the petals of a flower.

The inscription stated:

EVANGELINE LAYIA ELEANOR
2001-2017
Whoever changes one life, changes the whole world

The figure knelt and touched the grave with both hands. It was smooth and cool.

"See?" he said in a whisper. "I kept my promise. I took care of his dream, becoming part of it. And now, I will keep another promise. One I made to him."

He drew a small container from his pocket, opened it, and studied its contents: a fine white powder. Without hesitation, he threw the contents into the air.

For a couple seconds, the light of the moon was able to penetrate the clouds, and the ashes in the air were lit up by a cascade of silvery glow.

Stardust, he thought, looking at the last fragments swallowed up by the night.

"Rest in peace, you two," he said, sealing the container.

A gust of wind rustled the hood back, revealing his face.

Tiago Silva Abreu Melo looked around. The two bodyguards in power armor waited at a respectful distance under a large red maple tree; their gazes scanned the sky constantly.

Tiago put a hand in the inside pocket of his coat and pulled out an infinity-shaped pendant. He touched the phrase engraved on it: *Change the whole world*.

A smile rippled across his face. He glanced up at the starry sky and said, "Will do my best, my friend."

He heard a beep coming from his communication unit.

He accepted the call. "Max?"

"Hey, kiddo," replied the familiar baritone voice of Max Lewis. "You done?"

"Almost."

"Good, 'cause we need the First Omnibus back in the fold."

"What's going on?"

"We've detected biomech activity; a lot more than usual. I don't like it one bit. I have a couple teams ready to go, in case we need to flex some muscles."

"Got it, I'm on my way."

Tiago closed the connection, put the pendant back inside his pocket, and walked toward the guards. He stopped, turning to look toward the tomb.

"Sir?" a guard said, frowning. "Is there a problem?"

"Not at all. I just forgot to say hello to someone."

Tiago's eyes lifted to the sky, where there were countless stars and just a hint of the moon peeking through a thin layer of clouds.

He put a hand on his forehead and with a wide smile saluted the bright vastness of the firmament.

The End

GET PROJECT VALHALLA FOR FREE!

Polaris was just the beginning. In an unknown location north of the Barents Sea, a research center as tall as the Eiffel Tower hides the greatest scientific discoveries of the 21st century.

The few who know of its existence call it Valhalla, but none suspect why it was built.

There is a secret buried in this outpost of progress hiding a catastrophic scenario: destruction on a planetary scale never before seen in human history.

Wei prepares for war as Valhalla holds the only defense capable of repelling the coming apocalypse.

Get your free copy of *Project Valhalla* by signing up to my newsletter.

CONTINUE THE OMNILOGOS SINGULARITY SERIES...

Legacy of Ariul, the second book in the Omnilogos Singularity series, is now available in eBook and paperback format!

GET LEGACY OF ARIUL ON AMAZON OR ON YOUR FAVORITE ONLINE STORE

ACKNOWLEDGMENTS

Thanks to Alessandro, Alberto, Chiara, Raffaella, Mana, Lena, Laura and Mark, for reading this story and providing amazing feedback.

You helped me make *Rise of Polaris* what it was meant to be.

ABOUT THE AUTHOR

I grew up writing of falling empires, space battles, mortal betrayals, monumental decisions, and everything in between.

I wrote and published my first English book, *Lord of Time*, in between waiting tables and exploring the world.

I now spend my days traveling through time and space and, more often than not, writing about impossible but necessary worlds.

When I'm not busy training dragons or mastering the Force, you can find me at MicheleAmitrani.com or hanging out on Facebook at /MicheleAmitraniAuthor.